Under a Warped Cross

Steve Lindahl

Under a Warped Cross

by

Steve Lindahl

I dedicate this novel to the friends who have supported my writing throughout the years. Thank you to all who have read the stories, attended readings, and encouraged me to explore my passion.

Chapter One
Waso

Ten days after the priests cut off her nose, Abigail disappeared from the village. Waso didn't know what was worse, watching his sister suffer or not seeing her at all. What he did know was this: the church was responsible.

Goda, Waso's twin brother, also disappeared. He was last seen in the village the morning of Abigail's punishment. Waso wasn't surprised Goda didn't stay to watch.

***

"Go out with your father." Their mother once instructed Goda and Waso. "He will slaughter one of the pigs today and you need to learn." They were four.

Waso stepped outside immediately. He had grown tired of helping with the churning and was looking forward to watching his father work. But Goda argued. He preferred spending time with the women and liked to play with two-year-old Abigail while his mother worked.

After a while, he came out and joined his brother.

Goda didn't look like Waso. Although they were both the same height, about as tall as their father's waist, Goda had dark hair, almost black, while Waso had light brown. Goda's jawline was narrow compared to Waso's and his arms were weaker. He was also thinner than Waso and a little big in the belly despite the small amount of food they ate.

It was cold, but not unusually so for winter. The water in the pig trough had a thin layer of ice where the pigs had not broken through, but the creek below the farm was running hard and loud, like Waso's heart. There were only a few patches of snow left on the ground, since most of what had fallen a week earlier had melted. The grass was a mixture of brown and green, matching the trees that were either bare or evergreen. There was plenty of exposed pasture, so the decision to butcher a pig was based on the needs of Waso's family not on the scarcity of food for the animals.

"He hasn't picked a pig yet," Waso told Goda.

"I hope he doesn't choose the little one."

"Mother said they taste best."

"You are horrible, Waso."

"Our mother said it."

Waso knew when he saw Anund, their father, loop the rope over the smallest pig in the yard, Goda would disobey their mother's instruction. Waso watched the animal as his brother turned and, although Waso kept his eyes on the pig, he could feel his twin go behind the house to hide. Goda was weak in many ways.

Anund made a harness out of the end of the rope by running a line behind the pig's front legs, over the top, then in front of the same legs. He tied it on top, so he could use the long end to lead the pig to the place where it was to be slaughtered. He tied the rope to a post with as short a length as possible, pulling the pig until the animal touched the wood.

When the animal was in place, Waso's father looked in his direction. He appeared surprised that Waso was alone and glanced around the yard, but didn't stop long to look for Goda. He picked up an oak club from the place where it was leaning against the fence. It had a spike in one end. Then Anund turned and hit the pig's head. The blow didn't stun the animal, so Waso heard it squeal and saw it try to back away, while his father took another swing. Blood was squirting out of the first gash and the second blow opened another wound. Waso's father hit the animal a third time. The pig fell against the post and hung there. It was no longer squealing or moving, but was still breathing.

"Where's your brother?" Anund asked.

"He left."

"I can see that. Where did he go?"

"I was watching you, but I think he went behind the house." Waso started to shiver a little, as he often did when his father spoke to him about Goda.

"He's not where he belongs, so it's up to you to help me with this meat."

Waso flinched, but quickly hid his fear. He looked at his father and shrugged.

"There's a knife on the ground near where I dropped the club. Pick it up for me."

Waso did as he was told, bringing the knife back to his father and handing it to him carefully, hilt first.

"I am going to finish the job," Anund said, "and I want you by me where you can see how to properly kill and clean an animal. Someone other than me has to know how and I don't think it will ever be your brother."

Waso glanced back at the house then walked to his father and the pig.

Anund got down on a knee next to it. "We need to clean this animal, but first we have to bleed it or the meat will go bad. I'll show you the cut. We have to be careful not to kill it, because the beating heart is important for the bleeding." He pointed to a spot underneath the fat neck. "I always start here." When he finished opening the pig's neck, he used rope to lift the back end. "When the blood stops, we need to open the belly, take out his guts, and bury those. Understand?"

Waso nodded and braced himself for a long afternoon.

***

The killing of the pig wasn't the only time Goda had run from something unpleasant. It also wasn't the worst. The worst was when his sister's face was butchered.

Goda and Abigail had been lying near a pond on a scorching summer day when a local farmer had discovered them. Goda was naked from the waist up and Abigail was wearing only a chemise. They were both soaking wet. The farmer reported the sin to a priest and explained that he didn't see them touch each other but thought their behavior was odd and immoral, since they were no longer children. Goda was fifteen and Abigail thirteen. They told the priest they were drying in the sun after swimming. They were brother and sister, had grown up together and were used to swimming together.

The church declared them guilty of incest, its religious leaders decided the woman, who was the natural seducer, needed punishing. Prior to the cut, one of the priests declared that the church was still not fully established in Britannia and could not risk letting any citizens slip back into pagan ways. Four men held Abigail down in the churchyard while a fifth cut off her nose with a dull, iron knife. When they were done they gave her a rag she could use to stop the bleeding and sent her on her way.

After Goda and Abigail left the village, Waso was alone. Two years earlier, Waso's father had died when a tree he was taking down fell on him, causing a thick branch to pierce his chest. Waso's mother followed her husband into the afterlife a month after his death.

One of their pigs bit her leg during feeding time. The bite hadn't appeared serious at first, but the wound infected. Foul smelling pus began to ooze from the lesion, she grew feverish, and died a few days later.

Waso searched for his siblings alone, for more than a month. He didn't find either of them and didn't hear anything to help his search until one afternoon when the village potter came by the farm.

"I have word of your brother," the potter said. This man had married a village girl a few years earlier and had built a house near Waso's farm. Waso didn't know him well, not even his name. He didn't trust a man who had spent most of his years in York, a town controlled by the Danes.

"How do I know I can believe what you say?" Waso asked.

"My wife knew your sister before the punishment. If we had been here, she would have sworn an oath to Abigail's innocence. It might have made a difference."

"Where were you?"

"In York."

Waso shook his head. There were too many neighbors who had sided with the priests when they claimed Abigail had sinned. He was willing to pay for knowledge, but not for lies.

"We were with my mother," the potter added. "She's been sick."

"I am sorry to hear that," Waso said, but he didn't ask more. Instead he said, "How much do you want for the information?"

"I don't want anything, just to help."

Waso paused for a moment, considering the offer, then said, "Thank you."

"Goda is near the monastery in Nendrum. There are people in that area who can help him, and your sister, if she is still with him."

"The Kingdom of Dublin?"

"To the north and off the coast. I asked if your sister was there as well, but the man I spoke to didn't know."

"Do you believe this man?"

"He's a Dane, so he knows about the monasteries."

"I'm sure he knows where they are and how they're fortified," Waso said, thinking how the Danes found the monasteries to be weak targets. "But how does this man know the name of someone taking shelter there?"

"I can tell you what I think," the potter replied. "He knows our language and isn't ashamed to speak with slaves. That's how he knows who is there to defend against the raids. I believe one of those slaves told the Dane about a man whose sister lost her nose. There are plenty of people in Nendrum, but only one with a story like his."

**

Seven days later Waso appeared at the gate to Nendrum. He had walked a great distance and boarded a boat to get there, but despite the tiresome journey he didn't appear weary. He was eager to learn if what the potter had told him was true and refused to allow exhaustion to interfere.

The monastic site was a community on a hill surrounded by a thick stone wall. Inside were orchards, large gardens, a few small buildings and a second wall. Inside that wall were more buildings with thatched roofs like the first ones he'd seen, but round. He thought they were the places where the monks slept and wondered if Goda might be in one of them.

There was a good chance Goda was held against his will. Any other reason seemed strange, since he had sought sanctuary in a place controlled by the Benedictines, the same sect that had mutilated Abigail.

Waso didn't want to wander around the monastery grounds looking for his brother, because someone might question his reason for being there. Instead he went to the top of the hill, inside the third wall, where there was a church, a tower, and a round house, which had to be the home of the Abbot. Waso sat on the ground, leaning against a wall of the church. From that position, he could watch the Abbot's home. Waso didn't know if the Abbot would lead him to his brother, but if Goda was in the monastery there was a good chance the religious leader would check on him, hopefully sooner rather than later.

A thin man who looked to be in his early forties came out. He was wearing a long, tan robe with his hood pushed to the back of his neck. The man had a shaved head and a long beard with streaks of gray among dark blonde hair. He carried a long walking stick in his right hand, but Waso was more interested in what he had in his left. Although it was difficult to be certain from such a distance, it appeared to be a necklace, very much like one his mother and his sister used to share. This was a good sign. The strung beads might have been brought to the monastery by either Goda or Abigail.

There was a chance this man was a monk or a slave visiting the Abbot, but given the cleanliness of his clothing, it was more likely he *was* the Abbot. Waso decided to follow him. Perhaps the man was bringing the necklace to one or both of Waso's siblings.

There were few trees on the grounds, which made it difficult to hide while following someone. Waso kept his distance. He was lucky the presumed Abbot never looked back. Waso followed him through the gate of the innermost wall, directly to one of the small huts.

Waso wondered what to do next. He could go in and confront the Abbot to find out what he knew of Goda and Abigail. But the chance of success with such a reckless plan was slight, so he decided to wait and watch. Waso waited until the thin man exited the hut, noticing that he no longer held the necklace. If this was the religious leader of Nendrum and he had left the beads in the hut, then there was a good chance Waso's brother and his sister were in there. When the Abbot had crossed the yard, Waso slowly wound his way down the hill. He watched as the man crossed through the middle wall into the lower section then

Waso went to the small structure. Now that he was so close, he was not sure what words to say. He wasn't even certain what to think.

He burst into the hut, hoping to find either Goda or Abigail, but found a dark-skinned girl who appeared to be about twelve or thirteen, sitting on the floor. She quickly rose to confront him. She dropped the necklace as she stood.

"What are you doing here?" she shouted at Waso. She glanced at a cloth near the necklace on the dirt floor. She didn't reach for it, but seemed concerned. "Please look away."

He thought this was an odd request, but averted his eyes. "I am sorry, my lady. I was hoping to find someone else."

"Why would someone else be in my home?"

He paused a moment then turned back to see she had picked up the cloth and had used it to cover her hair. It was a scarf, long enough to wrap over the top of her head and cover one of the shoulders of the simple brown dress she was wearing. The scarf had a dark blue pattern around the edge. It was very clean and neat compared to her rumpled, long-sleeved dress, but she wore both with a sense of confidence and dignity that caused Waso to admire her.

Now that her head was covered, Waso felt an urge to see under the covering. He didn't understand his desire. The image of her dark hair seemed to be fixed in his mind, yet he couldn't shake the need to see it again. He looked away from her, down at the necklace, still on the ground.

"Women live in Nendrum?" he asked, trying not to think about the thick soft waves that framed the light brown skin of her face or about her black, close-set eyes, as deep as the ocean.

"I am the only one," she told him. "Men are not allowed to be here, in my house."

He thought about the Abbot, who had been in this woman's home and had brought her the necklace, which, apparently, she cared about less than she cared about her headscarf.

"I was looking for my brother and sister. My sister wore a necklace similar to that one." He turned his head and nodded toward the jewelry on the ground.

"It's not unique. Is that why you chose to look here?"

He wanted to tell her what the Benedictine priests did to his sister's face, but held back, unsure that he could trust her not to think the worst of someone who had been punished so brutally. "I believe my brother is seeking refuge from guilt."

"Guilt? Many here would answer to that description. Tell me his name."

Waso stepped toward her. "First, you tell me why you're here."

She held her hand high to stop him. "I don't have to tell you anything," she said, shaking visibly. "You're in my home." She stood straight and stared at him. "And I'll scream for help if you do not leave immediately."

The threat didn't surprise Waso. He was surprised, though, she hadn't cried out when he first appeared. He turned to leave, then thought better of it and looked back. "My brother's name is Goda."

"The one who sinned with his sister?" Her voice raised up a pitch.

Waso clenched his hands and said, "They have not sinned! And it's *our* sister, not *his* sister."

She smiled and told him. "Don't be upset with me." Her tone had changed suddenly, causing her to seem less offended. "I have met them both," she added. "I know the horrors the church can do in the name of God."

He hoped she was being honest about knowing Abigail and Goda, but he worried about the horrors she was referring to. Was it something more the church had done to his sister and brother? Or was it something she had experienced herself? Even if this woman looked well fed and lived in a dry, comfortable home, it was possible she had suffered.

The woman bent down and picked up the necklace. "The man who brought this to me called it a gift, but I knew he took it from someone. It meant nothing to me before. Now I know it must have been Abigail's..." Her voice faded as she turned the necklace in her hand. "I don't know where they are now, but there's a man who might help you. He lives outside the monastery where he works as a smith's assistant. I only tell you this because I know what your sister and brother have been through."

He nodded to acknowledge that he understood. "Can you tell me how to find this smith's assistant?"

"I will introduce you." She looked up at the roof of the hut as she seemed to be planning her next move. He noticed how her long straight nose gave her a strong appearance that suited her. "But we cannot leave together. I will go first. You will wait here until you think I have had time to leave the grounds. After that, you should turn away from the gateway and spend some time looking over the gardens. Take as long as you can without raising suspicion. I will meet you at the foot of the hill near a large elm tree. Understand?"

He nodded again.

Waso paced about the hut as he counted to keep his time estimate as accurate as possible. When enough time had passed, he walked into the yard and turned toward his left without looking to either side. His goal was to appear as if he belonged there. When he reached the garden, he got down on one knee and began to study the plants. There were peas, beans, leeks, cabbage, lettuce, and a few plants he did not recognize growing in a square plot of land, about twice his height in both length and width. The garden was well tended, with only a few, tiny weeds. His own garden had never been this clean.

When it was time to head out of the monastery, Waso stood to find the gateway in the wall. What he saw forced him to stop. While he had been focused on avoiding the attention of other men in the monastery, he hadn't noticed they were all running about like frightened lizards, grabbing weapons, and heading for positions beside the wall. He found the gateway and headed toward it. It was locked and there were five monks guarding it, all carrying swords. He glanced out at the water, so he could see what was causing the panic.

There were boats in the water below, a hundred Viking long ships swarmed like hornets. The raiders headed for the shore with their weapons drawn.

Chapter Two
Abigail

"I don't want to have an ugly face, but if it's the face I have then it's the face I have to live with." Abigail was on one knee near a peaceful creek she visited every day, looking at her reflection among the tiny ripples. She loved the spot because the sound of the flowing water and the fresh smell helped her deal with the sadness that could overwhelm her. She was talking to a wren in a nearby bilberry bush. "It's the staring that bothers me."

Before the punishment Abigail had many close friends and was well liked by the citizens of their old village. Now she kept hidden in the home she shared with her brother to such an extent that the other tenant farmers began to ask Goda if his wife was dead. Elfgar had told them that pretending to be married would keep them from having to explain their choice to live together. He had not told them how to avoid questions about Abigail's face. People would look at the wound where her nose had once been and assume she was a whore. Why else would she be punished so severely?

Goda seemed to need nothing more than Abigail's friendship, but she needed more. She found solace by confiding to the small animals that lived near their home. At first, she felt awkward, speaking with creatures who couldn't understand her words, but the way they looked with curiosity rather than disgust made her comfortable. And when she had been near them for a while they went back to foraging for seeds, darting behind bushes, building nests, or whatever other tasks consumed their days. They never gave Abigail's appearance a second thought or wondered what she'd done to deserve such a punishment.

Goda was the only human who saw her regularly. She stayed with him because she loved him, but his reactions to her were more painful than the expressions of the others. He didn't look at her when they talked, instead he would wrap his arms around himself and stare down at his feet. On that awful day, it had been her suggestion to go for a swim, her decision to strip down to her chemise, and her choice to lie beside him. Maybe Goda felt guilty because he was two years older than her, but she'd always loved the way he'd treated her, never trying to push his decisions on her the way Waso had.

It was fall when Abigail found the stoats in a shallow warren. The mother was limp, a bone protruding out of its neck. It was possible she'd been attacked by an animal such as a fox who had been scared off before he could eat his prey. Abigail wasn't certain about the turn of events. What she was sure of was that the mother and five of her kits were no longer alive. Only one of the kits had survived and it wouldn't live long, hungry and attempting to nurse from its dead mother.

Abigail picked up the living baby and studied it, noticing that it appeared more confused than frightened. It was about as large as Abigail's thumb and, unlike the dead kits, had some hair. Its dead mother looked a lot like a weasel, only larger and with a black tip on her tail.

It was obvious that the right thing to do would be to put the poor animal out of its misery. It was so tiny that all she had to do was put it down on a rock and step on it. But one thought filled her mind. *This baby is fighting to stay alive.*

She felt her heart beat faster and her smile grow while she pulled her palm closer to her eyes and watched the delicate kit wiggle about. Abigail understood the constant struggle survivors face every day and she saw some of her own will to live in this little animal. There was no way she could leave it alone to die. Goda would understand. He always did.

They didn't own goats, but they had goat milk, part of the supplies they received from their landlord in exchange for portions of their crop. Abigail would soak a bit of wool and let the little animal suck. The time Abigail spent with her young ward meant she couldn't help as much with the farming, but once again Goda seemed to understand what she needed.

Abigail named the stoat Dev, which was short for either Devon or Devona. Only after the kit was old enough to flip over and examine did she know her baby girl's full name.

Once Devona could eat some solid food, Abigail fed her chopped mouse meat. They had plenty of mice in their home. Goda, who still wouldn't kill a pig, caught the small pests with snares made with string and pegs. He was pleased that such a slight change in routine could make Abigail happier than she'd been since the punishment. And she might have stayed happy, if Devona hadn't grown.

By spring Devona was old enough to be on her own. Abigail had been as good a stoat mother as a person could be, but Abigail didn't know if the stoat could take care of herself in the wild. Would she know how to hunt? Would she know what predators to avoid? There would be instinct, of course, but was it enough?

Abigail fashioned a small harness and a leash out of rope then carried Devona to the edge of the woods where she'd found her. Abigail looked in the old warren, but there were no longer any signs of Devona's mother or siblings. The forest scavengers had taken care of their bodies.

"This was your home," Abigail said. "I'm going to sit here while you get to know this place."

She loosened as much of the leash as she could, so Devona could explore the tall grasses and bushes that bordered the forest and even poke her nose behind a tree or two. Abigail could smell the sweet scent of old leaves on the forest ground. She wondered if Devona noticed the same smell then watched as the stoat stood on her back legs, sniffed at the air, jumped, flipped over, and stood back up on her back legs. It was a dance-like move Abigail had seen other stoats do, but never Devona. Something was waking inside the young animal, probably from the smell and feel of the field. Still, Devona hadn't seen one of her own kind since she was too young to notice. They stayed there, enjoying the warm, sunny day, until Abigail grew hungry. They would need to return.

On the third day, Abigail finally found what she was after, another stoat. She knew the animals were solitary creatures, but this one seemed very interested in Devona. And Devona also seemed interested. Abigail loosened the leash and watched as they sniffed at each other then began to wrestle and spin around. She wasn't sure if the two stoats were fighting or playing. She didn't think they were mating, but they certainly seemed to be getting along. "It is time," Abigail told herself, as she used the leash to pull Devona toward her.

"I love you as if you are my own flesh," Abigail said. "I don't believe anyone could love an animal more, but it is time for you to go back with your own kind. I'll never forget you and I hope you'll never forget me."

She untied the harness as she spoke and released the animal. Devona's eyes were two, dark orbs, focused on Abigail. She held herself upright and leaned toward the woman slightly as if lessening the distance between them could help her understand. Abigail reached out to scratch her behind her ears. The familiar touch seemed to reassure her.

Devona took a few tentative steps toward the tall grass then turned and stared. Abigail knew what she had to do. She stood up and started to walk away. When she glanced back, she saw that Devona was following. She couldn't allow that, so she bent over, found a stone, and tossed it close enough to her stoat to make the message clear. Devona turned and darted away.

***

Abigail and Goda took care of each other as well as any married couple could. Abigail helped in the fields during the planting and the harvest, contributed by grinding flour, cleaning fish and poultry, and preparing their food. She also cleaned their home, and wove the cloth for their clothes. Yet in the days after she set Devona free, she felt diminished, as if most of her value had gone into the wild along with the stoat. Devona had depended entirely on her, something she couldn't say of Goda. He was an unusual man, not at all helpless in the home. As a child, he had preferred women's work and now, as an adult, he had learned to do what he had to do. He could survive without her, while she would have problems without him.

The life she led with Goda was similar to the way they had lived as children, causing Abigail to feel they'd changed location, but nothing else. They had the same routines, the same conversations dominated by talk of weather or signs of fungus on the crops, and the same lack of physical contact. Their father had been mostly silent in their house, preferring the company of his hogs to that of his wife and children, while their mother and Waso had limited their conversations to advice on the best ways to complete tasks. In Waso's case these were opportunities to demonstrate his superiority over Goda. Yet only Goda had listened to Abigail's dreams. It hurt to have him act like the others now that they were living alone.

Abigail knew Devona had never understood any words beyond her name, but it had felt good to speak to the stoat. And when she had pet the animal, the sensation of her fingers touching a living being felt better than the warmth of summer sun on her shoulders. Abigail's disfigured face was what kept her away from others, but it was the loss of Devona that made her aware of how much her loneliness hurt.

"The Aphids are bad this year," Goda told her at a dinner about two weeks after she'd freed her stoat. Abigail and her brother were eating chicken and drinking enough mead to loosen both their tongues. Goda had traded bread for the chicken and some cloth Abigail had woven for the mead. Trading was another task Abigail couldn't do without Goda's help, since she couldn't face her neighbors.

"Will they hurt the wheat?"

"Some of the seedlings perhaps, but most of the crop has grown enough."

"Good."

"I suppose, but I'd rather see clean stalks."

She took another drink. She was tired of hearing about bugs and fungus. She wished he would speak about something else, about how the sense of loss she felt would not always be so painful.

"Goda – I don't feel loved."

His head jerked up and he stared at her for a moment. "I've always loved you," he told her. "You must know that."

"Maybe I used the wrong word. I should have said needed. I don't feel needed."

Goda stood, pressed his lips together, then looked straight at Abigail and spoke in a steady voice. "There are different types of need. I need you because I love you. I wouldn't be able to get through a day out in the field if I didn't know you were here, waiting for me. But you're talking about Devona, right?"

She nodded.

"She needed you for food and security. I'm sure she wanted your company as well, but it wasn't anything like my need to be near you. Now that she's with her own kind, she'll adapt and find a substitute – a stoat. But me? I'd die without you."

"I believe you would." Her heart raced as she realized Goda meant what he said. He would do anything to make her happy.

***

A few days after that conversation, while Goda was out in the field. Abigail cleaned herself as well as she could, washing away the field dirt from her arms and legs. She used a rag to clean the hole in her face. It wasn't easy to do because it wasn't just a wound. It had healed, but it constantly leaked mucus. It wasn't just ugly. It was disgusting. Hopefully, Goda didn't think so.

"I still miss Devona," Abigail told her brother when he came into the house. "But setting her free was the right thing to do."

"Yes, it was. I know you loved the animal, but she'll be better off living out her years with her own kind."

"There's something else, something more than just missing her."

"What?"

Abigail looked away from her brother, sucked in a breath and looked back. "I hope you'll understand. I can't help how I feel."

She felt a flutter in her stomach then noticed that more snot was running down toward her lips. She wiped her face again with the rag. Goda was staring at her. He tilted his head slightly and ran his fingers through his hair. "I always respect what you say," he told her. "So, speak up and I'll listen."

"I love you, Goda. But Devona made me realize we're not enough. I need a life with more."

"You're leaving me?" Goda gasped.

"Of course not. You are my blood and soul. I would never do that. You treat me so well that sometimes you make me feel as if I'm not ugly." He seemed about to respond to her words, but she signaled for him to be quiet as she kept speaking." What I am saying, however, is that I also need someone else. This isn't enough, just the two of us." She took another breath then said, "I want a baby. I want to have your child."

Goda took a couple of steps backwards, as if he was trying to keep his balance. He waited a moment then spoke in a shaky, soft voice. "We'll be damned to Hell."

"I don't believe that," Abigail said. She wiped her hole again then stared in his eyes. "Look at me. Look at my face. If God didn't want this to happen to us, He wouldn't have let them do what they did. We've already paid the debt and our lives have already been changed forever. The sin, if you want to call it that, is ours to commit."

Goda suggested other men, ones who could keep a secret. He would pay, if necessary. But Abigail didn't want a stranger inside her. She wanted Goda, whom she loved even if he was her brother.

"I see how men look at me, gawking and laughing as if they'd come upon a two-headed turtle. The only way I can live my life is by hiding from them. So, no, I don't want one of them to father my child."

Goda appeared as if he was about to speak, but no words came. Instead he just rocked back and forth like a boat in a storm.

"God wants this for us," Abigail said.

"How can you believe in the God of those priests?" Goda said through curled lips.

"Whatever god has made this world, has made it unfair. We have to live with that. But you can give me what I need."

Goda stared at Abigail's bare toes and indicated his consent by nodding.

Abigail turned to Goda and took a breath through the place where her nose had once been. Since her punishment she breathed mostly through her mouth, but couldn't smell that way and now she wanted to remember the acrid odor of his body after a day in the sun. His scent wasn't pleasant, but it was the true scent of Goda, the smell she'd grown up with.

They sat together and ate the rabbit she'd prepared along with boiled carrots and potatoes. They drank mead with their meal and each had an extra cup afterwards. Abigail hoped the drink would loosen her brother's reserve.

After dinner, she took him by his hand and led him to her bed. It was the only bed in the house, but he had never shared it with her before this. He slept across the room on a blanket spread out on the floor. She sat on the bed but he didn't follow, so she stood again and hugged him.

She had timed her seduction to when the daylight was almost gone by talking at the table more than usual. Goda was used to her appearance with space between them, but holding him this close was different. She needed the dark to hide her ugliness. She kissed the side of his neck, but did not move her mouth around to his lips. She could feel how tense he was and knew it was too early for a full kiss. She kept hugging him, moving her hands to massage his shoulders, his arms, his back. He started to speak, but she raised two fingers to his mouth to silence him. He was starting to relax and she didn't want words to get in the way. Time was on her side.

Goda began to stroke Abigail's back, returning the same type of touch she'd offered him. He was comfortable enough for her to make the next move. She twisted and gently pushed him to indicate she wanted him to sit. Then she lifted her skirt, so she was naked from the waist down, and sat beside him. He tensed again, not as much as before, but still a step backwards. She hugged him again and felt him relax into her body. His hand went to her thigh as her mouth went to his mouth then they lay down together in a single motion.

***

Abigail stayed on her bed for some time after Goda left, thinking about his seed now inside her, hoping it would grow. She prayed this would work, but knew enough about farm animals to realize she would have to join with Goda a number of times before she would be blessed with a child.

Chapter Three
Olaf
(Scandinavia, a year after the raid on Nendrum)

Olaf needed a quern stone to grind barley to flour. He had heard of a new type with a post to keep the top in place and a handle to spin it. This new stone would leave less grit in his flour. Olaf did not have enough trade-ready wool to make the trip worthwhile, but he had enough silver to make the purchase.

Olaf raised sheep, as his father had before him. He looked like his father had, muscular with red hair and a matching beard, although his father's beard had been full while his was still thin.

Olaf acquired barley, fish, and silver by trading milk, lambs, and wool. But, like all his neighbors, he was also a blacksmith, a tailor, a carpenter, and a miller. His other chores left him little time to tend his sheep, so he had bought a slave, Waso, to handle the menial work. He treated Waso as well as most men treated their thralls, but knew he could not be trusted. Slaves wanted what freemen had. To be certain there was no trouble, Olaf kept a battle-axe and was trained to fight. Laws existed, but each man had to enforce them for himself.

Birka, the place where farmers like Olaf sold their wares and bought their supplies, was located on an island in Lake Malaren. Olaf went there frequently to purchase iron for his tools and cloth, which was finer than what he could weave himself. Birka was also the place where Olaf had bought Waso.

Although Waso was the only slave Olaf needed, he took some time to watch that day's sale, specifically the women. There were always young ones and old ones, fat ones and skinny ones, tall ones and short ones, pretty ones, and hags. They all hung their heads and turned whichever way the merchant pointed, like submissive sheep in Olaf's flock. When he finally saved enough silver, he planned to buy a bed slave, but that day was still years away. Meanwhile, he could continue to dream.

The first slave's severe injuries would bring a lower price. One of her eyes had swollen till it shut, and her left arm hung uselessly at her side. Even if those problems weren't permanent, her age wouldn't change – over thirty at least. Olaf shook his head as he spat at the ground. He'd been hoping for a pretty one, someone he could think about at night.

He turned to leave when he noticed his stocky neighbor, Hakon, beside an exquisite female thrall with thick, dark hair that shined like a frozen lake in moonlight. This slave's beauty was ten times that of Olaf's sweetest dream. Her hands were bound and when Hakon and the girl approached Olaf, he could see the rope was wool, probably because it was softer than oak fiber, the most common rope material. Most likely the wool had come from Olaf's sheep, since Hakon traded with him more frequently than with their other neighbors. "Why are you here?" Hakon asked, after they had greeted each other.

"No reason worth mentioning." He didn't want to bring up the quern stone, but Hakon glanced at the contents of the small cart Olaf was pulling and smiled.

"A fancy millstone," Olaf's neighbor said, "I don't have one that nice, but I am sure my new woman can make bread with the old one."

Olaf looked from Hakon to his slave. Her hair was what he had first noticed, but her skin was also dark, the way he'd imagined the women of Persia. And so were her eyes, like the feathers of a black raven. He wondered what land she'd been taken from. Her clothes seemed to be like the dresses he'd seen on other slaves from Britannia, a light brown dress, very simple, without a single brooch. But her hair, skin, and eyes argued against that land as her place of origin.

Olaf was never good at guessing anyone's age, especially women, but the thrall seemed young. He thought she was thirteen or fourteen, a couple of years younger than Hakon, who was Olaf's age.

Her build was not as sturdy as other thralls Olaf had seen, which made him wonder how useful she would be on Hakon's farm. Olaf turned his eyes to her hands and saw they were smooth. He was certain Hakon wanted this woman for his pleasure and probably to birth other slaves he could use or sell. He did not want her for making bread.

Olaf glanced back at Hakon and knew from his neighbor's smirk that he'd let his jealousy show. Hakon nodded then led the woman away, while Olaf pulled his cart in the opposite direction. He decided he would wander around the market for a while before he headed home, just to be certain he didn't have to ride the same ferry as his neighbor.

The next thrall to be sold was a boy, a short, skinny, child slave who could not have been older than twelve. This was one who would cost more to house and feed than he was worth in the field. Olaf decided it was a bad day for the thrall market, except for Hakon's woman.

Hakon wasn't a rich man, just a wheat farmer, so there had to be another reason he got the pick of the plunder. The man had been on at least two raids a few years back. Perhaps he had helped someone during those voyages and was cashing in on favors owed. In any case, Olaf's neighbor now owned a woman who could change the man's life.

When Olaf reached the ferry, he found it crowded, but was relieved that Hakon and his thrall were not among the passengers. The clinker-built boat was flat bottomed, stable, and large enough to hold a few oxen or horses. The operator, who was the single rower, made Olaf pay a second passage for his cart, but he still made out better than he would have had he waited for the large ferry. The rest of the passengers only had a few items in their arms and were probably local people enjoying the market for the day. Most were women, sturdy Scandinavians, unlike Hakon's slave. But there were a couple of men, one of whom was carrying wool which might have been the same product Olaf had sold earlier that day.

There was a slight breeze, but the water was calm and the ride was pleasant. It was a warm sunny day, perfect for both the trip across the lake and the beginning of the long walk home. He hoped the good weather would hold for the next few days and the nights wouldn't be too cold for sleeping outdoors. He'd been able to make the trip to Birka in a single day back when he owned a couple of horses. But he'd lost the gray in the horse fighting at the Festival of Ostara and he'd sold the brown to help pay for Waso. So now it took three days, each way.

After the boat reached the shore and Olaf had his cart on dry land, he thanked the ferry operator and started on the path home. The cart's wooden wheels were solid and would easily last for the length of the trip, but they creaked and wobbled. The sound was constant and soothing along with the leaves rustling in the breeze. It was too early in the season for many insects, but the birds were adding their voices to the melody of the wheels. There were ravens and hawks gliding above the ash trees that grew along the path and perched on their branches were a number of songbirds. Olaf recognized the smaller birds, but didn't know them by name. Together their sounds were as eerie as a whistling night wind.

In the cart, along with the quern stone, Olaf had his battle-axe. Having the weapon nearby was a comfort. He had kept it within his grasp during the nights on the trip to Birka and he planned to do the same now that he was walking home. Olaf's father had owned a farmer's axe he used to cut wood and would have disparaged Olaf's desire for a battle-worthy weapon. But his life might have been longer if he hadn't felt that way.

At age nine Olaf found his father's body in the barn, cut open in a way that could not have been an accident. Apparently, the murderer was a thief, since three of their lambs were missing. It was true that Olaf's father could not have worked with an axe always in his hand, so the results might not have changed even if he had owned a true weapon. Still, Olaf wished his father had been trained to fight.

His mother had died when he was too young to remember. He had asked his father about her and had been told she started coughing, a deep cough that shook her whole body until it shook the life right out of her. The death of Olaf's father was extremely hard on Olaf. He became an orphan a few months before he was to turn ten.

Olaf had been working the sheep since he was five and knew his way around the farm better than most grown men. That was fortunate because the only way to survive was to keep up with everything he'd been taught to do.

A brown songbird with a white breast called from the branches of a Hazel tree a short distance off the path. Olaf was familiar with the sound, three or four notes repeated at a medium pitch then at a low pitch. After a pause, the pattern started again. Birds like this one frequented the fields by his farm. The sound reminded him of home.

Since the death of his father, Olaf had spent most of his days alone. Sven, a cousin of his mother, had arrived days after he was orphaned and had tried to take him in, but Olaf had resisted, running back to his farm four times. Sven eventually gave up on the idea of adding Olaf to his family, but insisted the boy live with them until he was trained to defend himself. Given what had happened to his father, Olaf agreed.

Olaf had been a quick study with Sven's battle-axe. The axe handle was long, so the weapon had to be wielded with both hands. This gave the fighter a long reach, but made it difficult to move quickly. Fortunately, Olaf was nimble and fast, so he could compensate for the clumsiness of the weapon. When Olaf was ready to go back to his farm, Sven gave him the axe saying, "You have earned it and have become better with it than I am. Always keep it by your side so you may use it if the man who killed your father returns." Olaf took the words to heart. When he was home, he slept with the axe in his bed closet, alongside his bed. Now that he was on the road, he cradled it at night and during the day he kept it in the cart he was pulling, positioned so that he could grab it if danger presented itself.

Olaf stepped over an exposed root, walked two more steps, then felt one of the cart wheels catch. He could pull harder until the cart rolled over the impediment, but he didn't want to damage it. So, he let loose the handle and stepped to the side where he could lift. It wasn't heavy, which was a good thing since he had to lift while shifting the weight forward. When the wheel was beyond the root, Olaf got back into position and resumed his walk toward home.

He thought about the slave girl again, imagining how wonderful it would be to have her for his own. She would cook, weave and clean. Thralls were always rebellious during their first few months in captivity. After they were convinced they would never see their homes again, they gave in to what was best. They'd all been taken by force and felt a mixture of resentment and fear, but the fear always won out. Surviving in the Scandinavian wilderness would be a difficult task.

Hakon had to have the same thoughts as Olaf had, but he would have the chance to make those thoughts real. If Olaf's father had lived just a few more years, Olaf would have gone on a raid or two and been a wealthy man. The slave, or another like her, would have been his, instead of his neighbor's.

Olaf had to make his way through a small stream that ran across the path and joined a larger creek. The creek had been running parallel to the path for a good distance and was very beautiful. He was passing through grasslands, so the water touched the shore where there were tall reeds and flowers, purple and yellow, like fine jewels on the most beautiful sword hilt ever made. He wondered if the flowers were also as useless as jewels. With his battle-axe, Olaf could take on any sword fighter, no matter how fancy a weapon he owned.

The day was hot and he thought about pausing for a while to wade in the water. He decided not to waste the time. But if he'd had Hakon's slave beside him, he would have stopped, just to splash water on her bare legs.

***

When Olaf reached home, he was surprised to find one of his ewes out of the pen, mingling with the wethers. The female was fine, but she was not where she belonged. He called for Waso, but the slave didn't respond. He turned toward the house and called again, but still nothing. Olaf muttered, "Just what I need," before setting the cart by the barn, grabbing his battle-axe, and approaching the sheep. His body shook and spat out, "I'll knock some sense into that fool!"

He poked at the animal with the handle of his axe, guiding her through the barn. When Olaf turned the corner to get to the entrance, he found the plank door left open. He cursed Waso again, as he kept leading his sheep. When he placed her back in the pen, he counted heads and discovered another still missing.

He thought, *"He'll pay for this. I swear he'll pay."*

The water trough was dry. Olaf deduced the herd was deserted for a good part of the day, at least. Olaf was surprised they hadn't all followed the two who escaped looking to quench their thirst.

Olaf closed the barn door and set out to find his missing ewe and wayward thrall. The herd needed immediate watering. If Olaf found Waso, he would have him fetch the fresh water from the creek. Unless, of course, the slave couldn't walk after Olaf beat him.

Olaf looked in the stalls, in the dairy section, and behind the barley stack. Those were the only places a man might hide, since the building was small. He left the barn and turned his attention to the house.

Hiding will make it worse. He should know that.

The house was a small, turf hut. There had only been one time when more than two people lived in it, during the period between Olaf's birth and his parents' death. Now, again, there were two residents, Olaf and Waso. The building was a wooden structure on a stone foundation with the outside walls and roof covered with turf. The only sources of light in the house were the front door, the single smoke hole, and the fire pit in the center of the long room. Other than the long room, the only rooms in the house were two small bed closets. Olaf and Waso shared one of those in the cold weather, with Olaf on the bed and Waso on the floor. During the warm weather, when Waso's body heat wasn't needed, the thrall slept in the loft.

It didn't take Olaf long to search the building. He did not find Waso. He did, however, make an interesting discovery. Olaf found a length of wool rope near the fire pit. He knew how rare wool rope was, which is why he was convinced it was the same line that had been used to bind the wrists of Hakon's slave. Hakon had been there. While Olaf had been dreaming of Hakon's thrall, Hakon had been plotting to steal Olaf's. *It had to be Hakon who did this,* he thought. *That swine stole Waso.*

After filling the water troughs in the pen and looking around for the lost sheep, Olaf would start on the path to Hakon's, holding his battle-axe high as he walked. His neighbor would not get away with this crime. Olaf would defend what was his.

But first he decided to check the latrine, to be certain he had looked everywhere for Waso. When he entered the outbuilding, he found a naked male body. The man was on his stomach with one foot in the waste trench. Olaf wasn't certain who the man was, only that he was too stocky to be Waso. He pulled the body toward the center of the room and flipped it over. It was Hakon. He was dead, a huge gash on his head.

Waso was gone, along with Hakon's thrall and his clothes. Olaf let out a screech like a wounded fox and beat the ground with his battle-axe.

Chapter Four
Waso

Stateira had Abigail's hair – thick and dark, like the fur of a bear. He hadn't noticed the likeness at Nendrum nor at Olaf's farm when Stateira came back into his life with her hands bound. All he knew then, before he had spent time with her in the wilderness, was that his heart beat hard and fast when he saw her.

Waso had struck out at the man who held Stateira. He had knocked him to the ground by swinging a shepherd's staff through Hakon's knees. Waso killed him by bringing the same pole down on his head. Waso had lost control, but when the attack was over and Stateira's master lay dead, he was pleased with what he had done.

"What now?" Stateira whispered, as she stood motionless and stared blankly at the lifeless body.

"We've got to leave. I'll hide him to give us extra time when Olaf returns."

"But where do we go?"

"Does it matter?"

She tilted her head and took in a deep breath. "It does if we want to stay alive."

"Help me put him in the latrine."

"What about food and shelter?"

"We'll find what we need."

Waso took a chicken and a ewe, whose teats were filled with milk. Once they were deep in the woods, he started a fire to cook the chicken. Only then, while they shared their first meal together, did Stateira reveal her true feelings about the death of Hakon. "He brought me to wait for Olaf," she said. "He enjoyed running into his neighbor at Birka and wanted to show me off again. At the marketplace Olaf looked at me with hunger, so Hakon planned to let him use my body in exchange for something Olaf had, maybe silver or wool or something else. He hadn't counted on you."

Waso felt pride that he had helped Stateira. Yet, when he tried to speak about her fate, his words stalled in his throat and twisted about like water in a blocked creek. The things she said meant Hakon was a cruel master, but the emotionless way she said them also told him she felt like a whore. He knew what the priests had done to his sister and wondered what they'd done to this woman. "You've been through a lot," he said.

She raised her head high. "So, have you. I thought you died the day we met, during that raid on Nendrum. I escaped because I was out of the monastery waiting for you. You never showed up."

"I had no weapon and wasn't fighting," Waso said, "which is why I ended up in Scandinavia and was sold to Olaf. And you? If you escaped why would you return to Nendrum?"

"I thought the Abbot had been killed, or at least taken in the first Viking raid, the way you were, so I didn't run. I stayed in the village outside Nendrum's walls. I thought that part of my life was over, that whoever survived wouldn't look for me. But one of the monks saw me in the village. Shortly after that I was captured and forced to return to the monastery. I was there until the next raid."

"That's horrible!"

"I hope you're different than other men I've known," she told him. She paused before adding, "I will protect myself if you're not."

It was good she still had pride, Waso thought. Yet he was stronger than she was and she knew it, so she had to be bluffing. She didn't know his hatred for the priests who hurt his sister, changed his soul. "I'm not like Hakon," he told her in a steady, soft voice. "I will never hurt you."

Stateira laughed and shook her head. "Those words of yours are the same words the Abbot said to me the first time we met. He went on to tell me he would bring the spirit of his God, which he claimed would give me a joy unlike any I'd ever experienced. The joy was his, not mine. And it was no different than the pleasure of the first one who owned me, a man who bought me from my father. But all that's over, isn't it?"

Waso nodded and looked back at the fire. Her voice had cracked when she spoke about her father, but she hadn't cried. He decided not to ask any more questions. He was happy Hakon was dead and pleased he'd been the one to kill him. He stared at the coals as the cooking fire burned out. He glanced at Stateira. She sat to his right side, finishing what was left of her meal. She appeared to be trembling. Her lips glistened in the firelight. He thought she was about to say something else, but she didn't.

He loved the pink of her mouth, especially where it met the dark, olive of her skin. He wondered how soft her face was and felt a bit dizzy at the thought. He forced his gaze back toward the fire. The Abbot must have felt a need for Stateira similar to what Waso felt, but he knew he had to resist. It was the only way she would trust him.

"Are you cold?" he asked, forgetting his decision to stop asking questions.

"I'm fine."

But he knew she wasn't.

He thought about his sister again. When she was young she had been a beautiful girl. Now the priests had made her into a marred and ugly woman no one would want to touch. There was a chance he'd never be able to see Abigail again, to tell her that he loved her no matter what. But he could see Stateira and he could talk to her, as long as she trusted him. "I promise I won't touch you," he told her, "I was Olaf's thrall for more than a year. I had no choice but to do whatever he told me to do, just like you with the Abbot..."

"Not quite."

"Let me finish. When people have power, they use it. But we're still alive and no longer under their control." He tightened his fist when, again, he thought about his sister. "Our scars will last for the rest of our lives, but not our open wounds. We're alive and we're strong. We'll get our revenge."

Stateira lifted her head up and stared at him. "Hakon's dead."

Waso stared back as he told her, "We're just beginning."

***

Stateira

Stateira and Waso hid for ten days in the dark Scandinavian forest – alone. Waso didn't act the way she expected a man to act. Although he sometimes touched her hair or brushed a hand against her skin, those gestures seemed innocent. Waso's restraint made her feel safe, but his behavior nagged at her. *Why doesn't he want me?* she wondered.

When they first met at the Hell called Nendrum Monastery, Stateira had been the mistress of the Abbot, a religious man who often stated how all children of God were treasures. Yet, the Abbot only valued Stateira as someone who could take care of his sexual needs. She thought of him as a monster, exactly as she thought of the other man who had owned her.

She hated all men, but Waso was different. Perhaps the time he had spent as Olaf's thrall helped him understand what it meant to be someone's property. That was a theory she had trouble believing. No man can fully appreciate what it is like to be a woman owned, she thought, not even a male slave.

"Does it bother you that I am a thief?" he asked.

Stateira couldn't have been more surprised by Waso's question. He was keeping her alive. To do so, he'd stolen bread, grain, rope, and a knife he used to make snares and to clean the prey he caught. But she'd also stolen. She had taken a bucket from a farm and had repeatedly returned to fill it from their well. Yet Waso never implied *she* had degraded herself by stealing.

"These are the people who took us from Britannia," she told him. "They are the thieves, not us."

"I stole from farmers."

After they'd eaten the ewe, they'd had no choice but to steal. She said, "They might be farmers one day and raiders the next. You don't know."

"That's the trouble. I don't know."

Stateira took Waso's hand. "What we do, we do to stay alive."

He took his hand away.

They were spending their nights in a small shelter Waso had built. He had used the stolen knife to cut branches for a small two-sided structure, just big enough for them to lie down. He'd covered the branches with twigs and the twigs with leaves, creating enough layers to keep the rain out. Their body heat kept them warm.

The first night Stateira had spent in the tiny shelter she was wary of Waso, believing he would be like the other men she'd known. She trusted him to keep her body alive, but not to care about her emotions or her mind or her soul. She slept under the night clouds until the rain started and forced her to crawl in beside him.

"I won't hurt you," Waso whispered, while she lay beside him. "You need to believe me."

"I believe," she replied, turning on her side to face away from him. She wished she could turn her thoughts as easily as she turned her body.

Although they continued to sleep next to each other, their daytime conversations remained focused on two subjects – how to survive in Scandinavia and how to get back to Britannia so Waso could continue his search for his sister and brother.

"What if we posed as Vikings looking to join a raid?" Stateira suggested.

"It would be unusual for a woman who looks like you to go on a raid. And you aren't trained to fight."

"But you could join," she told him. "You're the one who needs to get back to Britannia. My home is in Persia."

Waso shook his head and scowled. "I'm not leaving you. We'll figure something out."

Stateira didn't pause. "We could steal a boat," she suggested.

"And row the entire way?"

"Wouldn't it make more sense to take one that has a sail?" Stateira smiled as Waso nodded.

"But I'm not a pilot," he told her.

"When I was young my father used to take me and my brothers sailing on the Caspian Sea. I know how to catch the wind and I know how to navigate by the sun and the stars." She held her breath as she tried to stifle a small grin.

"You continue to surprise me, Stateira." Waso said. "Where are we supposed to find a boat like this?"

"Birka," Stateira told him as she stepped close. "The marketplace where Hakon bought me. He took me on a ferry to the mainland and I saw a couple of others there as well. Those boats are all large enough for open water yet small enough for the two of us to handle."

Waso paused for a moment then brushed Stateira's hair away from her face and looked at her closely. It might have been her imagination, but she thought his eyes had a shine she hadn't noticed before.

***

Olaf

Although Olaf was a shepherd, not a tracker, finding two runaways leading a ewe didn't seem to be a difficult task, not at first. He found footprints, sheep scat and crushed weeds in the field they had crossed. But the thralls had taken a direct path toward the forest and once their trail entered the woods, he lost it. He found signs indicating well-traveled paths, but pointing in all directions. Most of those signs must have been from the animals of the wilderness.

It didn't take Olaf long to realize that finding Waso and the woman would be a difficult and time-consuming process. His sheep couldn't survive without him for more than a day and there was a dead body in his latrine. He had to turn back. But Waso had made a fool of him and that shame couldn't stand. He would have to come up with a better plan.

The following day Olaf went to the home of Bisi, the leader among his neighbors known as the *first among equals*. Olaf explained that Hakon's body was in his latrine, killed by two thralls: Waso, Olaf's own slave and a woman Hakon had just purchased. Olaf didn't know the woman's name, but believed the two slaves had come from raids on Nendrum Monastery.

"And what do you want from me?" Bisi asked.

"I want them both declared outlaws. But I plan to look for the runaways, so I won't be here for the next assembly. Would you declare my wishes?"

"Of course. I assume you'll take care of Hakon's body?"

"Yes. I'll burn it."

Olaf waited for Bisi's response. When it didn't come, he realized he hadn't offered enough.

"I'll go by his farm for clothes and jewels to burn with him."

"Yes. It is good to offer him as much respect as you can."

"There is something else," Olaf said. "Do you know of anyone who might take care of my sheep while I hunt for the outlaws?"

"How long will you be gone?"

"Until I find them. I will *never* give up."

"So, you don't know?"

Olaf nodded.

"Hakon was your closest neighbor," Bisi continued, "and you know how long it takes to travel from your farm to his. It would take a lot more time for anyone living further away."

"Do you know anyone who might want to live there – until I return?"

"I do know someone," Bisi said. He smiled and added, "A thrall who saved enough of his living expenses to purchase his freedom. He needs work and a place to stay."

"Can I trust him?"

"I believe you can, if you pay him fairly."

Olaf wasn't certain what "fairly" was, but he thought he could negotiate with the man. "What is his name?" he asked Bisi.

"He calls himself Payne and he, like your Waso, came from Nendrum. He might help you in other ways. There's a chance he knew either the woman or Waso."

***

It didn't take long for Olaf to determine that Payne's life hadn't changed much after he bought his freedom. He still dressed in thrall clothing, except for the slave collar, and he still worked the most menial tasks. Payne arranged to continue working for his former master in exchange for room and board because he had nowhere else to go. His days and nights were no different than when he'd been a slave.

This arrangement did not seem fair, which convinced Olaf he could get the best of this man.

"I have to leave my farm while I look for two runaways," Olaf told Payne. "I need someone to take care of the sheep, but I don't know how long I'll be gone."

Payne raised his head slowly and narrowed his eyes. "You want me to leave this farm? Why would I do that?"

"You can gather and sell my wool while you're there. You won't have a master looking over your shoulder and you might earn enough silver to get your own place, if I'm gone for a long time. All I ask is for you to watch over my farm."

"Yes. But if you find these thralls quickly you could be back in a day or two. If that happens, you would kick me out and I wouldn't have anywhere else to go."

"That's not likely."

"But possible."

Olaf took a step closer to Payne and stared. "I lost their trail because they're hiding in the forest. It will take some time to find them."

"Maybe." Payne cocked his head. "Or maybe they're dead and all you'll have to do is follow the crows to their bodies."

"Waso was with me for more than a year. I know him well. He's sharp and wily. I'm certain they're both still alive and well hidden. It will take time to find them."

"Waso? How about the other one? You said there were two."

"Yes. A female from Persia, dark skin and dark hair, very beautiful."

"Ah, yes," Payne said, grinning. "I know the Persian. Stateira's her name. She was the Abbot's bed slave."

"So, it is true. You were in Nendrum?"

"I was. And I know Waso as well. I met him on the longship when we were brought to this God forsaken land. The poor soul had arrived in Nendrum just in time for the raid. He wasn't there even a day. He was looking for his brother and sister."

"Brother and sister?" Olaf stepped back.

"I thought you knew him well."

"So, did I."

"The brother and sister were punished for incest. The priests cut up the sister's face. I guess they won't be committing that sin again." Payne smiled.

"He told you that?"

"I heard most of the story before I met him. I just had to hear his name to know who he was. But what's important is that Waso would still want to look for them. To do that he's got to get back to Britannia."

"Thank you. That helps." Olaf spoke in a voice that was a little too loud. He was excited because the only way Waso would know to get to Britannia was through Birka. "Here's what I'll do for you, Payne. If my thrall lives through the beating I plan to give him, I'll sell him. That way I will need you, so you can stay on if that's what you want."

He seemed to consider the offer before speaking. "Interesting, but not good enough." Now it was Payne who took a step toward Olaf. "What I want is this. I get half your land and a third of your flock as soon as you head out. Of course, I'll take care of yours as well as mine. But if you don't come back in two years, I get it all."

Olaf looked down at the filthy straw Payne had been carrying out of the barn and knew he could get a better deal if he took time to negotiate. But then he looked up and saw the sun crossing the clear, blue sky. It reminded him that time was passing and the longer he waited the greater the possibility he would never again see Waso or the beautiful thrall, Stateira.

He felt his neck tighten as he silently cursed his murdering slime of a thrall once again. Then he spoke out loud saying, "Give me three years to get home and you've got a deal"

Chapter Five
Waso

A quarter moon poked out from between the clouds every so often, just long enough for Waso to see where they were going. Stateira had taught him a trick, to look around when it was light then to close his eyes when it was dark. She said he could capture the light and hold it under his lids. He didn't think that was true, but her method did seem to help him get around without bumping into obstacles or stepping into the water.

Waso could easily pass for a local freeman, if he didn't speak. But anyone who saw Stateira would know she wasn't from Scandinavia, which could mean trouble if word of their escape reached someone they encountered.

They weren't planning to cross the lake to Birka, since the ferries they were looking for were kept on the mainland side, near the homes of the pilots. Stateira had a specific boat in mind, but the trick would be to get its sail and oars. Most of the ferry operators brought the loose equipment into their homes at night to prevent anything important from blowing away or falling into the lake.

The boat they were after was tied near the ferry Stateira had been on the day Hakon bought her. It was among the smallest of the boats kept in that tiny port. They went toward the waterfront first, to check out the boat where it was beached.

"This is the one?" Waso asked.

"No. The one next to it, with the mast."

Of course, it was. The sail they were planning to steal wouldn't be of much use without a mast and rigging. Three of the five boats had masts, but he had pointed at one that didn't. He felt stupid.

The boat was narrow enough for one person to row, with a hull that curved up at the bow and the stern and was as long as four men lying head to toe. A single rope tethered it to a tree about ten paces away from the water. The other boats were tied in a similar manner, all to the same tree. When they were ready to leave he would need to follow the rope, to be sure he was untying the right one.

He thought he heard a crack, like someone stepping on a stick, so he grabbed Stateira's arm and pulled her down beside the boat. They stayed crouched there, listening to more footsteps. Nestled together, trying to make themselves as small as possible, Waso could feel Stateira shaking slightly and breathing in tiny bursts, almost matching his own. He could smell her hair. It was like an aphrodisiac, causing him to turn his face toward her and to touch her ear with his nose. She didn't move nor make a sound. Was her silence from fear of discovery or fear of his intentions? *I won't touch you* was the promise he had made. He'd already broken it on a minor level and hoped she wasn't aware of how much he wanted to break it completely.

After he was sure the person they'd heard had passed, they stood slowly and moved apart. Stateira straightened her skirt, crossed her arms, then looked away from Waso, toward the homes. He noticed that her breathing was a little quieter and more even.

They spied on the area for three days before they learned where the pilot lived. They needed to know so they could be certain they would steal the correct sail.

The night was clear with a slight breeze, about as close to perfect as possible. It would be calm enough to row without much resistance, but windy enough to make some progress once they were in open water and raised the sail.

"You're sure the pilot came in on this boat?" Waso asked in a whisper.

"You saw him, too, didn't you?"

Waso shook his head.

"Oh." Stateira looked away then raised her chin and turned back. "He left this boat here and went to that house." She pointed to the furthest building in the cluster of homes.

"All right then. Let's get what we need."

The house was stone and turf with a log frame around the entrance, very much like Olaf's home. They found the oars on the ground beside the entrance – a stroke of luck. But the sail was nowhere to be seen, most likely kept in the pilot's home since rain soaked wool would be heavy and hard to handle.

"You get the oars," Stateira said. "I'll get the sail."

"Why should you take the risk?"

"Because you plod like a bull moose when you walk," she said through the corner of her mouth. A sly smile slipped her lip.

Waso felt his face flush. He opened his mouth as if to speak then thought better of it and looked toward the water. He took in a breath, exhaled then turned back in time to see her stepping into the pilot's house. Nothing he could do now but wait and hope.

He stood as still as he could, trying not to make even the slightest sound. The oars were still at his feet, but he wasn't about to pick them up while she was in the building. He pulled out his knife in case he had to rush in to defend her, but heard no indication of trouble. Stateira emerged from the house, as quiet as a butterfly landing on a flower. In her arms, she held a long pole wrapped in cloth.

It was time to head to Britannia.

Chapter Six
Stateira

Typically, the wind calmed when the sun was down, but that night it was strong enough to warrant hoisting the sail. Waso was in better condition than Stateira had imagined and could row well. But they would go faster under sail and although they were in open water now, they were still on the lake. He needed to save his energy for the long stretch of sheltered waterways they would have to pass through before they could reach the Baltic Sea.

"Help me unroll the sail so we can tie the yard to the ropes and raise it up the mast."

Waso seemed confused, so Stateira explained she was talking about the long pole the sail was rolled around.

"I'm not a sailor," he told her. "Yet, I've seen enough ships to know the pole will be used to keep the sail spread out when it's raised up the mast. But shouldn't we get further away before we stop to do that?"

"The sooner we get the sail up, the sooner we start to put distance between us and the man whose livelihood we just stole." She hoped her words hadn't sounded too forceful, but they did have to move quickly. Waso grabbed the half of the pole closest to him and helped her unravel the material.

When the sail was in place, Stateira pulled on a few ropes. The cloth billowed and the boat began to move.

"Take the steering oar, while I hold the sail," she told him, "We're moving."

"I came this way on the longship that brought me here," Waso told her, "but that was a long time ago. I'm not sure which way to steer."

"Right now, we need to put some distance between us and the man who owned this boat. After that, we need to go east. And after that, when we're in the narrows, we'll have to turn south." Stateira looked up. "But the stars aren't out to guide us, so we'll have to wait to see where the sun rises. We need to find a place to beach the boat."

"You think that's safe?"

"Nothing we're doing is safe." She started to scan the land. "We'll need water and food once we make it to the Baltic, so look for a place near a house. We might as well do some thieving while we're waiting."

Waso smiled, nervously. "Right again." They continued to sail.

The moon poked out after they had passed a couple of small islands, which seemed more like shadows than tree covered land masses. The area around the water was visible long enough for Stateira to see a huge building on the mainland, up a hill from the lake. She pointed it out to Waso who said he'd heard of similar buildings, but had never seen one.

"Olaf used to talk about how much he wanted a huge home and I'm certain this is what he had in mind. He talked about rich people a lot."

"Rich, you say?"

"Very rich. Olaf had silver, but not as much as he wanted."

"Head in that direction. The landowner is bound to have what we need."

"He'll own animals and wheat fields, but also many thralls. Some of them may be awake."

"Then we'll have to be quiet. But if we don't get supplies, we'll die while trying to make it back to Britannia."

They pulled their boat onto shore at a place where the land sloped down to water level and the shrubs had been cleared. There were three other boats pulled up and tied with ropes to nearby trees. They were all smaller than the one Stateira and Waso had stolen.

"Wait here," Waso said. "I'll see what I can find."

She watched him walk toward the house, his head down, watching his feet to avoid any twigs or dried leaves that might make noise. Stateira took advantage of his departure to relieve herself beside one of the boats. She'd been with Waso long enough for him to know most things about her, but she still tried to maintain a little dignity. She realized she'd have to hang over the side of the boat once they were in the Baltic and the idea worried her. She had trouble believing anything good could come from Waso watching her as if she was a farm animal.

Stateira stood up, straightened her shift, and looked at the enormous house, hoping to see Waso returning with his arms full of supplies. She had been thieving with Waso for some time now and had a general feel for how long the process should take, but this was an exceptionally large home built on terrain he didn't know well. It could take longer than she expected. She found a patch of grass beside the tree where the boats were tied and sat, keeping her head down in case someone might be looking when the moon peeked out from behind the clouds.

She was wearing the brown dress she'd had on when she arrived at Birka. Waso had stolen a set of men's clothing for her, which she wore when they were thieving to make it easier for her to sneak. This time she was dressed for sailing rather than crawling, but fortunately the color would hide well against the numerous trees and shrubs on the farm.

When light from the sun began to peek over the horizon, she knew something had gone wrong and she had to act. She looked in the boats, the ones that were pulled up on the beach beside the one they'd stolen. She found a small, cast-iron knife someone had left in one of the hulls.

She held it in her left hand and pulled the sleeve of her dress over it. She started to slowly walk around the property, sticking by a ring of trees where she could hide if necessary.

Stateira could see five buildings on the property, the long house, the latrine, and three other buildings, all of which appeared to be barns, smaller than the ones she'd known at Nendrum. It seemed odd that they were so tiny since the landowner was wealthy.

She wasn't sure where she should look, but knew she had to find Waso soon or it would be so light they would be caught before they could get back to their boat. She thought she'd start by the barns. The thralls would be getting up soon. There was a good chance that some of them slept with the animals, but even so the barns were a safer choice than the longhouse. The latrine was another possibility, but it was unlikely Waso would be there. She thought of Hakon's body in Olaf's latrine and cringed.

She was more than halfway up the hill when she saw two people walking down toward the lake, carrying things in their arms. Stateira moved back into the woods and hid behind an ash tree until they were close enough for her to identify Waso. The other person was a young woman with a round face, exaggerated by high cheekbones. She wore a light brown shift with a dark brown dress over it and a white headscarf, not the full kind that Stateira used to wear, just a kerchief, covering her dark hair.

When they were closer, Stateira realized that the woman looked familiar, but she couldn't place where she'd seen her previously. Then it came to her. She was Wulfgyfe. The woman had lived near Nendrum, someone Stateira had barely known. The poor girl was a slave now, which means she must have been taken in one of the raids. Was Waso bringing her back with them? If so, this would make the voyage to Britannia much more difficult.

Stateira followed and watched them from a distance. When Waso reached their boat, he stood tall and looked around. Clearly, he was looking for Stateira, so she came out into the open and approached them.

"What's going on?" she asked.

"This is Wulfgyfe. She was on the boat from Nendrum with me."

"I remember you," the woman said. Her tone didn't sound friendly.

"I remember you as well. Are you coming with us?" She hoped her opinion didn't show.

"No. I'm happy here."

"But you're a slave?"

"People called me free back there, but I was every bit as much a slave as I am here. And here I have a good master. You wouldn't understand. You had the Abbot in Nendrum."

"It wasn't like that. He had me. I had nothing."

The corners of Wulfgyfe's mouth rose in a tight smile. "Yet you want to go back?"

Stateira thought she heard something behind her. She spun to see five ducks splashing about on the lake's surface, diving down in search of their breakfast. Morning was near. They had to get going. She turned again to face Wulfgyfe. "I hope someday to make it home to Persia. But for now, I'm going with Waso."

"I'm certain he appreciates the company." Stateira could tell Wulfgyfe wanted to add "like the Abbot did" to her words, but she didn't. Instead, Wulfgyfe put the supplies into the boat and turned to Waso. "It was good seeing you again," she told him. "May God be with you."

Waso put the supplies in the boat next to what Wulfgyfe had carried, so only Stateira watched as the young woman walked back up the hill.

"You weren't in danger?" she asked Waso.

"Wulfgyfe saw me before anyone else and kept me hidden while she collected what we need. We were lucky."

"I hope that luck holds," she replied.

They pushed the boat halfway into the lake, then Stateira got in before Waso made the final push and hopped in. She looked up at the sky as Waso raised the sail. Now it was clear which way was east and they were blessed with a steady, gentle wind. Also, they had plenty of food and water, if they didn't run into any unexpected delays. But as she sat back in the hull of the small boat and tried to count their blessings, Stateira couldn't help but wonder about one unexplained part of the stop at the rich Viking's farm. Since Waso had a friend helping him gather what they needed, why had it taken him so much time to get back?

Chapter Seven
Olaf

Birka was built on rocky land that stuck up out of Lake Malaren like most of the other islands. As Olaf approached the pier on a ferry, the buildings at the center of the marketplace impressed him again. They always did. There were over twenty structures, more than any other village he had seen in his lifetime. And in front of the structures there were countless places where people were displaying their wares.

In the past, Olaf had always gone straight for whatever booth or booths had the items he needed. This time the purpose of his trip was different. The best chance for Waso to make it back to Britannia would be to sign on with a Viking raid. Waso could do that in Birka, but it was rare for the raiders to accept women outside their clan. He needed to dump the Persian woman in a way that was to his advantage.

Olaf tried to think of what he would do if he was Waso and had decided the best plan would be to convince Stateira to come along with him. Then once they were in Birka, he would sell her. Given her foreign appearance it would be easy for Waso to pull that off and, if he did, he'd have his passage and money to help him when he arrived back in his homeland. *A good plan, if Waso was cunning enough to pull it off.*

The boat landed at a thin pier made of boards supported by wooden pilings. Olaf climbed out along with the other two passengers. He hadn't spoken to either of them or to the ferry operator during the entire ride, although he'd eavesdropped on their conversation. It seems the two passengers were brothers who had known the operator for their entire lives. They were coopers. Most of the barrels they made were already at their stall, although they'd brought along a couple to replace ones they'd sold the day before. One of those barrels didn't make it out of the ferry because they traded it for passage to and from Birka. Olaf felt they were cheating the ferry operator, but he wasn't about to get involved.

Olaf had brought his cart and the quern stone back with him. His first stops were to find buyers for both items, because he needed silver to complete his plan. Losing his new quern stone was another crime against him he'd have to take out of Waso's hide.

The marketplace smelled of grilled lamb because there was a place to buy salted meat. There was also another stall that sold salt, for the farmers who cured their own. The salt was in wooden bowls as were the onions, leeks, and radishes for sale at another stall in the same aisle. Olaf passed all the tables and turned a corner. On this aisle were baskets, cast-iron pots, axes, and shields, as well as quern stones.

"Anyone organizing a raid?" Olaf asked the Viking who had sold Olaf his stone when he was last in Birka and bought it back now, for half the price. Olaf chose to ask this merchant with hopes that he'd be recognized and would get an honest answer.

"They're down by the waterfront. Look for the large pier, south of the ones the small ferries use."

Olaf thanked the vendor then headed back toward the lake, trailing his empty cart behind. He located a man who was organizing a raid and told him his story.

"Two runaways, you say?" The man had thinning dark blonde hair with a thick beard that matched the hair on the backs of his hands. He was built like Olaf, only taller, and had a hard smile that had made Olaf think twice before speaking to him.

"The girl is unusual and easy to recognize. She's Persian, dark skin, dark eyes, and dark hair, almost black. But if the other runaway decided to split from the girl he could be alone. He's taller than me and thinner, but muscular. He's got light brown hair and narrow shoulders."

"'I'm afraid I can't help you. I haven't seen the girl and none of the men who are joining my raid have come alone."

Olaf paused before asking, "None?"

The man turned toward his boat and started to retie one of the ropes holding it to the pier, pulling the line tighter. He spoke while facing away from Olaf, who had to lean in to hear. The day was windy enough to cause a constant stream of noisy waves to break against the pilings. "A raiding voyage can last half a year and the fighting can be brutal. Most men want someone they can trust with them. But I break them of that. It won't be long before they learn I'm the one they need to trust."

"Anyone else I can talk to here?"

"What for?"

"Maybe somebody else signed a man who fits Waso's description. Or maybe someone saw the girl."

"Does the girl look good?"

"She's beautiful." Olaf regretted his answer as soon as the words came out. He felt like walking away, but stayed because he didn't have other leads.

The man turned back to Olaf, grinning now. "I'd have noticed if a pretty one was anywhere near this pier. I've got a sense about that. And as for the man, I don't sign runaways and don't know anyone who would. Most aren't worth the trouble, since they generally try to escape while the rest of us are fighting."

"He stole the clothes, so how would you know what he is?"

"I can pick out someone raised in Britannia from halfway across the lake. But I'll tell you who you need to talk to."

"Who?"

"The ferry operators. They can give you the name of one of their own who just had his boat stolen. Most runaways are thieves and if I was trying to escape I'd sail on my own before I signed onto a raid."

Olaf thanked the man, then stepped off the pier onto solid ground and grabbed his cart. Olaf started back toward the docks where the ferries landed, but changed his mind when he realized the operator who'd had his boat stolen probably did not live on the island. Each day the first ferry would travel to Birka and the last to the mainland, so a mainland house was more practical. Olaf wasn't about to leave Birka until he had explored every lead he could think of. He headed back to the market stalls, still trailing his cart.

He wanted to talk to the pig vendors because he knew Waso had been raised on a hog farm. The runaway might have used his experience to earn some silver from one of them. Olaf wove his way around the tables until he came to a stall where pork and salted ham were sold. This wasn't the live pigs he'd been looking for, but it would do. Waso knew how to butcher and he might have worked here. He stepped toward the table to speak with the vendor, but a man wearing a Mjölnir pendant was blocking his way while waiting for service.

Olaf was familiar with the Mjölnir pendant, because his father had worn one just like it. It was supposed to protect the wearer. Obviously, that hadn't worked for his father, but it was still powerful. The people of Britannia had a new religion with buildings used for men whose only jobs were to pray. It was said their god was a strong god, but He had failed to protect the people of Nendrum. Olaf wondered which god would win in battle. He didn't know the answer, but he knew together they would be a force beyond compare.

The pendant was patterned after Thor's hammer, hung upside down from around the man's neck. He studied it carefully. The widest place represented the hammer head, while the handle was short and narrow and the pommel spread out again, to about half the size of the head. The medallion was silver with a red jewel in the middle and relief swirls rising from the metal to surround the precious stone.

The sound of a gruff voice snapped Olaf out of his thoughts. "What are you looking at?" Olaf looked up to see the man staring back at him.

Olaf took a step back, but held his head up. "Your medallion is the same as one my father used to wear," he explained. "He wore it in his funeral fire and we buried it with his ashes. Now I'd like it back. Would you sell yours?"

"How much?" the man asked slowly, cocking his head to his left as he spoke.

"Two English coins, silver."

"Ha!" the man shook his head and shrugged. "There's more silver in this Mjölnir than in two coins."

"I'll let you have my cart."

"Along with the coins?"

"All right."

"Done."

As Olaf walked from the stall he thought how the freed thrall taking care of his farm had said that Waso was angry with the god of the religion in Britannia, because his sister had been unjustly punished by one of their priests. That god was already on his side and with this pendant, Olaf would have them both.

The man paid for the meat he wanted with one of Olaf's coins and pocketed the other. He glanced at Olaf as he pulled the empty cart past him, grinning. Olaf turned to the vendor and asked about Waso.

"I haven't seen anyone fitting that description, with or without the dark-skinned thrall."

"Any other hog farmers in market today?"

"None that I know of."

As Olaf walked on, he tried to think of another person he might ask about the runaways. He decided to head to the slave market. His luck seemed to turn when he saw that the man he'd bought Waso from was in the stall, hawking a couple of females who looked to be in their late teens.

"It was a long time ago," the salesman told him. "I remember the name, but I wouldn't be able to say if I've seen him around here. And the only Persians I've seen in the last half a year have been men."

"You're certain?"

"I know the difference between a man and a woman."

"Of course."

"Now this is a fine female here." He grabbed one of his slaves by her wrist and pulled her toward Olaf. "She'd make a nice wife, strong enough for farm chores and look at her hips, perfect for bearing sons. She could keep you warm at night and replace Waso during the day."

"No thanks."

"You're wasting your time," he told Olaf. "It's too big a world to find one lost slave. You should buy this one and get back to your farm."

"I have reason to believe I'll find him," Olaf said, fingering the medallion as he spoke. "And when I do I'll teach him that no one runs from me."

He wandered around the market for a brief time more, but didn't stop at any other stalls. The vendors seemed to have their own concerns and after asking a few customers if they'd seen either Waso or Stateira, he determined that his questions would be unlikely to lead to any useful answers.

It was time to find the ferry boat operator. He walked back to the small pier and looked for someone to talk to, as the raider had suggested. The first man Olaf spoke with knew the operator whose boat had been stolen. He told Olaf the man's name was Maarav and lived, as Olaf had suspected, by the shore on the mainland side.

Olaf paid to ride across the water. When they reached the shore, the pilot pointed toward Maarav's home. It was smaller than Olaf's house, with a latrine to the side, but no barn. The family might have a milk goat living in the house, but they couldn't have many animals.

The house was built in a wooded area, close to their neighbors. There were thick sticks scattered about the land, branches that had fallen from the surrounding trees. A path had been cleared to the building.

"If you're trying to get to Birka, you've come to the wrong place," Maarav said when he opened the door. "I'm out of business." He was a stocky man with a large head and a crooked nose. He looked strong, but not as muscular as Olaf.

"I'm looking for a couple of runaway thralls," Olaf said. "I was hoping you could help."

"Everything I have in this world has been stolen from me. I'm in no position to help anyone."

"That robbery is what I want to know about. I believe my thrall might have stolen your boat."

"What are you telling me?"

"He is trying to get back to Britannia with another slave, a Persian woman."

Maarav lunged at Olaf, who screamed, "Aaagh!" and fell backwards. The ferry operator reached for a branch and swung at Olaf's head. He missed when Olaf rolled. The

Viking sheep farmer had no idea why this man had attacked him, but he was ready now.

Olaf grabbed a large branch. This weapon was thick enough to do real damage. He jumped to his feet. "Think of yourself as a man, do you? That little stick of yours wouldn't impress your sister." He started to circle Maarav. He was laughing, taunting, and speaking in a soft, mocking tone, "Come at me again, why don't you?"

Maarav dropped his stick, stepped behind a tree and picked up another, this one as big as the branch Olaf wielded.

Olaf cursed himself for not attacking quicker. He assumed a fighting stance and glared. He was alert, his muscles ready to spring, while Maarav was showing weakness. The ferry operator's head jerked back. His eyes grew wide.

"You're nothing. You know that, boatman?" Olaf taunted, shifting his stare between his opponent's eyes and weapon. "I can beat you."

"You stole everything!"

"What are you saying? You don't even know me."

Olaf could hear a quaver in Maarav's voice. The man wasn't a trained fighter. He watched as Maarav's weapon dropped ever so slightly then he swung his branch down at the man's head. But the ferry operator moved and blocked Olaf's stick with his own.

"Tell me what I stole," Olaf said. As he spoke, he pulled back then swung up. Maarav blocked his move down low. Maarav swung his weapon at Olaf's head, who stepped forward while raising his stick. The two staffs crossed in the center with a loud thud. Olaf dodged to the side while he thrust the end of his stick at Maarav's chest. Maarav fell back, landing on his wide posterior. Olaf stepped on his staff, ready to strike the man's face.

"What was that about?" Olaf asked, looking down at Maarav. The beaten man's chest heaving, his breath blowing the strands of hair out of his face.

"You own the thrall that stole my boat."

"What does that have to do with anything?" Olaf stepped back and allowed the man to sit. "Stay there for a moment, then explain yourself."

"You owe me retributions," the man answered, still breathing hard. "You owe me a new boat. You couldn't control your slave well enough to keep him at your home. This is your fault."

"Once Waso ran, he became an outlaw. I'm not responsible for anything an outlaw does and you know it."

The man clenched his fists, but looked away from Olaf, down at the ground. "I can't make a living. I can't even afford food for my wife and my son."

"There's a way around this," Olaf continued. "I'll buy a boat and it will be yours after you do something for me."

"Do what?"

"Sail with me to Britannia and help me find Waso. When we bring him back you can keep the boat."

"I would have to leave my family? How would they survive?"

"You're not helping them without a boat. This gives them a chance. But if you return alone, you will all die. I'll arrange for that. I don't want you deciding halfway to Britannia that it would be to your advantage to put a knife in my heart while I'm sleeping."

There were more lies than one in what Olaf had promised. First, there was no person he could trust enough to kill for him, especially to kill the family of a freeman. Secondly, he was running low on silver. He did not have enough to buy the boat outright. So, he would find a boat owner who needed money, but instead of paying him its value, he would offer enough for the use of it for a month or two. By the time the owner wanted the boat back, they'd be long gone. Olaf would be a thief, an outlaw like Waso, but this was the only way to get to Britannia.

What difference does any of this make, Olaf thought, *as long as Maarav doesn't know.*

***

Waso

It took four days to reach the narrows, longer than Stateira had predicted but at least they were on their way.

"I can read directions from the stars and the sun," she told Waso. "The problem is that *travel east* is all I have to go by and this lake is huge."

They turned into coves, traveled around islands, and were blocked by a few peninsulas before they finally reached a place Stateira recognized and could turn south. They could now see land on both sides and were able to follow the shores.

"We will face a couple of branches in the waterways," she told him. "When we have to make a choice, I'll pick the passage that points in a direction closest to the east. Eventually we will reach the Baltic Sea."

"How do you know these things?"

"I'm tracing the way I was brought to Birka – backwards."

"Amazing!" Waso's breath caught in his throat as he considered the power of her memory. He'd been brought along the same route as she had and all he could remember was his own anger and fear.

The wind was gentle, but constant. They didn't have to tack. Since Waso could handle the steering oar and the sail at the same time, he offered Stateira a chance to sleep. The only rest either of them had taken was short moments when there was no wind. She took him up on his offer and said, "It will be your turn next."

Stateira moved to the bow of the boat. She emptied supplies out of one of the longhouse baskets then positioned it between two cross beams to keep the wood from digging into her body so severely. When she'd finished her makeshift mattress, she lay down on her back. It only took a moment for her breath to slow to an easy, regular rhythm that matched the sound of the waves against the side of the boat.

Waso watched her and thought of how this serene moment compared with the horrors forced upon her during so much of her life. Their time together had not been easy, but he had tried to treat her as well as he could. *Perhaps there may be a time when Stateira and I might share a life filled with the joy of normal experiences,* he thought.

As if in answer, Stateira squirmed in her sleep, turning her face starboard. Her legs separated and her shift slipped up, exposing her ankles and calves as well as her right knee and part of her thigh. Waso trembled a bit and tried to look toward the shore, but the draw of Stateira's naked legs pulled his gaze back. Since the day he had killed Hakon, she'd shared his world, like grass and stones, but this was different. In her sleep she didn't turn away from his gaze, the way they both did when they needed to relieve themselves over the edge of the boat. Her vulnerability made the moment illicit, immoral, and impossible to resist. He wanted to leave the steering oar and go toward her. He wanted to touch her, to place his own body against hers, to tell her he loved her. But there was that horrible promise.

Stateira moved again, twisting her face back toward the sky. He stared, but Abigail's damaged face was where Stateira's should have been. *How could that be?* He shook his head, gazed at the clouds, then back at the woman before him and things were right again. Her skin was dark, her hair black, and her face had the perfect Persian features that had been etched in his mind since he had first met her at Nendrum.

My mind is playing tricks, Waso told himself. *I am too tired.* But he knew there was more to what he'd just seen than simple exhaustion. He needed to find his sister and his brother or thoughts of them would always consume his life.

***

Stateira and Waso kept heading south once they made it to the Baltic Sea, although Stateira said they would eventually have to go west and north again. The plan was to follow the southern edge of Scandinavia until they reached the North Sea.

Stateira grew hungry shortly after they left the inland waterway. Around the same time the wind calmed, an event Waso took as a sign. He released the sail. "This is good. I'm as hungry as a bear on the last day of winter."

"Most of our food would suit a bear." She pulled a small blanket out of one of the baskets and unwrapped a couple of cod fillets, smoked and salted. "Wrap your paws around this." She smiled slightly then handed one to him and kept the other for herself. They both started to eat.

Waso was tired of cod, but was glad to have anything to fill his belly. This saltwater fish was a common food, but one that surprised him since they had taken it from the lake house. The landowner must have traded for it, probably to provide food for his thralls during the next winter. Waso hoped Wulfgyfe would not be discovered, since taking from winter supplies was a serious offense.

Waso swallowed a couple of bites of fish then looked at Stateira. "How do you know how to guide us to Britannia?"

"I read the stars at night and the sun during the day."

Waso looked in Stateira's eyes and tilted his head slightly. "I know that, but who taught you?"

She stared back at him then up at the sky as if she was thinking of how to start. "My father was a wealthy textile merchant who loved to sail and shared his love with my two brothers. I was jealous, so I whined and complained until he gave in and offered me a lesson as well. I was a natural sailor, better than either of his sons. We kept it up and we both began to enjoy our time on the Caspian."

Waso reached for one of the oars, which he used to turn the boat slightly. When he settled down, Stateira continued. "In addition to a certain skill with a sail, I had a thirst for knowledge about the sea. I went through my father's collection of maps, planning imaginary voyages. I never shared my fantasies with him or anyone else, but he did catch me looking at drawings of the world's oceans. He must have had some idea of what I was thinking.

"One night, when I was asleep in my room, some men came to our home and took me from my family." Waso's eyes opened wide as she continued. "I was locked in the home of a man named Omar, a man who told me that my father had sold me to pay off a debt and that I now belonged to him. He said silk had become more popular than cotton, which I already knew. But then he told me my father had lost his fortune and had borrowed to keep up a life he couldn't afford."

Waso flinched. "Your father sold you?" he blurted out.

"That's what Omar said, but I don't believe him. My father was an honest man who always treated me fairly. He would never have put me in a such a position."

"And Omar? Was he honest?"

"It's hard to say. I could have been with a worse man. Omar never hurt me, but I was his slave and knew what I had to do. There was a child, a girl who was born dead. Omar never seemed to blame me for that, but soon after I was sold to the Abbot and sent off to Britannia."

They paused for a moment and stared at each other. Waso noticed her eyes had grown wet. She was a strong woman, but the death of a child was as hard as life gets. When they finished eating, she pulled the rope in so the sail swelled with wind and the boat moved forward. Waso returned to the steering oar.

"Now tell me something about the life you led," Stateira said when they were moving again. "What were you like, when you were a child. Were you happy? Did you get along with your brother and sister?"

Waso looked away from Stateira, at his own feet. He took a breath before speaking then said, "I did not think much about happiness when I was young. I do now, because of you, of what you taught me about keeping on after living through hard times. But back then I thought I knew what had to be done and I tried to do it. I was more worried about pleasing my father than what Goda and Abigail felt. I let them down and when I find them, that's what I intend to say."

Chapter Eight
Olaf

The wind was calm during Olaf's second night on the Baltic sea. The gentle rocking of the boat should have eased him into hours of much needed sleep, but Maarav was cracking his knuckles. It wasn't the sound that kept Olaf awake, since the open air seemed to swallow most of the noise. It was that he couldn't stop thinking about the reason behind Maarav's nervous twitching. There was anger in the way his fingers seemed to move involuntarily and if Olaf slept, there would be an opportunity for Maarav to act on his anger.

Olaf knew that a strong offense could protect as well or better than an alert defense. So, he watched Maarav first to protect himself and second to learn how to navigate the boat. If Olaf acted before he was ready, he would sail in circles until he died.

The boat was small and shallow, plenty of room for two men, although with no seats they were sitting or lying on the wooden hull. They had brought a pail, a cup, and rags they used for bailing. They couldn't get all the water, so they were always squatting in puddles, which irritated Olaf. He focused his irritation on thoughts about Waso's betrayal, increasing his determination to make his thrall pay for his crimes, no matter how long Olaf had to live side by side with the fool, Maarav.

That night passed slowly, painfully so, the way time had when Olaf used to wait for a lambing ewe. He couldn't close his eyes or something might happen. But as he watched he could hear his own heart and it seemed as if there were days between each beat.

When the sun finally rose, Olaf was exhausted. However, his weariness didn't last long. Maarav pointed toward the south at a dark cloud approaching quickly. His adrenaline kicked in. Sudden storms are common on the Baltic, so this one wasn't a surprise, but there is a world of difference between expecting harsh weather and encountering it. Maarav shouted "Help me here," as he started to lower the sail. Olaf jumped, rocking the boat more than he should have, yet not enough to take in water.

Maarav had the sail down less than a third when the wind picked up. The cloth billowed. The boat lifted then started to skim across the water, speeding toward the northeast, away from where they wanted to go. A hard rain began to fall moments after the wind picked up. Olaf could barely see to help Maarav, who was trying to loosen the sail without losing it into the sea.

Olaf released another rope, but that was the wrong thing to do. It broke free of the sail, forcing him to let it slip from his hands. This left the rope Maarav was holding as the only tie keeping the sail and their shared future from disappearing into the turbulent water. Olaf jumped behind Maarav and helped him hold on. They worked together, managing to pull the cloth back on board but snapping the yard in the process.

The boat began to spin. Maarav crawled to the back to use the steering oar to stabilize it. They kept turning, but at a slower speed. Meanwhile, Olaf used the bailing pail to keep the boat from sinking low enough to capsize until, finally, the wind and rain diminished and a patch of blue sky poked through.

Overall, they'd done all right. They were still alive, afloat and in possession of an untorn sail. They rowed toward shore to find a place of safety away from the open sea.

"We'll need to find a replacement for the yard," Maarav told Olaf, "and we'll need to splice the rope. Or make more, if we can find a source. We lost the length you untied. But we have to hurry. We can't face another storm without the proper equipment."

Olaf nodded, but didn't apologize. He'd done the best he could. He realized it was good he hadn't killed Maarav before the storm. Still, it was a worry, since he'd given the ferry operator another reason to hate him.

There was an incline at the shore for as far along the coast as they could see. Maarav found a place where it didn't seem too steep to manage, but the grade would still make it impossible to beach the heavy boat. He instructed Olaf to row near the shore then he tossed the iron anchor overboard and tied its chain to the stern.

Maarav told Olaf to point the bow toward land then he stepped out of the rocking vessel and scrambled onto the rocky shore. "Toss me a rope," he shouted.

Olaf found a length tied near the bow. He threw the free end to Maarav who scrambled up the incline until he reached a tree. Once the rope was secured, the boat was held where the waves couldn't toss it against the stones, more than a full length away from the shore.

"We need tools," Maarav told him. "Can you toss an axe to shore? Without landing it in the water?"

Of course, I can, Olaf thought. *I am a farmer, which means I'm a lot stronger than any ferry operator.* After the axe, Olaf tossed two knives where Maarav could retrieve them. Then he rolled the broken yard up in the sail and tossed it into the water beside the boat. He shoved the floating sail toward shore, so Maarav could grab it and drag it onto land.

Now Olaf needed to step out, but the boat wasn't as close to shore as it had been when Maarav got out. It was still shallow enough to walk, but Olaf got soaked up to his waist. *Things could be worse.*

The hill at the edge of the sea was covered in grass and rocks. After Olaf scrambled to the top, he sat beside Maarav and looked around. There were a few trees, like the one Maarav had used to tie the boat, but they were all twisted from the sea wind. The closest thick forest seemed to be a distance inland. This wasn't good, since they needed to replace the yard and that meant finding a straight tree, neither too thick nor too thin. He looked down at the carefully anchored boat, the broken yard with the roll of sail around it, and the pile of tools near the water's edge. Olaf was exhausted and certain that Maarav was the same, but every moment they rested hurt the chance he'd ever catch Waso.

Olaf stood. "What's next?"

"You hike to the forest to find a replacement for the yard."

"Me? Alone?" He wondered if Maarav might be thinking of abandoning him on this isolated shore.

"I've got to make rope."

"I can spin a rope."

"Can you?"

"That's right. Wool or oak fiber. You name it."

"How about grass?"

"Is that the plan?"

"It's what we've got. And plenty of it." Olaf shook his head, so Maarav added, "It will be strong enough if it's made right. Have you ever woven a grass rope?"

Olaf shook his head again. "It's about the only type I haven't made. Never saw the point since grass rope doesn't last long, especially in wet places, like on a boat."

"It will last long enough to get to Britannia. Once we're there, we can replace it for the voyage home. For now, we take what we've got and make the best of it."

Olaf scratched his head then, without thinking, tried to run his fingers through his knotted hair. He had to pull his hand out of the tangled blond mass and move it back to his side.

"You need to go for the yard," Maarav said. "The rope has to be tight and strong and I'm the one with experience braiding grass."

Olaf thought the process couldn't be so different from any other type of rope, but he gave in. It didn't make a difference who did what if the repairs to the boat were made and they could get under way again.

He carried the two jagged pieces of the old yard, to be certain he could find a straight tree of the proper size. The halves were pointed staffs which could work as weapons, but he also carried his axe. Although he hadn't seen any signs of people in that area, it didn't hurt to be careful. Besides, he needed the axe to cut the tree.

As Olaf hiked toward the woods, he thought about Stateira, the Persian slave girl. Before Olaf discovered Waso had the initiative to kill and run, he couldn't have imagined his thrall satisfying a woman, even a fellow slave. The man had appeared too weak to provide a firm hand, seeming more at home with such tasks as cradling a newborn lamb. But now Olaf's image of his thrall was of a dominant and violent man. Because of this and the knowledge that Stateira had been a bed slave, Olaf could not shake the image of the two slaves wrapped around each other like wild dogs – a mental picture which both excited and repulsed him. Olaf felt his stomach tighten and realized he was jealous of his own slave.

He was about halfway to the forest when the tightness spread through his chest to his neck and shoulders. He picked up his pace and tried to shake the feeling, but it wouldn't leave. This was more than jealousy. This feeling came from the realization that Waso might raise his situation, that his former thrall could get to Britannia and build a new life. He might even have land someday, if he knew someone who would help him. And, since Olaf had given up so much to pursue the two runaways, the Persian girl might not want to leave. She might see Olaf as a step down.

"I will make her see that she doesn't have a choice," Olaf said out loud, as he imagined her sitting on the ground, watching as he swung his axe into Waso's chest. "She'll come home with me and be what I want her to be."

When Olaf reached the forest, he studied the trees. He was after a straight trunk, longer than his height with his arms raised and about as wide in diameter as his fist. He thought the birch trees would be his best option, thin and mostly straight. But the ones he saw were either too thick or crooked in critical places. He studied the area again, this time considering other types, and found a young poplar that would work. He took his axe to it, felling the little tree in five strikes.

Once the tree was down he measured by placing the pieces of the old yard against the trunk and cut it to length. Then he removed the branches, stood up and looked at the perfect replacement. Now he just had to bring it back to the boat and tie it in place.

Thoughts of Waso and Stateira had occupied Olaf's mind since he had started his search, but that changed as he began the hike back to the boat. His small worries about Maarav grew into a full storm by the time he'd walked a few hundred steps.

"What if he didn't need this yard?" Olaf asked himself. "What if he just wanted me out of his way long enough for him to repair the sail and steal the boat. He could head back to his home and say I died in the storm. Who would know the difference?"

Like most of the unmarried farmers in Scandinavia, Olaf was a loner. Since there had been no one on the farm to speak with from the time his father was killed until the day he brought Waso home from Birka, Olaf had learned to speak with the gods and goddesses whose names he had learned as a young child. But he was no longer a sheep farmer, appealing to Freyja for the health of his flock. His needs were more confusing than they had ever been before. Waso had run out on him, so did he appeal to Vali, the god of revenge? Or should he try to reach out to Forseti, the goddess of justice, peace, and truth? Back on the farm, Olaf could often feel the spirit of his own father, but the man's presence had not followed him on this quest.

Olaf felt a sharp sting on his leg. He dropped the yard and his axe then brushed off the offending insect. But as soon as he'd knocked off one hornet, a second was stinging his arm and another was on his neck. He brushed those off and ran a few steps. Then he turned around to see over twenty buzzing by where he'd just been standing. Clearly, he'd stepped on a nest.

He needed the yard and certainly didn't want to lose his axe. So, although he hated returning to the place where the angry hornets were still circling, he had no choice. He crept back slowly, hoping they wouldn't notice. They did. In the process of retrieving the yard, he received more stings, at least five, but managed to pull the long pole away. Things would be all right if he could also get his axe. He left the yard where it lay and went for his weapon. His effort succeeded, but caused the hornets to attack again and left Olaf with a few more wounds.

When he was far enough from the nest, he set down what he was carrying and tended to the stings. He dug some dirt with his fingers, then spit in it to make a paste. He rubbed the mud on the stings on his face and neck. Then he took off his tunic and dropped his trousers, so he could tend to the wounds on his arms and legs. When he was dressed again, he picked up his axe and the yard then continued the walk back to the woods.

The hornet stings hurt and were getting worse with each step. He'd been stung enough over the years to know the pain would turn to an intense itch in a few days, but after that he'd heal. If he'd broken a bone or had suffered a serious cut, he'd have a real problem. He knew he should be grateful, but he couldn't help cursing his luck. The field he was crossing was open and wider than a river. Why had he chosen a path that led over a hornet's nest?

He tried to pick up the pace as he got closer to the place where he'd left Maarav, but his feet felt so heavy. His stomach was turning and he was thirsty. He felt stupid he hadn't brought fresh water with him, but the hike hadn't looked long, not until he was on his way. The back of his neck was tight. He needed to rub it, but his hands were filled. He transferred the axe to his right hand, where he also carried the yard, and used his left to massage his neck. He stopped to do this, then shook his head and started walking again, breathing even heavier now.

"What took so long?" Maarav asked as Olaf entered the camp. He was standing near the length of grass rope he'd woven, scowling. "I could have made it to the forest and back three times. Truth be told, my three-year-old boy could have cut that yard and had it back here faster than you," Maarav stepped toward Olaf. "Let me see what you've got. The wood looks the right size. I just hope you picked a strong one. We can't wait here forever."

Olaf hated this man. He hated his superior attitude. It wasn't as if Olaf didn't know his way around the sea just because he'd spent his life on a farm. He was still a Viking. Boats were in his blood. And how dare Maarav criticize. Olaf had been working on his farm since he was four, while all Maarav did for a living was row a boat to Birka and back each day. Now there was something a three-year-old boy could do.

"Follow me to the boat," Maarav told Olaf. "We need to tie the yard in place and get back on the water. At this rate, I'll never see my family again."

Maarav started to walk toward the water, but Olaf didn't follow. After a few steps, the ferry operator stopped and turned. Olaf could see the man's irritation in his narrow eyes. All Maarav's talk of his family scared Olaf. If Maarav wanted to get home that much, he'd take action sooner or later. Olaf had to make a choice and he had to do it quickly. He was tense and irritated from being on land when he should have been on the sea chasing Waso and from the stings that were still fresh and from his distrust of Maarav. This couldn't go on.

Olaf grew angry as he thought again about Maarav's family - his boy. "My father had a son," he said quietly then he shouted, "And no one cared!" He dropped the yard, grabbed his axe with both hands, and swung it at Maarav, splitting the man's chest open and killing him instantly.

Chapter Nine
Stateira

There was a steady breeze from the southeast and a clear sky, mostly perfect for sailing, except for a few storm clouds toward the northwest. Since the wind was blowing in the opposite direction the storm presented little threat. The weather reminded Stateira of the days from her childhood, when her father used to wake her with an offer to get out on the Caspian. She was feeling rich, contented, and privileged, even though she was a runaway slave risking her life for a man whose situation was as bad as her own.

Stateira stood to see if the distant clouds were moving. Since Waso had control of both the sail and the steering oar, she could stretch and move around the tiny boat. The gentle rocking of the boat caused her to feel safe, like a baby resting in a cradle. She looked back at Waso, who smiled, revealing a contentment he hadn't shown previously.

The boat rocked, stopped with a jolt and twisted toward the right causing Stateira's feet to shoot out from underneath her. When she landed the side of her forehead smashed against the gunwale, opening a wide, bleeding wound in her head.

"What...?" Waso shouted.

Stateira scrambled to her knees, looking back at Waso as he released the sail and pulled to no avail at the steering oar. She turned toward the bow and saw the problem.

"You're stuck on a tree trunk. It's floating just below the surface." She crawled forward where she found a branch had punctured the hull. She didn't know why they hadn't noticed the limb sticking up like a heron's neck. Maybe the trunk rolled? "We need to rock the boat free."

"You're bleeding!"

Stateira reached to her forehead and brought back a blood-soaked hand. "Never mind that. Rock the boat!" They freed the boat from the log and Waso managed to push away using one of the oars. Stateira tried to stand, but couldn't. "We're taking in water."

"You look like you hurt your leg, too," Waso said.

She wished he hadn't noticed. He didn't need to be worrying about her. "I'll be all right, but I'm not sure about the boat. We have to land. I'll bail while you work the steering oar and hold the sail. The most serious damage appears to be above the waterline, so we want to keep the bow up as much as possible and avoid waves." She realized how impossible that sounded, so she added, "We're lucky the ocean's calm."

"You've got to stop the bleeding on your head before we do anything else. Hold your sleeve against the wound."

"I can't. Not now. We need to sail before we take on more water than I can bail!"

She grabbed a wooden bowl and used it to get as much water out of the boat as she could. It was small enough to hold with one hand, so she used her other hand to keep pressure on her wound while she worked. But a few waves tossed the boat and taught her that she had to hold on to the boat side for balance or she'd hurt herself more.

They had been following the coast, which meant they could see land. But Stateira knew the shore could be a greater distance than it appeared. It would have been hopeless if they'd been out in the open sea, but they probably would not have hit a waterlogged tree trunk if they'd been out there. She kept bailing.

They were lucky in another way; the wind was blowing toward land. Waso turned to the closest shore and let the sail carry them. In a short time, they were moving fast enough to lift the bow. Stateira put down the bowl and rested. She tried to rip some cloth from her tunic, but she was too weak. She used her sleeve, as Waso had suggested, tilting her head down and lifting her arm to apply pressure as well as she could. It didn't help that the cloth was wet. When her arm grew tired, she shifted her body to lie on her back.

***

Waso

The shore was a sandy beach, backed by tall grasses with small, scrawny evergreen trees. The trees were isolated at first but merged into a forest further from the sea. Waso hopped out as soon as they were close enough to stand, then he pulled the boat onto the beach far enough to be certain it wouldn't drift away. The bottom was filled with water, up to Waso's ankles. Stateira, who was lying on the floor, was soaked. She opened her eyes when he put his face next to hers, but she didn't speak.

He examined her wound, which had stopped bleeding, due to the pressure she'd kept on it. Waso carried her out of the boat and on to the beach. Stateira mumbled a thank you, but seemed too exhausted to say anything else. He needed to clean her cut, which meant he needed clean water. He went back to the boat to get the bowl she'd been using to bail before she grew too weak. He filled it with salt water and brought it to her, along with some of the smoked cod. The bleeding started again after he rubbed her with the salt water, but he could stop it with a slight bit of pressure.

Waso had to lift Stateira to feed her. He managed to get some of the fish in her system, although it appeared she wanted to sleep more than she wanted to eat. He left her resting while he went back to the boat for one of the kegs of fresh water. He woke her long enough for her to drink a half a cup.

To have any hope of healing her, Waso had to provide water, food, and sleep. He'd accomplished all that, but they also needed shelter. She was just beginning to dry out from the wet trip to shore and it rained often in the North Sea. He had to make something quickly. He looked to the forest, a few hundred paces away. There didn't appear to be settlers in this area, so it probably had not been picked for firewood. He could get logs, but how much time would it take to build something to keep the water out? He looked at the sky. There were still no dark clouds nearby, but how long would their luck last?

He shook his head, stared at his sleeping friend then over at their boat. They were still struggling with water. They had successfully kept out the sea, but would eventually be dealing with rain. An idea came to him. If he flipped the boat, the hull would make a solid roof, much better than any temporary shelter he could build.

He had to drag it far enough from the sea to avoid storm surges. It would be their home long enough for Stateira to heal and who knows what would happen during that time. The ferry wasn't a huge boat, but dragging it would be hard work. Before he could try, he needed to empty it, to move all the supplies to where Stateira was resting. After that, he would bail out the water remaining in the hull.

Waso grabbed hold of the boat by the tall hull at the bow and pulled it for a couple of small steps. The boat slid forward, but there had to be an easier way. He moved to the stern and pushed, discovering he could shift the boat further that way, but with trouble keeping it straight. He learned he had to shift to the bow to pull it in the right direction, then back to the stern to get a little distance and only with this constant switching could he move the vessel where he wanted it to go.

The sun was near the horizon by the time he had the boat halfway to the spot where he planned to place it. He wasn't going to stop for rest, but a weak, familiar voice caused him to look up from his task.

"What are you doing?" Stateira asked. She had half limped, half crawled to where he had pushed the boat. She sat back in the sand, panting visibly. She was almost unrecognizable from the woman he had first met in Nendrum. Her torn, brown dress was ten shades darker, filthy with sweat, dried blood and dirt. Her matted hair lay flat around her neck and shoulders like a layer of pond muck. Only her dark eyes remained the same. They reminded Waso of the promise of a night sky and how lucky he was to have found this woman.

"You should be resting." Waso's tone was sharp and commanding.

"When I opened my eyes, you weren't there."

"I had to take care of the boat." He got down on one knee next to her and touched her shoulder. "You lost a lot of blood."

She sighed. "I'm tired, but not so much I can't sail."

"I'm going to build a shelter by flipping the boat. We're staying here long enough for you to heal. I can fix the hull while it's upside down. When you and the boat are better, we'll move on to Britannia."

"But why move it any further than here?" As she spoke she took a breath between every two or three words.

Waso looked out at the sea and saw he was further from the water than he had realized.

"The tide's out," he said, shaking his head. "When it's back in we'll be too close. I want the boat near where you were resting."

"This is far enough," she told him. "What's your plan?"

Waso looked at the ground then at the dark clouds over the sea. They seemed to be moving more than before. He bit the inside of his cheek, rubbed the back of his neck, and said, "I'll collect logs then flip the boat onto them."

Stateira slid back in the sand and studied the situation. "It's too big, especially the bow and the stern. You'll never turn it over alone and I'm too weak to help. But we can still live in the boat if we make a roof out of branches."

"Branches won't hold the rain."

"They'll hold, if you use enough. I can gather them while you find food and fresh water. We need to replenish our supplies and get back on the sea."

"No," Waso told her. "You need to rest at least until your head wound heals. We'll see about your leg."

To maintain any hope of finding Abigail and Goda they needed to get back on the sea. Stateira was right about that, but now he had to concentrate on fishing, hunting, and finding a source of fresh water. They needed shelter before anything else, but it had to be quick and easy. He would go to the woods with his axe to find branches for a lean-to. The boat wouldn't be a roof, but it could be a foundation for whatever he built.

Waso watched as Stateira crawled into the shadow cast by the boat. "After I've built enough of a shelter to get you out of the sun, I *will* find fresh water."

"Thank you. The keg won't last forever."

"No, it won't and I also need water to wash your clothes, clean your wound, and get the blood out of your hair. You can't get better unless you feel better."

Chapter Ten
Olaf

Olaf thought he knew enough about sailing to survive what the sea would throw his way, but only time would show if his confidence was true or a fool's wish. His life had fallen apart. He felt some shame in the way he'd become a murderer and a boat thief, like Waso. Yet he felt much greater anger than shame. Waso was more than a runaway thrall, more than the man who had attacked Olaf's pride, more than Hakon's killer, even more than the man who had stolen the woman Olaf wanted for his wife. Waso was Nidhogg in human form. Like the dragon of the gods, Waso fed on human corpses. "I will find the monster and make him pay," Olaf said to himself. "I swear an oath that nothing will stop me, nothing!"

Olaf believed he was chasing Waso and Stateira, but he wasn't certain. He knew they were headed to Britannia, but had no idea if they were far ahead or just around the next peninsula. They might even be behind him, if they'd had to stop to hunt or find fresh water.

A gust of wind brought his mind back to the boat he was trying to control. Sailing alone wasn't as difficult as he'd thought it would be. A single person wasn't enough ballast for a hard wind, but Olaf compensated by not moving too fast. He sailed across the wind even when he didn't have to, and each time the force seemed to be too much, he released the sail enough to settle the boat. Patience was the key.

Navigating was a different issue. He thought he could find the north star, based on a few pointers he'd picked up from Maarav. But Olaf wasn't confident enough to travel after dark. So up to this point he'd been following the shoreline during the day and had beached his boat each night. Following the shore was tedious, because it was filled with sand and trees, which all looked alike from a distance. Once in a while there might be a rock that had a unique shape, but even those seemed to fade together after a short sail.

Olaf had looked for a map in Maarav's pockets, but the dead ferry operator didn't have one. Maybe the man thought he'd be safe if he kept everything in his head? If so, Olaf had proven him wrong.

Olaf couldn't rest and sail at the same time, so he headed to shore each evening. He would anchor and swim if there was no safe place to pull the boat, but most of the shore had beaches. When the weather turned bad, he headed in early.

Like all Vikings, Olaf worried about the weather. He knew the signs for changing conditions and had a good sense of how long it would take for a distant storm to arrive at his doorstep. But the sea was different. Sudden storms could appear in an instant and disappear even quicker, which is why, when he saw darkness in the northern sky, he turned toward land.

What he saw as he approached the beach surprised him. There was something on the sand that appeared to be a simplistic structure with signs of human activity around it. He turned his boat east, believing he could land further away and explore on foot. Maybe there were supplies he could steal, at least a rope or two.

Olaf lowered the sail and rowed to a narrow strip of sand backed by a rocky area mixed with tall grasses. He was able to pull the boat out of the reach of the waves, but in case the threatening storm brought larger waves, he carried the anchor to the rocks and secured it there. He looked to the north, checked on the dark clouds, and decided he needed to find shelter.

Olaf liked depending on himself alone. At sea, he might have asked Maarav what to do, when he was still alive, but Olaf was on land now, back in his own domain and capable of coming up with his own decisions.

He could either walk along the beach toward the ragged hut or he could seek cover in a wooded area, a few hundred yards inland. He decided to head for the forest, to approach the signs of life later, when he had time to check out any potential threat. Olaf kept thinking about Maarav as he walked. The man had been unarmed when Olaf killed him. If it had been a fair fight, Olaf would have felt better about what he had done, but pride in one's actions wasn't as important as surviving. Olaf's father had taught him that by dying.

Olaf found two fallen trees in the woods, one about as wide as the length of his thigh and the other half again as large. The smaller had fallen across the larger, leaving a narrow accessible area, a foundation for a structure. He thought how since he'd begun the quest to find Waso, the sheep he kept at home lived better than he did. Branches, leaves, and mud from a creek would make a place where he could keep dry, one that would serve him for a day or two, but he'd still be sleeping on the ground.

When the shelter was done and the sky was turning dark, he ate some of the dry cod he had with him, then set out to check on the other camp. His boat marked his place well enough to find the shelter when he returned. He would walk along the beach until he was close enough to sneak a look. Maybe those people had something better than what he'd been eating, something he could steal. Olaf brought his axe for protection, and started along the shore.

***

Waso

Five days after they had made their boat into a campsite, Waso and Stateira noticed the small boat sailing near the shore. They had been close enough to see a lone man sailing the vessel, but not close enough to distinguish his features, except for his blond hair which looked familiar.

"Do you think it's Olaf?" Waso asked.

"I don't know," Stateira replied. "We have to be careful no matter what."

"Maybe, but it looks as if this man isn't planning to come ashore." Waso smiled. "I think we scared him off."

"Not if he beaches his boat further along and comes back when we aren't prepared."

"Then we need to stay prepared."

She nodded in agreement, but kept her eyes on the boat as it rounded a bend in the shoreline.

Stateira and Waso walked to the forest, or rather, hobbled to it, since Stateira needed a makeshift crutch to move anywhere. They would watch from a safe distance, hoping there was nothing to see, but staying in a place where they could hide if necessary.

They turned toward where the boat had gone, following the edge of the forest, their progress slow. By the time they saw the man walking along the sand in the direction of their camp, the sky was dark. They couldn't see his features, but Waso noticed how he was carrying an axe and walking with a gait similar to Olaf's. He believed this man was the Viking who had once owned him.

"You think he would still look for us after so much time?" she asked.

"Oh yes," Waso told her. "Olaf is as stubborn as any man I've ever met. Yet I don't understand how he could have found us after we crossed so much water."

"If he's chasing you to Britannia, he would follow the shore, like we did. And our boat wasn't hidden."

"But there's no way he could associate it with us."

Waso pressed his lips together and held his head high as he watched the man he believed to be Olaf walk further along the beach. He saw Olaf practice with his axe more than once. The man was as brutal as any of the Vikings who had raided Nendrum. Perhaps Waso was worried unnecessarily, but he decided not to confront him. They would let this person walk toward their camp while they examined his.

"He went into the forest here," Stateira told Waso. They were at the edge of the woods, near the other beached boat. "He built a shelter there." She pointed to two fallen trees covered with branches. "Like us, he's stopping to replenish his supplies and wanted to hunt and fish, but may find it easier to steal our food."

Waso felt the muscles in the back of his neck tighten. He kept his eyes on the sailor as he spoke in a soft, steady voice. "If that man is Olaf, then he's here to kill us." They needed to confirm his identity, before he confirmed theirs. If he *was* Olaf, even a single identifying item left at their camp would turn him into a hunter and them to his prey.

"You need to stay here, while I look through his supplies."

Stateira looked away from Waso, at the small shelter they'd discovered. "What should I do?"

"Keep an eye on the beach and hide if you see him turn around."

"All right, but if I see he's headed toward you, I'll wave my crutch."

As Waso walked to the sailor's boat, his feet sank in the loose sand. He counted fifty steps between glances at Stateira, resisting his urge to look back more, because he knew it would slow him down. His stomach twisted in a knot and his jaw clenched. He tried to get his mind off his fear, by thinking of what he would find in the boat.

Olaf had a few items he treasured. One was his axe, but there were smaller possessions as well. It was likely he'd have brought cups and bowls or maybe some recognizable iron cutlery, if he didn't want to eat with his fingers.

He reached the boat and turned to look at Stateira once more before going through the supplies on the vessel. She was standing tall where he could see her, but where anyone else could as well. He wished she would be more careful. She was still staring along the beach. Waso looked in the direction the sailor had walked and couldn't see anything. Stateira was just being cautious. When he turned back to her, she didn't raise her crutch, which meant he had time to search the boat.

The boat appeared to contain the normal supplies: oars, rope, and the sail, wrapped around the yard as well as fishnets and what appeared to be a single change of clothing. He opened two barrels, one containing dried fish, the other holding carrots and onions. Waso needed to be careful as he went through what was in front of him. He didn't want to leave a clue that anyone had been searching through the sailor's things, especially if the sailor was Olaf.

He looked around some more and saw a small box which he opened carefully. It was a sewing kit, containing thread along with a mixture of wood, bone, and iron needles. Waso and Stateira did not have anything like this, so it was good their sail hadn't torn. Next to the sewing kit there was a pile of knives, seven in total, of various sizes, and next to the knives was a whetstone. Waso felt his skin tingle when he saw the stone. He picked it up, turned it over, and saw familiar scratches: a line as long as the width of his pinky with a four-sided figure attached to the right end and, above that, a squiggle of about the same length with a bend toward the other scratch. One of his tasks when he was Olaf's thrall was to sharpen all the tools. He'd spent days with this stone and knew it better than any other tool he'd ever used. This was the confirmation he needed. Olaf was here and they had to deal with him.

By the time Waso was back at Stateira's side, he had a plan. "It will be dangerous and could backfire on us," he told her, after he'd explained the details, "but it's worth the risk."

"You know best," she told him, shaking her head slightly. She appeared ready to say something else, but didn't.

"Before we do anything, we need to find a place where we can watch Olaf's shelter without him noticing."

"There's a small hill," she said, narrowing her eyes. "We'll climb it and look down on him. We'll hide behind a couple of trees." Dark clouds covered most of the stars, but they could see silhouettes, especially one as large as Olaf. "And your plan starts once we're sure he's asleep?"

Waso nodded.

"What about me?" She asked, looking down at her injured leg.

"I'll go to our old boat when he's asleep for the night. After I'm gone, you'll have plenty of time to get to his boat. Make a wide circle around his shelter and crawl. He'll hear you if you try to stand, especially if you fall."

***

Stateira

They were on their stomachs, side by side, unsure where Olaf was, unable to speak for fear he might hear their whispers and unable to move for fear he might hear the scratching of their bodies against dry leaves and sticks. Their sides were touching. On the boat, they'd been forced to reveal the most intimate parts of their bodies to each other, but they hadn't touched, not like this with such a long, gentle joining of their sides, not since they were first hiding from Olaf. They knew each other now and somehow that made it more intimate.

Stateira closed her eyes and listened to the sound of the waves breaking on the sand, gentle and constant, like the earth breathing. That strange idea made her aware of her own breath, and of Waso's. She hadn't noticed before, but the rhythm of their breathing was synchronized. Was she imitating him, reacting like a young girl with her first love?

She tried to slow her own breath, but kept hearing him, kept falling back into his rhythm. She opened her eyes. His eyes were open, too, staring along the beach, scanning the shore for Olaf, which was what she was supposed to be doing. Her body tingled, especially her thighs and her chest. She didn't think she was shivering, not in a way he could detect, but it was hard to tell.

She needed to control her thoughts, to think of something other than Waso, who was still breathing in and out, still touching her side, still making her body quiver. It had to be something mundane, like cleaning fish, a skill her father had insisted she learn. She had hated that task as a young girl, so dirty, slicing the fish's belly to remove the guts, then cutting off the head, tail, and fins, and, finally, cutting along the back to pull the bone. She had to hold the fish to the table while she used her knife and afterwards her hands smelled for days.

Waso moved slightly, pulling her thoughts again. He signaled that they needed to keep quiet. She looked along the dark shore and saw a shadowy figure walking toward them.

It started to rain, just a few drops at first, but soon enough there was a downpour drenching them both. Waso reached over and put his palm on her back, clearly trying to reassure her. He didn't need to. The rain didn't upset her. In fact, the sound of drops on the ground provided additional cover for any accidental noise they might make.

Olaf went to his boat instead of coming straight toward the shelter. The rain made his choice seem odd. His shelter was constructed well enough to keep the rain out, but he was taking his time getting there. By now Olaf had to be as soaked as a swamp. Stateira started to worry he might ruin Waso's plan by heading out to sea again. It seemed strange to leave at night, but perhaps something had scared him.

Olaf stopped at his boat for a moment then turned toward the forest. The reason he'd gone there hadn't taken him long and he was now coming their way.

When Olaf reached the entrance to his shelter, he first put his axe under the branches, then peeled off his clothes and crawled in, carrying what he'd been wearing in a crumpled ball. Waso started to move immediately. Stateira had expected him to wait for a moment, to be certain Olaf didn't emerge again. The rain must have changed his decision about the timing. It was time for Waso's plan to begin.

***

Waso

Waso picked up a stone as he left the woods. It was about the size of his palm, perfect to grab and hold. He also found a stick about as thick as three of his fingers and tore off a couple of thin shoots, creating a club. He carried the stone in one hand and the stick in his other. He was ready to do some damage.

The rain was starting to let up a bit, allowing Waso to pick up his pace. It was easier to walk on the wet sand than it had been on dry, so he could move faster than he had earlier that day. He started to jog. As he ran he thought of Stateira, trying to move to the boat without being heard. He needed to get back to her as quickly as he could.

***

Stateira

When Waso was almost out of sight, Stateira decided to leave her hiding place. She shifted to her knees and began to move across the wet leaves, out of the space behind the tree where she'd been hiding. She would use her crutch after she reached the sand, but for now she would carry it in her right hand while she crawled, as Waso had instructed. The rain had stopped, but drops were still falling from the trees. She looked over her shoulder at Olaf's shelter. There was no sign of movement from his little structure.

She had changed to Waso's clothing when they beached their boat. The material of the dress she normally wore while sailing would have made crawling difficult, but the trousers and short tunic she had on were perfect. She didn't hurt her knees when she climbed over fallen trees or crossed the one large rock that lay between her and the beach. When she made it to the sand, she stood, then hobbled the rest of the way to Olaf's boat, using her crutch the way it was supposed to be used.

***

Waso

When Waso reached the boat he and Stateira had beached, he looked around for anything he thought might be useful during the rest of their trip. There was nothing worth carrying to where Stateira was waiting.

He climbed into the boat and knocked at one of the boards with the rock he'd brought along. He chose a board that had been damaged by the waterlogged tree they'd hit at sea. He banged on it a few times with the rock he'd brought along, matching his strokes to the rhythm of the waves to partially block the sound. After a few hard strokes, he managed to loosen it. He tried the one next to it and discovered it was easier once there was a gap. When he had three loose boards, he stepped out of the boat and used his stick to pry one of the boards off. Then he used that board to pry off the other two. He took the three boards to the sea and tossed them as far as he could, hoping the current would carry them off.

Waso returned to the boat, found a knife he could use as a chisel and began to tap it into the side of the boat with the rock. After he cut five holes in the hull, he stood back and admired his handiwork. They'd beached the boat to repair the hole from the floating tree trunk, but instead of repairing it, he'd compounded it. This vessel was no longer seaworthy and, without the proper tools, it would be impossible to repair.

Chapter Eleven
Olaf

Inside the clothes Olaf had been wearing was a knife he'd found at the other beached boat. It had a handle made of apple wood with a design near the butt – two double lines separated by the width of his pinky and connected with a series of jagged, diagonal lines. He'd made that design, burned it into the wood with sticks he'd turned to hot coals in a fire. The knife was his, which meant the people who'd made a shelter from a boat were Waso and Stateira.

Olaf thanked the god of the priests of Britannia, then touched the medallion he still wore around his neck to thank Thor. He was breathing hard now, picturing Waso with his head separated from his body, a glorious scene. "Oh yes," he said. "Oh yes."

They must have been hiding when he walked to their camp. It was likely they suspected he was the one who had found them, since hiding was a sign of fear. If so, they were probably watching him now. He rolled to his side and began to work at the dirt between the branches covering the side of his shelter. He dug and bored until he made a small peephole. The rain clouds were still thick enough to leave a dark shadow over the area, especially when combined with the trees. But the shelter was not deep in the woods, so some light peeked through the clouds, enabling him to see silhouettes.

Olaf studied the area around him, but didn't see any suspicious movement. He rolled over and went through the same process, creating a peephole to view the other side of his shelter. After studying that second scene for a while, he rolled back and looked through the original peephole. This time he noticed movement, something down on all fours, like a bear cub only thin. *Could it be Waso? If so, why was he crawling?*

The animal seemed to be carrying something in its right hand, a long stick, but an animal would use its mouth to carry, not its paw. Only a person would hold a stick that way, a stick that could be a weapon. He looked more carefully. It had to be Waso.

Olaf climbed out of his shelter in time to see Waso reach the beach. He watched him as he used the stick to stand slowly, then proceeded across the sand using the same stick as a crutch. Waso was injured. Olaf touched the Thor's hammer medallion and thanked the gods again. He put on his wet clothes, grabbed his axe, then walked toward the boat to confront the slave he'd grown to hate more than anyone, even the faceless murderer who had killed his father.

As Olaf gained ground on Waso, he watched the slave slide behind the boat and lie down. Olaf wasn't sure if the man was tired or looking for a place to hide, probably a little of both. He was, however, certain that Waso had not noticed him following. The slave hadn't glanced around even once. The element of surprise was on Olaf's side.

Olaf lifted his axe in his right hand, circled close to the boat, and jumped out at the figure in the sand. He stopped short. Waso wasn't the helpless person lying in front of him. It was Stateira. The Persian slave was dressed in Waso's clothing, dirty as a lamb in a mudslide. Her head had a huge scab and her leg was covered with a filthy bandage. He wondered if her wounds were infected.

Stateira held the stick she'd used as a crutch in front of her, as if that weak branch might offer protection against his powerful axe. He knocked it to the side with a single stroke then looked at her eyes. He enjoyed the fear in her stare, her dark eyes more like forbidding caves than the liquid pools he remembered. She closed them as if preparing to die, but death was too quick, too easy. He would have some fun with her first.

Stateira's skin was smooth, except for the scab and her hair looked as soft as black lamb's wool. Olaf was quite certain that underneath Waso's dirty clothing she would still look pretty.

***

Waso

The knife Waso had used as a chisel was the only tool he took from the boat he and Stateira had called home for many days. He didn't feel nostalgia, although he had enjoyed growing close to Stateira, especially after they beached the boat and he took care of her wounds. Waso also took a leather sack filled with what was left of their smoked cod. He promised himself he would never eat that fish again once he was back in Britannia, but for now any food prepared for a journey was a blessing.

Waso took a few steps before deciding he should have a weapon. He went back and found the stick he'd used to pry the first board off the boat, before setting out for the final time. Hopefully, he wouldn't run into anything unexpected, but if he did, the stick and the knife in his belt would have to be enough.

He felt his legs tighten as if his muscles were telling him to run, but that would be a mistake, too noisy and too exhausting. The plan was good. He had to keep to it. Thinking of why he might need a weapon was borrowing trouble, which was never a good thing. He could trust Stateira to sneak to the boat as quietly as a water spider. He was certain Olaf was sleeping soundly. Soon they would be back on the water and rid of him forever.

Whatever happened next, Waso was better off than he had been a year ago when he was a slave on Olaf's land.

He remembered leaving a gate open once, when he was learning about life as part of the lowest class on a Viking farm. None of the sheep wandered through the open gate, but Olaf was furious. Olaf made Waso remove his tunic then lashed him, striking him across his back until he collapsed. When the punishment was over, Waso's wounds were open and bleeding, but Olaf did not tend to them. Waso had to care for his own lesions. He often wondered if Olaf had been looking for an excuse to punish him, to use the new leather whip he'd bought in Birka.

The boat was very close now, close enough to see despite the dark of a cloudy night. Waso was surprised because he couldn't see any motion near it. Stateira might hide despite the knowledge that Olaf was still asleep in his shelter. Maybe she was being cautious, but there could also be something wrong.

***

Stateira

Olaf's hand was on her mouth, the weight of his body on top of hers. Stateira tried to bite him, but his hand was cupped, keeping space between her teeth and his flesh. She squirmed underneath him until he poked her with the knife in his other hand. She knew this wasn't the first time Olaf had held a woman this way. He was a violent man who wanted to keep her quiet. He planned to surprise Waso, to kill him before he had a chance to fight back.

He was keeping her pinned down, stopping her from banging into the boat or making any other sound that might warn Waso. She could hear the wet sand squishing beneath Waso's feet. Soon it would be too late.

Olaf's axe was close. He'd dropped it to pin Stateira down, but she couldn't pick it up because Olaf was holding her down. She started to squirm again and managed to move one of her legs across the axe handle. He didn't seem to notice what she'd done. He was probably too preoccupied with keeping her quiet and listening to Waso's approach. This meant Olaf would have to move her body before he could use his favorite weapon. Maybe the extra time would help Waso.

She heard Waso moving closer, then felt Olaf tense and roll. He reached for his axe. As she had planned, her weight kept him from picking it up. He jumped around the boat. She couldn't see him, but was certain he had decided to attack Waso with his knife rather than wrestle her for his axe. He was thinking like a man, assuming once he killed Waso, he could easily take her down, even if she had his most dangerous weapon in her hands.

Grunting, swearing, and the sounds of bodies rolling were coming from the other side of the boat. She was thrilled with the noise because it meant Olaf hadn't killed Waso, not yet. Waso had probably pulled his own knife as he had approached the boat.

Stateira grabbed the axe, then darted around to the fight. She watched Olaf lunge at Waso, who countered the Viking's knife arm with his own, then Waso pushed the man down to the sand. Olaf spun to his back, so when Waso tried to take advantage of the fall by attacking with his own knife, Olaf was able to bring him down with a sharp kick.

They were both on the sand now. Olaf rolled to his knees and started to stand when Waso jumped him. Two brutal men wrestling body to body, trying to stab each other wherever they could find an opening as Stateira watched helplessly. The men were so close she couldn't attack Olaf without risking Waso, until finally one of Olaf's legs stuck out from the mass of their bodies. She swung down, leaping as the axe fell to put all the force of her body into the weapon. The Viking screamed, then both men went silent. Olaf dropped his knife when Waso cut his throat.

Chapter Twelve
Abigail

"Dev," Abigail called out, speaking toward the grass in front of the woods. It had been more than a year since she'd seen the little stoat. It was possible the animal had forgotten her. It was also possible Devona hadn't survived life in the wild, but Abigail shook her head at that thought.

Holt was with her, wrapped in white linen with dark bands holding the swaddling blankets in place.

***

It had taken twenty-one tries before Goda's seed grew inside her. They hadn't had sex since, not even kissed. She wasn't sure if Goda felt shame in their relationship, but he stuck by her when she needed him, providing food, shelter, and someone to listen when she needed to talk. He loved her in the ways that counted.

When it was time for Holt to arrive, Abigail refused to call for a midwife. She birthed him with help from Goda and no one else. They used the knowledge they'd gained growing up with farm animals, which turned out to be enough.

***

A stoat stepped out, weaving about sporadically until it stopped to stare at Abigail. Devona had a small, thin line of dark in the white fur under her nose, like a mustache. The animal was too far away to see if it had the same unique marking, so Abigail wasn't certain this one was hers. Its body appeared longer, but leaner than the young stoat she'd dropped off a year earlier.

"Devona?" Abigail pleaded as the stoat turned to step into the cover of the grass. It stopped again and turned back, appearing to think over the danger of this situation.

"I brought Holt, my child," Abigail said. "I wanted to show him to you."

The stoat stepped toward her and tilted its head. It *was* Devona. Abigail thought she could see the dark line and, even if she couldn't, Devona was showing recognition by her lack of fear.

"You appear healthy and you've grown so much. Do you have kits?"

Abigail didn't expect an answer. She understood animals enough to know Devona could only ever recognize her name and a few other words. She would feel foolish speaking with any other stoat, yet somehow, she felt comfortable with the one she'd raised. She believed the tone of her voice was a way of communicating that worked with Devona.

"He has a nose, a beautiful nose. I worried about that – thought the sin I share with my brother might have passed to our child, leaving him with a mark like my own. It didn't and I was thrilled. Goda was not. He said Holt has our father's nose. He said we will always think of the unfeeling man who raised us whenever we look at our child. The nose is strong and straight, but not as large on Holt's face as on our father's. Besides, time has already made us think less of Father. Now that our family has grown, we will change our focus again."

Devona stood up tall and wiggled her muzzle. Abigail took this to mean the stoat was considering moving forward, trying to sense possible danger before making her final decision. Abigail set Holt down on the ground and moved toward Devona, crawling so she wouldn't frighten the stoat by appearing too tall. Devona kept wiggling as

Abigail approached, then the stoat darted forward, but at an angle toward Holt.

Devona jumped on Holt with an experienced hunter's calm attitude. The child screamed and Abigail jumped to protect her baby but it was too late. The stoat had latched onto Holt's nose, clamping her teeth into the baby's flesh and refusing to let go.

Abigail grabbed Devona's thin body, using all her strength to tear the animal off Holt's face. She tossed Devona toward the forest without turning to see her hit the ground. Blood was pouring from the bite, mixing with Holt's tears. Abigail picked her child up, pushed his nose against her shoulder to stop the bleeding, and ran for home.

Tears flowed out of Abigail's eyes, making it hard to see as she ran. *What was I thinking? Is there no end to this punishment?* She wanted to scream, but she knew Holt was terrified and didn't want to scare him more. Even childbirth had been easy compared to holding back her wail.

She had never loved an animal the way she loved Devona, but that was over. She hated that stoat for what she had done to Holt's nose much more than she hated the priest who had cut her own.

Abigail thought she would return alone and kill Devona, but as she ran reality poured into her thoughts. It was her fault, not the stoat's. They're hunters. They leave people alone most of the time, but Abigail had raised Devona and in the process, had taken away the stoat's natural fear. They attack rabbits not much smaller than Holt and can sense helplessness in their victims. No one could have been more helpless than Holt, too young to move even if he hadn't been tied in his blankets. Abigail was a fool. She should have known better.

***

Goda was in his field, harvesting the chickweed growing between the rows of wheat. He stood when Abigail screamed. She watched him look around and yelled again. When she caught his eye, he dropped the basket he was holding and ran to her.

"Holt's been bit," she shouted.

"By what?" When Goda reached them, he took Holt from Abigail and dropped to his knees. He rubbed the child's nose with his sleeve. "The nose is torn, but only a small chunk is missing. We'll clean him and wrap the wound."

"Devona attacked him." Abigail's voice cracked as she spoke.

"Why would you let her anywhere near him?" He looked up as he spoke, but not at Abigail. He turned his attention back to Holt. "He should heal. You lived through worse."

She clutched the cloth of her shift under her neck and breathed in. "We have to take him to Elfgar. I would have died without his balm."

"You don't know that."

"You don't either and we can't take that chance."

"Any idea what was in it?"

"Honey and herbs, but I don't know what kind of herbs. Like I said, we can't take that chance."

Goda tilted his head and looked at the sky. "Elfgar was a priest."

"*Was.*" She touched the space on her face where her nose had been. "He left the church because of what they did to people like me. He is an honorable man, who found us a place to live."

"He doesn't know we have a child."

"I know, but Holt needs him," Abigail said. She knelt beside Goda, but didn't touch her brother. "Our child's nose was perfect and now this. It's our sin. He's paying for our sin."

"Animals are animals," Goda told her. "If there's a sin he's paying for, it's your refusal to recognize that fact."

"I thought Devona would sense how much I love our baby."

"Maybe she did."

Abigail leaned back. "You're saying she did this because she was jealous?"

"Hungry rather than jealous, but we can't know how animals think or what they feel."

Goda picked up Holt.

"His nose was perfect," Abigail repeated, more to herself than Goda.

"I never did like his nose, too similar to father's. Holt can be his own man."

"Like you are?"

Goda frowned. "More like Waso, I suppose." He paused a moment before adding, "We'll go to Elfgar."

Chapter Thirteen
Elfgar

Although Elfgar gave up the priesthood, he kept a life of philosophy, ritual, and drunkenness. He consumed alcohol all day, lining up glasses of mead, wine, and ale, in honor of the trinity. Mead was the oldest type of alcohol available, so he chose it to represent the Father. Wine, the drink Jesus once enjoyed, was the Son. Ale, the drink of day to day life, signified the Holy Spirit present in each person. He explained all this to the Benedictines who kept an eye on him after he left the order. They didn't care about Elfgar's philosophy, but liked the impression that his drinking had left him helpless.

Elfgar was reading a letter, instructions for the placement of two more people persecuted by the church. His work was rewarding, but not solely altruistic. Elfgar was paid by most of the people he helped into safe homes. The two women referred to in the letter were pagans who could pay with silver, which was a lot better than receiving another pig or a few chickens. It was also an easy placement. There was a community in southern Alba where pagans could live in relative safety, if they were inconspicuous.

"Elfgar," someone called out, pulling his attention from the letter. He didn't recognize the sound of the man's voice, so he hid the letter under a pile of dirty clothes and stepped outside to see. The man appeared younger than Elfgar, by about ten years. A woman stood beside him. Her age was harder to determine, but Elfgar knew her immediately by the open hole in her face. He couldn't remember her name, just that the man was her brother.

She carried a baby.

"We need the balm," Abigail said. "Our son was bitten by an animal. Can you help us?"

Our son? Elfgar thought. He'd told them to pretend to be man and wife, so no one would suspect her punishment was for incest. But he hadn't expected their *pretending* to create a child. An abomination, he thought, but he laughed at the idea he might burn in Hell for helping them.

"Come in," he said. "Have a drink."

"It took us a day to get here," the man told him. "His wound is starting to infect."

"Did you bring something for me?"

"Four loaves of bread and a slab of salted pork."

"Good enough. Let me see the little one." Goda hesitated before handing the baby over and Elfgar wondered if they could smell the liquor on his breath. "Bit him on his nose, yes? Think there's a reason for that?"

"Because of our sin?" Abigail asked, a slight tremor in her voice.

"I'm just talking, that's all. What are your names? I'm afraid I can't remember. And the boy, well, he's new to me."

Goda leaned to the right slightly, shifting most of his weight from both legs to one. He introduced himself, Abigail, and Holt. Abigail stared at Elfgar as Goda listed their names.

Elfgar wondered how Goda had sex with such a woman, her being his own sister and with a butchered face as well, but he had. And the proof was in Elfgar's arms. He remembered how he'd been paid by the Persian woman, a favorite of the Abbot's. That woman must have taken pity on Abigail, paid with jewels the Abbot gave her. He laughed again, at that irony, then noticed Abigail looking at him with a confused expression.

"I've got the medicine you're after right here. I'll put a little on his nose and some in a pot for you to take home. Put a dab on the cut every morning and every evening, until it's gone. He should heal, but he'll always be missing part of his nose. Better than the whole thing, right?" Elfgar giggled and looked at Abigail again. "Sure, you don't want to drink with me?"

"We'd best be heading home," Goda told him. "We don't want to be walking the trail after dark."

Abigail lifted her head and spoke to Elfgar, who was still holding Holt. "We can stay a little while longer. We brought a wineskin with us, and we'll share it with you, if you tell us what's in the balm."

"You'd never come back if you knew how to make it."

She smiled. "Other things will go wrong, especially after Holt's walking. The big wounds will bring us back, but it would be nice to have the balm for little scratches. I'm talking about the day to day cuts, the ones all boys get."

"A little honey alone will do for those. I can't tell you anymore than that."

Elfgar would have enjoyed their company for a little while longer, but Goda seemed eager to head home, and once he made it clear he wasn't about to give out his secret formula, Abigail didn't push to stay. Elfgar liked these two and hoped for the best for them and their son.

"The bite on his nose will be fine," Elfgar told Abigail as he handed Holt back. "I'm not sure about God's punishment for your sin. Maybe this bite will be enough, given that you've already suffered so much. Only God knows for sure. I will add you to my prayers for forgiveness."

Abigail looked at Goda as soon as she took the baby in her arms. She must have seen her brother's eyebrows draw together, like an abandoned dog. It was a worry, one they had to recognize. *They have to pray, too,* Elfgar thought. *God won't listen to me alone.*

Elfgar turned away from the door after they had walked a short distance, wondering if his tongue had been too loose. He took a drink of mead, and went back to reading his letter.

Chapter Fourteen
Stateira

Stateira was sold, imprisoned, enslaved, and raped, leaving her with numerous reasons to kill, but not without guilt. The Abbot had spoken to her about sins worthy of eternal damnation. Clearly, he didn't think fornication was one, but murder? She was sure what he would say to that. She wondered if his God would hold her accountable for her part in the death of a miserable Viking like Olaf.

They were on the North Sea, far enough out there was no longer any sign of land on any horizon. They were steering for the east coast of Britannia, a target large enough they couldn't miss. Waso had told her he planned to head for Nendrum once he reached his homeland. There were people near the monastery who had helped hide Abigail and Goda. If they were willing to talk, Waso might learn where to look for his siblings. The thought of returning to Nendrum terrified Stateira. She had no idea if the Abbot was alive, but if so, he still thought he owned her and would take whatever steps he needed to get her back.

The wind was strong and steady, perfect for sailing west. Yet Stateira couldn't relax. If the wind stopped abruptly, they would both need to shift their weight quickly or they might capsize the boat. Waso was relaxing, leaning back, looking over the water as he held the sail. He smiled blissfully unaware of how quickly a steady wind could turn gusty. "Are you paying attention?" she asked.

"Don't you see how beautiful the world is?"

"Careful, or you'll be seeing the world under the sea, instead of the one above."

"What are those?"

Stateira turned her gaze to the place where Waso was looking and saw what captured his imagination. There were at least ten sea creatures following their boat, jumping out of the sea, arching their backs. "Dolphins," she told him. "I've seen others like them." They splashed through the water like a flock of seabirds, then reached the side of the small boat and appeared to race. The wind was strong, but Stateira knew she and Waso couldn't keep up, even under the best conditions.

The scene brought memories of the time Stateira and her father had spent on the Caspian Sea. It had been their tradition to study the horizon as soon as they left the shore to look for Dolphins. She remembered how wonderful it felt to be the first to locate a pod.

The peace of the day and the strong wind left Stateira with the impression that they had been blessed rather than punished for what they'd done to Olaf. This good fortune brought a feeling of warmth and lightness throughout her body, until she looked beyond the dolphins and saw a cluster of dark clouds rushing toward them like a pack of hungry wolves.

"Storm!"

Waso looked up.

"There!" she shouted, gesturing at the approaching clouds. "Lower the sail."

Waso released the sail, causing it to flap in the wind, then shifted to the rope used to raise and lower the yard. Stateira moved to help him as quickly as she could, considering her injured leg forced her to crawl to the middle of the boat. Together, they rolled the sail and stored it lengthwise on the boat floor. They placed the oars there as well. Guiding the boat wouldn't do any good. Their best chance of surviving the approaching storm would be to hang on.

Stateira sat in the bottom of the boat and let Waso tie her to a couple of support boards which ran from side to side. When he was done, he did the same to himself and, finally, used the remaining rope to tie their bodies together. The smell of the rope told Stateira it was made of grass. It could be picked apart, but seemed strong enough when woven together. She thought it would hold.

The storm approached with the sound and force of an enormous waterfall. When it reached the small boat, the steady wind increased and started to swirl. Stateira felt a few drops, then, before she had a chance to take another breath, a torrent of rain fell. The boat began to spin and the waves grew so huge, they seemed like moving mountains. The boat went up and down. It twisted around while the rains filled it. Waso and Stateira didn't try to bail, because it was obviously a losing battle. They just held onto each other.

Rain soaked through Stateira's clothes before her heart beat twice, pouring so hard she had to tilt her head to avoid breathing water. The spin of the boat pushed her body against Waso's. They were as close as pine tar on boards. And her fear caused her to wrap her arms around him tighter than the ropes that bound them. Was this a punishment for Olaf's death? At first, she worried it was. Somehow, despite the fear that came from riding out the storm in such a small, open boat, her thoughts turned to Waso. There was no one else she'd rather die with.

Waso's body was a shelter to Stateira. He pulled her against his chest as she pushed her face into the crook of his neck. The rain fell like stones thrown from the sky. Stateira pleaded with the God of the Abbot. At first, she begged for both their lives, but as the storm grew in intensity, she begged exclusively for Waso's life. She called to the wind and the rain, saying "Take me. Take only me!" Waso was also shouting, but though their bodies were wrapped around each other, she couldn't hear what he was saying.

Then, as suddenly as it had arrived, the storm passed.

Stateira pulled her head back and was face to face with Waso. She could feel him breathing and his heart beating. They were both alive! She felt her face tilt closer to his and touched his lips with her own. Waso responded immediately, forcefully pressing his mouth on hers and lifting her wet skirt to touch her thighs and backside. She wanted more from him, everything, but they were tied in an awkward way and although their hands were free and they could kiss and touch, Stateira couldn't push her skin against his. She couldn't wrap her legs around him. She couldn't make their bodies one. She was as frustrated as a starving woman begging outside a feasting hall.

They both began picking at the grass rope, tearing through it piece by piece until Stateira began to laugh. "We're alive," she said, then kissed him again. "We need to bail the boat and raise the sail."

"I hate this rope," he told her as he broke free and moved away.

"It kept us safe, but now we have to work to get going again."

"I've never felt..."

She looked in his eyes then turned her gaze down as he looked back. "Nor have I, but we have to bail and set the sail."

He splashed back over to where she was sitting in water, working on the part of the rope that still bound her to the bottom of the boat. He kissed her one more time before moving to the other side, where he started to use a bowl to remove the water at their feet. When she finally broke her bindings, she grabbed her own bowl and joined in the task.

***

Goda

Elfgar's warning, that God's punishment might not be done, kept bothering Goda while he was back in his field, harvesting more chickweed for soup. He thought better when he was working his normal routine, tearing off the new growth until the sun set.

"I have to do penance," Goda told Abigail when he returned home for supper and took his normal place on the bench behind the cooking fire. "Elfgar said more punishment might come. It has to be for me. God won't stop until we've both suffered."

"You think that's so? What do you plan to do?"

He pressed his lips together. "I should cut off my nose to be like you."

Abigail gasped. "That's a horrible idea."

"But God..."

"If God wants that type of penance, let Him work out the details the way He did with Holt."

"And with you?"

"Yes."

He nodded then spoke in a steady voice. "But I need to plan something. I can't offer public confession. That would ruin both our lives. Should I fast?"

Abigail used her large wooden spoon to dip out the beans and cabbage she'd prepared for him. "I have a better idea. Forget penance. We'll go back to Nendrum and take one of the relics. God will keep us safe if we pray to a lock of the Virgin's hair."

"They have that there?"

"The Abbot does, along with a splinter from the cross. Eat, Goda, and think of a way to steal one of the Abbot's most prized possessions without getting caught." She placed a cup of mead beside him, then tore the loaf of bread and handed him the larger portion.

Goda thought how he was glad he wasn't fasting. Yet even if he didn't have to punish himself physically, Abigail's idea wouldn't be easy. He hesitated before taking his first bite, then he ate quickly, hardly chewing his food.

Chapter Fifteen
Waso

Waso and Stateira couldn't see any people on the shore of Britannia, just a long beach with grassland and small trees a short distance inland. Still, they knew they were in the right place.

"Where else could we be?" Stateira asked him, smiling broadly.

Stateira dropped the sail and Waso helped her roll it up. When it was properly stored he started rowing, with more strength than he'd thought he had left. He noticed Stateira looking at him rather than the shore. Her eyes were wide and she appeared to be crying.

"What?" Waso asked.

"You are home," she told him. "I'm happy for you."

"I'm not home yet. We've got to reach land then we've got to walk across the entire country."

"Still, I know how much this means to you. We did it! We're here, in the country where you were born, and we're alive."

"I would have capsized and drowned out there without you, so I say *you* are the one who did it."

Waso hopped out when they were near enough that he could stand in the shallow water. He then pulled the boat toward shore until he was on dry land. Stateira crawled out, then limped through the waves. Her ankle hurt too much for her to be of any use with beaching the boat.

"Where do we go now?" Stateira asked when Waso had pulled the boat up entirely onto the narrow beach of sand and smooth stones. They had known they'd reached

Britannia as soon as they saw the land from the boat. But they didn't know how far north they were.

"We don't go anywhere, not until you heal."

Stateira eyes grew soft as she smiled at Waso. Her expression caused all his worry and tension to ease away – but only for a moment. His chest quickly tightened again, as he realized her gratitude meant she had believed him capable of leaving her alone or even forcing her to walk on an injured leg. *How could she think him capable of such uncaring selfishness?*

They were experienced at setting up a campsite, so while Waso pulled the boat far enough from the water to keep it dry during high tide, Stateira went to the woods to find branches the right size for a lean-to shelter. She was limping, but managing to walk slowly. When she made her return to the boat, she was using a stick for support and dragging a few branches with her left hand.

"You need to take care of your leg." Waso told her. "Just sit there. I'll collect what we need when I'm done here."

"I want to help."

"I know you do, but you need to heal."

Their clothes were still wet from the storm at sea, but quickly dried in the sun. By the time the sun set, they had built a shelter against the side of the boat and were prepared to rest in a place Waso considered imperfect, but more comfortable and secure than what they'd had in the boat on open water.

Waso and Stateira both had to squirm about a bit after they crawled under the fresh cut branches, since the ground underneath them was a mixture of sand and stones. They removed most of the debris that made them uncomfortable, then they lay side by side on their backs.

Waso thought about holding her during the storm. He had been close to death and knew it the entire time, yet he hadn't been scared. It was as if touching Stateira made even death easier to face. He wondered if she felt the same way about him. Their kiss had certainly been passionate.

Waso lifted his hand and placed it on her thigh, on her skirt not her skin. She responded by resting her hand on his. He wasn't sure what this meant. He wanted to stroke her, to reach under her skirt the way he had during the storm. Was she stopping him or did she simply want to touch his hand? His feelings were confusing, but not as confusing as *hers*.

"What's next?" Stateira asked, speaking in a soft whisper.

He replied, "Nendrum," as he pulled his hand off her leg. "I'll find this Elfgar you told me about."

"I thought so."

"There is no other place to look, no other connection."

"But there is another, one I think would be a better choice. Elfgar was recruited and trained by a woman named Jolenta. They probably moved Elfgar, because it's dangerous keeping him near Nendrum too long. But I know where her home is and I am sure she would know as much about Abigail and Goda as Elfgar does."

"But wasn't Elfgar the man who relocated them?"

"Not by himself." Stateira smiled and began to speak louder. "To get to Nendrum we will have to sail across the Irish sea. But we can walk to find Jolenta, since she is in Britannia." She paused for a moment, then, returning to a softer voice, said, "Even if we try both places, there's a possibility we might not find them. Have you thought of that?"

"I will find them or die trying."

Stateira was quiet after Waso spoke, which was the way she responded whenever she was upset. She seemed to be frustrated with the difficulty of finding Abigail and Goda, but she knew how important it was to him. Besides, they'd been through the hardest part. They were finally in the right section of the world and knew what the next step had to be. This was the wrong time to give up.

It could be something else. The thought of Nendrum had to scare her after what the Abbot had put her through, so maybe he should listen to her suggestion about this woman, Jolenta. It was so hard to know the right thing to do. Everything about Stateira had become confusing after their time on the boat.

Stateira turned away from him, so he turned from her. He would try to sleep as well as he could.

They caught fish, which they dried and they trapped a few squirrels, which they smoked, replenishing their supplies and resting until a fortnight had passed and Stateira was walking without a limp. The sky remained cloudless and calm the entire time.

Waso knew Stateira wouldn't be happy when it was time to leave, but he had no choice. "It will take time to find this woman you spoke of." He talked as he packed a few supplies: a knife, some rope, two wineskins filled with fresh water from a nearby creek, and a change of clothes for them both. "If Jolenta can't help us, I'll go on to Nendrum. You don't have to go with me. I understand how you feel about that place."

"I go where you go," she told him, "but how do we get there?"

"We leave the boat where it is. We don't need it anymore. Then we'll walk along the shore until we find a well-traveled path and follow that path inland until we find people. We can't determine the way until we know where we are."

They decided to walk north and knew the direction because they were on the east coast of Britannia. The walk through the sand and stones was difficult and became worse when the sand turned entirely to slippery rocks. Yet

Waso was happy to be back on land with a plan to find his brother and sister.

The trees they saw along the way were short, scraggly plants and when they finally found a path to follow, it led them through a grassland. After all the good weather at their beach campsite, more rain came. Waso worried the turn in the weather could be a bad omen. Whatever it was, it made life difficult. He had thought he would catch small prey along the way, but the rain was keeping most of the animals in their burrows. They had to eat the food they were carrying sooner than he had expected. When that was gone, Waso started to grow hungry. Stateira, however, didn't complain or even suggest stopping to look for food. She just kept walking, churning her legs like the wheel of a watermill.

The path turned muddy, but they walked it anyway, because the grass beside it was long. It didn't take much time before they had stepped in puddles deep enough to come up over the edge of their leather footwear. Stateira lifted her skirt to get through the filthy water, but Waso just let the bottom of his trouser legs get dirty. He was wet all over, so what difference did a little mud make?

The land became hilly as they moved further away from the sea and soon the path wove its way through large stones, ten times as high as Waso. "There could be caves in those rocks," he told Stateira, "or at least an overhang where we might rest and dry out."

Stateira, who hadn't spoken for some time, made a weak sound that seemed to be a laugh, then smiled and nodded in the direction of the huge stones. Waso knew her well enough to understand she needed rest. He turned and she followed.

Waso reached back to hold Stateira's hand as they stepped off the path, but the rain was hard now and she tripped, twisting the ankle of the leg she'd hurt previously.

Waso helped her up and half carried her until they found an overhang, a place where other travelers had built a fire. Finally, some good fortune.

Behind the old ashes, they discovered a pile of dry kindling and small branches. Waso rigged a starter bow using a curved branch and one of the rawhide lashes from his shoes. It took a while, but he managed to get a fire going. When done, they stripped out of their wet clothes and huddled by the warmth. They couldn't change into their other clothes because they were drenched as well. This was like the storm at sea, but with the blessings of dry land and a fire.

Waso had trouble not staring at her naked body, because she was so perfect. He'd seen all of her before, but only in glimpses, never with all her clothes off. Her body was thin, her hips narrow, her small breasts firm with large dark nipples. Her light brown skin was like gold against the dark hair that flowed in waves over her shoulders and down her back. The hair between her legs was not as thick, but just as dark. He stood when he realized he'd stared too long.

Stateira was shaking slightly. They'd been wet for too long. Waso positioned himself behind her, rubbing her arms and shoulders. He reached around her body and touched her soft stomach, discovering it was warm. He lifted his right hand to her cheek and discovered her face was hot with fever.

The realization made his stomach tighten. He wanted to touch her with his body, to feel her smooth, soft skin against his chest and she wasn't stopping him. But she was sick, too weak to resist.

"You need to lie down," he told her, as he backed away. She did as he said.

"I'm cold."

"I know you are, but I can't cover you. Everything we have is wet."

"I'm cold," she repeated.

Waso thought for a moment then crawled on top of Stateira, covering her with his own body. She'd said she was cold, but she felt as if she was burning. He held himself up with his forearms, to keep his weight from hurting her while he pressed his skin against hers. This was what he'd dreamed of, but it wasn't happening the way he'd imagined. He was caring for her, like a doctor, not a lover. But this is what he had to do. He felt a wave of guilt over the thought. She was sick, yet here he was thinking of how he wanted to be inside her body. Waso shook off that thought, knowing he would do what he had to do. It would be hard to stay in this position, but he would hold it as long as he could.

The fever had come on faster than he'd thought possible. She must have felt bad while they were walking and had kept going by force of will alone.

Waso switched back and forth between covering her with his body and massaging her with his hands. When he had to feed the fire, he returned to her quickly, touching her with the gentleness of a butterfly, although she was sleeping so soundly it was doubtful he could have woken her if he'd tried. He watched and tended to her throughout the night, never sleeping, but Stateira slept and in the morning, she was sweating. Her fever had broken.

Their clothes had dried by the fire, although their shoes were still wet. Waso helped her put her shift back on, then dressed himself. "We'll stay here for as long as it takes to be certain you're well enough to travel."

Stateira's eyes grew damp and she placed her hand on her chest. She didn't say anything, but Waso knew she was grateful to have a chance to rest. "I know I'm a burden to you. I'm sorry I tripped."

"You tripped because you're sick," he told her "I pushed you harder than I should have. And you're not a burden. I would have died at sea without you. You rest now. The weather's better today. I should be able to catch a squirrel or two."

"That would be nice," she said, closing her eyes as she spoke. "I am a little hungry."

Chapter Sixteen
Abigail

"Nendrum will be swarming with Benedictines," Goda told Abigail, as they started their walk. "If they see you, they could hurt you again."

The trip would be long, across Britannia and almost as far north. Then they would have to find a way to cross the Irish sea. Abigail was carrying Holt as they began, but Goda would take his turn. She wished she knew of another place where they might find a Christian relic.

Abigail shifted her baby, so she could clench her right hand. She was trying to stop it from twitching.

"You'll have to take precautions." Goda's voice trailed off as he spoke. "You'll need to stay out of the monastery and wear a mask to cover your wound, but you can't look like a robber. That would bring problems of a different sort." They had brought material and a sewing kit, for patching torn clothes. He suggested she use a square of the fabric as a hood. She would have to keep her head down, until they reached the village outside the monastery walls. After that, he would wrap her head in bandages, covering her eyes as well as her wound. He would lead her through the streets, so no one would suspect the injuries weren't real. She and Holt would stay with one of Eflgar's friends.

They left early the next day. Abigail was walking beside Goda who was carrying Holt. They were comfortable with the easy pace of their walk, heading northwest toward Deva Victrix, when a man stepped from the woods, blocking their way. He was tall and burly, with a thick, brown beard and dirt smudged over his face and hands. He wore buckskin pants with a brown wool top.

His clothes were torn and as dirty as his face. Abigail stopped and reached for Holt, but Goda hung on to their son. Both sheltering him from danger.

They turned to run from the robber, but their path was blocked by two other men, both with spears pointed at them. They turned back to face the first thief.

"Surrender your weapons," the man shouted. "This is *my* land."

"We're travelers," Goda told him. He set Holt down. Then Goda pulled out his knife, tossed it on the ground and kicked it toward the man.

Abigail had been looking down since the man appeared, hiding her face, but she could still see their only weapon skid across the well-packed dirt of the path.

"I don't care who you are," the robber told them. "Hand over whatever you're carrying."

"We don't have anything of value."

"Give me what you have."

Goda started to answer, but his words seemed to catch in his throat as the robber picked up the knife and waved it at him. Goda took a step toward Holt, but the robber shouted for him to stop and he complied.

Abigail looked to either side of the thief and saw others hiding behind trees. There was no telling how many bandits were in the woods. She had to do something.

"Set your bag on the ground, then back away," the thief instructed Goda.

He did as he was told. Meanwhile, Abigail faced the robber and lifted her head. She pulled down her hood, revealing her scarred face.

The robber looked at her, smiled wide and yelled, "Scitte!" The other bandits reacted as if the curse were a command. Between ten and fifteen men came out of the woods.

"You ever see anything so ugly?" he asked his men. They laughed and shouted other curse words. "That's one face we'll have to keep covered." They all laughed more.

Goda ran toward Abigail, but two men grabbed him and struck him with the blunt ends of their spears until he fell to the ground. The leader instructed them to tie Goda and to place Holt near him. "Put the boy behind the tree, but let the man see what happens when travelers pass through my woods with no tribute."

Abigail had been dressed plainly, in a brown shift with long sleeves and a skirt that reached her ankles. Her hood was a separate garment. It fell off as the robbers grabbed her. They forced her to the ground where they pinned her, with two men holding her arms and two more holding her legs. They lifted her dress over her face. She tried to fight, but there were too many. She had no choice but to lay there with her head and arms covered by her dress, her feet covered by her shoes, and all the rest of her exposed to her attackers.

When the first man climbed on top Abigail was overwhelmed by his stench. He smelled like day old, dead fish combined with the scent of a freshly used latrine. That was just his body odor. His breath was like the stink of her father's hog farm on slaughter day. When the man raped her, the pain was both physical and spiritual. She screamed through the material of her dress, causing another man to cover her mouth, pushing some of her skirt between her teeth as he tried to stop her yelling. "It's hard to know which hole is her mouth and which is her nose," the man said, causing everyone to laugh.

"No problem down here," the rapist yelled as he scrambled to his feet and pulled up his trousers.

They laughed again.

Abigail gave up fighting. She let the other robbers have her body, but pushed her spirit out and went into a memory of the day when Waso and Goda had shown her a hiding place among some giant stones near the creek behind their father's farm. They'd all pledged their loyalty to each other, swore to it for the rest of their lives. It was the second-best day of her life, second only to the day Holt was born. She knew Goda was the one who had decided to include her and had convinced Waso. Now he was tied to a tree, watching her shame.

***

Waso

"Are you certain you're ready?" Waso asked Stateira. They'd been resting for more than a fortnight, about as long as they had when they'd first reached the shores of Britannia.

"I believe so," she told him, "The soreness is gone."

Stateira's ankle no longer showed any swelling and she was no longer limping. Yet, Waso worried that she could be putting his desire to get back on the road over her own recovery. "We'll try to go forward slowly. If your leg starts to hurt again, we'll stop."

They walked for half a day before coming to a large town with at least a thousand residents. The journey seemed easy, especially when they compared it to what they'd been through previously. The weather was warm and dry and the path was well traveled.

Octha was the first person they met in Beverlac, a sheep farmer who kept his herd in a field outside the town. At first, Waso thought they should move on, saying, "Sheep farming was Olaf's trade. It's a bad omen." But Stateira insisted they needed a place to stay and should take advantage of the man's kind nature.

"We want to get to a town near Croyland Abbey," Stateira told Octha. "But we lost our way."

"You're a long way from there."

She smiled at the farmer. "We were hoping you might tell us the roads to take."

"I'm not a traveler, never spent a night away from home, but you're headed in the right direction. I know of the place."

Octha offered supper to the couple, whom he assumed were married. He also told them they could spend the night in his barn, if they didn't mind sleeping with the animals. They accepted his generosity and, after helping him tend to a ewe with a wound on one of her legs, they followed Octha to his home.

Leola, Octha's wife, welcomed them and seemed excited to learn about their travels. She introduced them to her daughter, Gytha, who reminded Waso of his sister, Abigail.

The first memory Gytha triggered was of Abigail's thoughtfulness. Among the chores Waso and Goda had as boys was the maintenance of the thatched roofs, both the main house and the barn. Their surfaces needed to be cleaned of leaves and fir needles to prevent the spread of fungus and mold, which could degrade the thatching reeds. Also, the branches of trees close to the buildings had to be cut back regularly, to keep them from rubbing against the reeds and to limit the leaves they dropped on the surface.

Roof care wasn't the hardest job they had, but in the summer the sun would beat down on their necks, making both boys hot, thirsty, and tired. On those days, Abigail would come out of the house with bowls of berries: raspberries, loganberries, strawberries, currants, bilberries. The berries would often be topped with fresh goat milk, creating a treat Waso could taste to this day.

Although that memory was a pleasant one, it came with a sense that something was wrong. Soon Waso's warm thoughts were replaced with memories of the suffering

Abigail had endured at the hands of the priests and of losing contact with her and Goda.

He had trouble speaking with Octha, Leola and Gytha, because his mind was overflowing with other thoughts. Fortunately, Stateira jumped in and filled the void in the conversation with tales from their time at sea until Waso recovered his focus. The dinner and the rest of the visit went well. Afterwards, Octha led the two travelers to where they could spend the night.

Octha's barn was a triangular building with walls and doors on the front and back. Instead of sides, the structure had a thatched roof that began at ground level and reached a height at the peak as tall as two men. The back opened to a fenced area, so on nice nights Octha's small flock could rest either inside or out. Fortunately, the weather was clear on the night Waso and Stateira spent at the small farm. It would have been crowded if they'd had to share the building with all the sheep.

There was a good deal of dung and urine inside, with a bitter, irritating smell. Yet, Waso decided they'd been through too many outdoor nights to suffer another. They would each find a spot, clean it of scat if needed, and rest until sunrise. When he took his place on the straw, Stateira laid beside him. Her body felt good, since they'd slept next to each other so often. Still, this time there was no need for warmth or shelter. Stateira was beside him because she wanted to be there.

Waso was on his back, while Stateira lay on her side, facing away from him. He lifted his right arm and placed his hand on her hip. She responded to him by wiggling slightly closer, rubbing her backside against him. Her move seemed an indication she might feel something for him, the first sign since their kiss in the boat.

He lifted her shift, then placed his hand on her exposed leg, near her knee. She slowly rolled to her back and reached for that hand. He worried for a moment she would push him away, but she pulled his arm across her, so his hand touched her thigh. She turned her head to face him. He also turned and they kissed.

She moved closer, wrapping her left leg over his body. He responded by stroking her leg, running his fingers all the way up her thigh until his hand found the soft flesh of her backside.

It had been years since Waso touched a woman, but the memories were strong. He expected the feel of Stateira's flesh would trigger a pleasure at least as intense as what he felt a few years earlier when a butcher's daughter found him attractive. Yet he couldn't stop thinking of the Abbot, couldn't free his mind of how the chief priest had forced himself on her. He wondered what she thought when that man touched her. Was it the same for her then as it is now?

Waso knew he wasn't the first to touch Stateira. He was in a line behind the Abbot, the rapist who claimed he'd bought Stateira from her father, and possibly Hakon, the ugly Viking Waso killed. He opened his eyes to discover hers were open as well. They stared at each other for a moment.

"What's wrong?" she asked, her voice shaking. She pulled her head back and looked away, yet kept her arm around his waist.

"Nothing," he told her. "I don't want to hurt you." She looked back. He could see a hint of tears in her eyes.

"Hurt me?"

"You've been through so much."

"Is that it? You're concerned about the others?"

"I don't want to be like them. You're too important to me."

"I knew what I had to do to survive and I did it. With you it's different. You can hurt me more than any of those men could, because you have my heart. I thought you understood that."

"You have mine as well," he said, but the emotion he felt in his voice was not the love he felt in his heart. It was wary, nervous, as if his feelings were buried.

She pulled away from him and sat up. Her legs were crossed and her skirt pulled up to her waist. "You've shown me how you feel every day since we've been together. You've been dependable, loyal, caring, but I'm not your sister. I need you to show me your feelings in other ways."

Waso closed his eyes and swallowed. He was breathing too hard and fast, so he took a deep breath and let it out slowly. He opened his eyes when Stateira touched his face.

She leaned forward as if she was going to kiss him again, but moved her head to the side, so she could whisper in his ear. "Forget about yesterday, about my history, about Abigail, about Goda, and about what we had to do together to reach this place and time. Don't think about tomorrow, either. Live for this moment, feel like a hungry animal, a wolf perhaps or a fox."

He reached out and touched her thigh again, this time her inside thigh and he felt her shiver. She pulled back once again, but this time it was so she could pull her dress up over her head and toss it to the side. They made love for the first time that night, on a dirt floor, in a tiny barn, among sheep, a goat, and a couple of chickens. To Waso, however, the place felt palatial.

Chapter Seventeen
Jolenta
(Years earlier – When she was a child)

"May I speak?" Jolenta asked, her voice cracking. Her mother was sitting on a stool with an infant pressed to her chest.

"Of course," Coventina told her, "but make it short. You need to prepare dinner soon."

Jolenta nodded then looked at the feeding infant. All she could see was the back of the baby's head. "Is this a new girl?" she asked.

"He's a boy. Clean the hearth before you cook. We're lucky you haven't burned down the house, leaving so many ashes."

"Yes, ma'am." Jolenta didn't know much about the babies. She had never asked their names. Instead, she referred to them by descriptions like: the new one, the fat one, or the smelly one. She hated how they took all her mom's time. Jolenta was ten years old, old enough to understand that her mother had to make a living. Still, the girl didn't like having to do so many chores. She did the cleaning, cooking, sewing, and most of the weaving.

"He's here to replace the one who died." Coventina spoke as she set the new one on the carpet where the other three were resting. She picked up one of the others, a girl this time, and started feeding her. "It's time I explained why the infants are here."

"I already know," Jolenta told her mother. "The church makes you do it."

Coventina shifted the baby to her other breast then patted the child gently on her back. "But what you don't know is that your father is a priest, which is why he couldn't marry me. Instead he offered me a chance to make a living wage, while helping other women who were in the same situation. It wasn't what I wanted to do. I had experience harvesting wheat, tending to livestock, and weaving blankets. But no matter how I pleaded my case, I couldn't convince any of the farmers I could work efficiently with an infant in my arms. If I had owned land, I could have started my own farm, but without money that dream was like wishing to be the queen. So, your father suggested I work as a parish wet nurse, which sounded easy at first. What I didn't understand was that I had to take in charges, three at a time, all who needed my milk as much as you did. When you were old enough for solid food, the number went up to four."

This was something new, Jolenta thought, *something her mother had never told her.* She lifted her head and stared.

"There's been little time in my life for anything other than tending to babies. I have to feed them, of course, but I'm also in charge of keeping them clean, safe, and well rested. Each time one infant is weaned, the church brings another. But I never complain."

That last statement was a lie. Jolenta's mom complained all the time.

Coventina narrowed her eyes as if she knew what her daughter was thinking, but she continued. "The priests keep most of the money the parents pay, but we get some and get to stay in this house. I treat the children well and only two of them have died, one a couple of years ago and you know about the recent one. I guess my milk is good. Sometimes I feel like a milk goat, but you and I are secure. As long as I don't dry up, I can be a wet nurse for years."

Jolenta nodded, but shivered at the idea of living a life like her mom's. She turned and walked to the doorway. Something had to change. She stepped outside.

It was a warm spring day. The sun shone through a cloudless sky and a soft breeze blew through the trees and bushes surrounding their home. The wind rustled the leaves, like God was whispering to Jolenta, saying follow me. She walked into the woods beside her house and kept going until she could no longer see her home. Jolenta reached her perfect place to sit and think, a fallen fir with an area on its wide trunk clear of branches.

This time, she was sharing the tree with a lark perched on one of the remaining branches, calling with three chirps, one long and two short bursts. He rested a moment and began his call again. The bird turned around, looking for a mate, but remained alone, like she was.

"I'm so tired," she said, talking to the lark. "I don't ever want to go back to that life, ever. Yet, my mother needs me and I need her. A priest is my father and only she knows his name."

The breeze picked up, rustling the leaves in the hardwoods around Jolenta. She thought she heard a small animal. When she turned, she couldn't find anything moving. "Dinner will be late," she told the lark, "and mother will not be happy." Coventina often said she had to eat well and on schedule to keep her milk pure. Jolenta wasn't certain that was true, but she tried to keep her mother happy.

"Goodbye, bird," she said as she stood. "I'd better go home."

When Jolenta entered the house, she expected her mother to yell. Scolding was Coventina's first response when Jolenta veered at all from the normal routine. Yet, the only noise she heard was the sound of babies crying. Her mother was still sitting on her stool, but slouched over. She didn't look up to see Jolenta.

The babies were laid out on the floor, on a carpet Jolenta had woven, with a raw wool color behind a pattern of black. It was an odd place for infants to be, since they had cradles. Jolenta walked to them, picked up the child who was crying loudest, and tried to console her. The baby stopped making noise as she turned her head and tried to suckle from Jolenta, who was too young to have breasts, much less milk. The other three babies were crying now, filling the small house with a shrill noise that made the girl nervous.

She stepped toward her mother and shook her shoulder. Coventina fell forward, landing on her head, then rolling to her side and staring at Jolenta. Her eyes were open, but without the light of her spirit.

"Mmmm...mother," she whispered, her voice bending and shaking like a branch in a storm. She wanted to yell, but couldn't.

Jolenta set the baby down on the floor then turned back toward Coventina. She shook her again and again until there was no doubt she was dead. Jolenta had seen plenty of dead animals. Her mom looked the same. She dropped to her knees and rocked back and forth. "No. No," she called out. "I left. I walked out on you when you needed me. It's my fault. You must have thought I was gone forever. I...." Then she noticed a red line around her mother's neck. It was straight across, a mixture of bruises and places where something thin had cut through her skin. Jolenta looked up from her mother's body and glanced around the room. There didn't appear to be a bloody rope nearby, but whoever did this might have taken it with him. She noticed the crying baby again, the one by her feet. She picked up the little girl and brought her back to the other three screaming infants. They needed to eat or there would be more deaths on her conscious.

"Oh Lord, what do I do now?" Jolenta asked herself.

The babies continued to cry, but two of them had softened their sound. They still needed food, of course. They must have worn themselves out, which wasn't good.

Jolenta had to make a decision. She looked at her mother again. She should find the doctor, to confirm her mother was dead and probably murdered. But if she set out in search of the wise-woman, some or all the babies might die. She had no idea how long they could last without food. And for what? Jolenta had seen enough dead animals to know what death looks like. She could care for the babies first, but how? The walk to her nearest neighbor would take all the daylight hours remaining and the chance the woman there would be nursing a child was about as likely as bringing her mother back from the dead. If she chose the children, she'd have to go all the way to Grimsby Nunnery. If she put off dealing with the children and stayed, she could pray over her mother's body, plead for her soul the way a priest might beg. She knew Coventina would have wanted that.

It only took Jolenta a moment to choose the living over the dead. She stepped out of the house to get her mother's cart. She knew right where it was, since she had used the sturdy, wooden wagon more than Coventina had, to carry supplies from the abbey. About a year earlier, when her mother took sick, Jolenta had walked the empty cart to the doctor's house then had used it to carry the lame wise-woman back to their home. Carrying the babies wouldn't be the first time she'd pulled live people along the rough path, with the wagon rocking like a boat in rough water.

She secured the cart's back in place, wrapped the infants in swaddling clothes to prevent them from wiggling about, then placed two with their heads toward the front and two toward the back. They started to cry immediately.

The journey to the nunnery would be long, but the women there would know what to do.

Years earlier, Coventina had made the cart wheels, constructed them from solid boards held together with other boards nailed across grain. Jolenta had noticed wheels on neighbors' carts with metal bands around the edge, but the only iron in these were the nails. Yet, the wheels were strong. There would be no problem getting the cart to the abbey. The babies, however, might not survive the rough trip. Their cries had diminished to weak whimpers, a sound like lambs waiting to be slaughtered.

The path crossed a gully, as wide as Jolenta was tall and half as deep. She slowed the cart's descent into the ditch, attempting to keep the children from rolling on top of each other. Shifting about hopefully wouldn't hurt their bodies, since they were bundled so tightly, but if one of their faces was covered, a child might suffocate.

When the cart reached the bottom of the ditch, Jolenta tried to pull it up the other side. It didn't budge, no matter how hard she pulled. She wasn't strong enough, but she had to keep moving forward while there was light. The forest was so thick that when the night settled, she wouldn't be able to see her hand in front of her eyes, even if the moon was full. Jolenta needed to get the cart out of the ditch and onto a flat section of the path before she was forced to stop. Maybe it would have been a better idea for her to wait at home until morning, but the babies had to be hungry and thirsty. Time was critical.

One of the girls began to cry louder than the others. Jolenta picked her up and rocked her, humming a melody she had often heard her mother use to calm her wards. When Jolenta moved to set the child back in the cart, a simple idea came to her. She carried the infant out of the ditch and set her on the path. Then she moved the other infants in the same way. Without the children, the cart was light enough to pull out. Once accomplished, Jolenta loaded them back in the wagon and continued the walk.

The odd little caravan kept moving forward as twilight settled, until it was too dark to stay on the path. When Jolenta stopped, she didn't attempt to pull the cart off to the side. She took three steps away from the cart, squatted to pee, then stood up and straightened her frock. She had needed to relieve herself before trying to sleep, but she also remembered her mother saying that peeing near a garden would help keep animals away. If it worked for plants, it might work for them now.

Jolenta carefully placed one foot behind and turned in place, so she'd be sure she was facing toward the wagon. The babies were not crying, but she could hear their breathing, which also helped her sense of direction. She walked back, slowly, with her hands extended, until she found the cart, then she lay down beside one of the wheels.

There were too many things on Jolenta's mind, for her to sleep easily. She was worried that the babies might not survive the night and fretful that she hadn't done enough to help her mother's soul find peace. The forest was dark, but not quiet, with a constant ringing and the hooting of birds she thought were owls. She worried about wolves, but didn't hear any howling. Jolenta wondered if wolves howled when they were hunting. It didn't make sense that they would, since the noise would scare away whatever animals they were after.

Coventina haunted her thoughts – one memory, among others, of Jolenta learning to swim. It was an odd skill to emphasize, especially since Coventina had to bring the babies to the pond and keep them in the shade. She would shout words of encouragement if her wards were awake. If not, she would sit on the grass, watching her daughter paddle with all fours, like an otter. On the day when Jolenta finally moved through the water without standing, her mother told her, "If you fall in a lake now, you'll survive."

Jolenta didn't believe there was much of a chance she'd fall in a lake, but she had appreciated Coventina's concern. This was before the babies' constant feeding wore out Coventina and left her sitting in their home, unwilling to do much of anything other than nursing.

There were good times, mixed among the bad, and Jolenta worried she hadn't done enough to let her mother know she had remembered those. She prayed, hoping God would understand the choices she'd made, both the ones when her mother was alive and the most important one when Jolenta had left her mother's dead body to care for the living infants. Jolenta wondered if her choice had been a revenge of sorts, for all the times Coventina had chosen her wards over her own child. That thought made Jolenta worry about her own soul as much as she worried about her mother's.

The rising sun woke Jolenta from what had been an erratic and fitful sleep, still exhausted, but determined to bring the infants to Grimsby. She pulled her legs out from under the small cart, then rolled over and pushed herself up. As she stood, she checked on the infants. They were asleep, but they would wake as soon as she started to pull the cart. One of the boys wasn't breathing as deeply as the other infants. It concerned her, so she picked him up. He didn't cry out and only opened his eyes slightly. She felt his cheek and thought he seemed cold, despite the blanket she'd wrapped him in. This wasn't good, considering they were only about a third of the way on their journey. She set him back in the cart, got back between the two shafts at the front, and resumed pulling.

The rest of the walk to Grimsby Nunnery was much like the first third had been, although the air seemed cooler and a sudden abundance of above-ground, tree roots rocked the cart enough to start the babies crying again. Jolenta had to cross two more deep gullies, then pull the cart up and down some hills that would have strained her even if she was walking alone. The sun was high in the sky when she reached her destination – tired, hungry, but hopeful she had made the right choice.

Jolenta left the cart outside the nunnery. She started to run up the steps to the large, open door, but quickly slowed, too exhausted to move faster than a walk. Jolenta was surprised when a priest greeted her rather than a nun, a bald man in a full length, brown robe with the hood pulled back. He scowled, as she explained, "Mother was a wet nurse, working through Croyland Abbey. I was in the forest by our home and when I returned, I found her dead. There were marks on her neck. I think someone killed her. I didn't know what to do, so I left her and brought her wards here, for food and shelter."

"You left your own mother?"

She nodded. "I didn't know what else to do."

"Where are the infants?"

"Outside. In my cart."

He barreled passed her. She followed and watched as he bent over to examine the babies.

"One is dead. Couldn't you have gotten help from a neighbor?"

"We don't have close neighbors. I came here for help."

He looked around then shouted back into the building. A nun came out, a woman in her early twenties, dressed in black with a white cloth covering her head and shoulders.

"Matilda, take these babies inside. Find someone who can feed them. Hurry before we lose another."

The nun squeezed her eyes shut, then opened them to look at Jolenta. Jolenta felt ashamed that the weak baby had died. She also felt sorrow, although she didn't understand why, since she didn't know the child well. The feeling was more frustration than grief. She had done her best, but had only succeeded with three of the four.

"Take care of the girl as well. She's killed an infant. We need to decide what to do about that."

When Jolenta heard the priest's words, she wanted to run, but she was worn-out and hungry. She stepped toward the nun. The world began to spin and, as everything went dark around her, she fell to her knees. She rolled over and lay on her side, letting her exhaustion overtake her.

Jolenta woke on the floor beside Matilda's bed, comfortable, resting on two thick blankets. Morning light was peeking through the narrow, open windows. She had slept a long time. It was her exhaustion from the previous day rather than the comfort of the small room that had kept her eyes closed throughout the night. She rose up on her knees to see the nun, sleeping as soundly as Jolenta had. The woman was on her back, snoring lightly, unlike Coventina whose snoring had been louder than ten chickens facing a wolf. Jolenta felt a wave of grief as she realized her mother would never snore again.

The grief turned to fear, when she remembered the words of the priest. She shifted her body and stood, then waited for a moment to be certain she hadn't woken Matilda. The man's accusation of murder meant Jolenta needed to get out of this place while they still had her in a nun's quarters rather than a prison cell. She stepped to the door and pulled on the handle. It didn't open.

"Where do you think you're going?"

The voice came from behind her. Jolenta knew it was the nun, but didn't reply. She didn't know what to say.

"I was beginning to wonder if you would ever wake up," Matilda said. "I hope you're feeling better. I also hope you pay no attention to what that bitter man told you. You have nothing to fear from Luken. There's even been talk that he will soon leave the priesthood. We know what you did. You saved three souls and did your best to save a fourth. You are most definitely not going to prison, but we do need to determine what to do with you. I sent two men to your home. If your mother's dead, as you say she is, they'll bring her body back here, so we can determine if she's to be buried in consecrated land."

The idea of a church burial for her mother relieved a little of Jolenta's regret. "She would like that," she told Matilda.

"Of course, she would."

"The men you sent, can they find the person who killed her?"

"They will try. Meanwhile, we have to plan your future."

Jolenta wanted to make her own decisions. This woman planning her future meant she would still be tied to someone. It was one thing if the someone was her mother, quite another if she was a strange nun.

"I can look out for myself," she asserted.

"Perhaps you can, but your house belongs to the church. You can't live there. Would you like something to eat?"

The realization that she was homeless surprised Jolenta. She nodded at the suggestion of a meal. She hadn't eaten much the day before and had slept longer than she should have. She could figure out her living situation later and if Matilda wanted to help, why would Jolenta refuse.

***

Breakfast was bread, water, and a slice of ham. She ate what they put in front of her and had a second helping when Matilda offered. She was at a table with five nuns, including Matilda, and none of them ate more than their single helpings. Maybe they were rewarding her for working so hard to save the lives of the babies. Or maybe they were living by rules she didn't have to adhere to. Yet they weren't living by a rule of silence. They laughed and joked among themselves like a gaggle of squawking geese.

"This isn't what you thought life would be like here, is it?" Matilda asked her.

She shook her head.

"After breakfast, there will be a time for prayer and contemplation, but at breakfast we enjoy each other's company. It is each nun's responsibility to learn everything she can about her sisters, so she can help in times of trouble and celebrate in times of joy. As our Lord said, 'Do to others as you would have them do to you.'"

Jolenta stayed the rest of the day with Matilda and, since there was no other place she could go, the subject of her leaving didn't come up until six days later when Matilda said, "We can't stay like this forever."

"Like what?"

"You on the floor of my cell. The Abbess can only look away for so long."

Matilda was starting to become like an older sister to Jolenta, listening to her complaints about day to day life and offering more smiles than guidance. It was a rainy, miserable day, which made the concept of leaving the shelter of the convent even more frightening. She didn't want it to end, but it would, unless one of them could come up with a solution.

And so, she became a postulant, which meant she hadn't made up her mind about living the life of a nun. Although, she hadn't been accepted into the order, she did get her own bed. Jolenta slept in the dormitory with nine other girls, in a long room with the door on one end and ten beds lined up against the side walls.

In addition to the chores she had to accomplish, each day brought eight separate devotions dedicated to reciting prayer. Since Jolenta could not read, the prayers she was given were simple. The recitations cleared her mind, rather than filling it with concepts she didn't understand.

Scrubbing floors and cleaning stables were particularly hard tasks, but Jolenta enjoyed some of her other labors, such as cooking and her work in the convent garden. The gardening had the added benefit of being under the supervision of Matilda. It was the only time she got to spend with the woman who had taken care of her during her first days.

On one warm summer afternoon, while Jolenta was harvesting potatoes, digging into the soil with her fingers, Matilda told her, "I've asked the Abbess for permission to teach you to read and she's agreed."

"Why?" Jolenta asked. This was a surprise because most nuns remained illiterate. Since she hadn't even taken her vows, it seemed odd she would be chosen.

"You deserve the opportunity. The way you thought quickly and acted wisely when your mother was killed impressed the Abbess as much as it impressed me. Three lives were saved."

"Can I stay here while I learn?"

"Yes, as a novice."

"So, I'd have to commit to a life like yours?"

"Not a bad way to live. I don't have a husband, but there are advantages to that. I like making my own decisions when I have problems."

Jolenta could understand that feeling. She had no intention of ever marrying. "It's been a while, since my mother's death," she said, changing the subject. "Has anyone discovered anything that might help us find the person who killed her?"

Matilda crossed her arms and looked down, but she didn't speak. Jolenta understood this to be her way of saying no.

***

The reading lessons were complicated because they were combined with a study of the Bible, in Latin. The unfamiliar words meant Jolenta had to learn another vocabulary. At first it was an arduous process, but she had a natural aptitude for languages. Only half a year after she started, she found she could research complicated religious concepts on her own. Her lessons with Matilda changed from drills to intellectual discussion and debate.

As Matilda taught Jolenta of Adam, Moses, and Jesus, the young novice kept the thought of her mother's killer in her heart. She still believed her father was the guilty one, but a contradiction grew within her as she studied and grew. The Bible verses which influenced her the most were:

Proverbs 21:15 from the old testament – "When justice is done, it brings joy to the righteous but terror to evildoers."

and

The Epistle of Paul and Timothy to the Philippians from the new testament – 2: 3-4 – "Do nothing out of selfish ambition or vain conceit. Rather, in humility value others above yourselves, not looking to your own interests but each of you to the interests of the others."

When Jolenta entered the convent, her anger over her mother's death was intense. She believed her father was responsible for her mother's death as well as the dismal way she had lived. Since she knew her father was a priest, her feelings extended to the church. Yet here was a nun treating her with kindness and teaching a philosophy based on love, touching both justice and charity. She spent years in the company of Matilda, until the Abbess asked her to decide, either take her final vows or leave. She decided to go out into the world, but to dedicate her life to the concepts she had learned.

Matilda met with Jolenta on her last day in the convent. "Where will you go?" she asked the young novice. "How will you survive?"

"God will provide," Jolenta replied, smiling as she spoke because Matilda had said the same words more times than she could remember.

"Your faith is strong. Why don't you take your vows and live here? Is a life with God so abhorrent?"

"We've been through this before."

"I know we have, but I worry. You may be surprised how difficult life is outside the convent walls, especially for a young woman."

"I can feel God's call. His will is pulling me into the world. I can help people who are suffering."

Matilda shook her head. "This is God's house, the place where women come to serve Him. I don't understand how your faith can push you away from this place."

"My faith is different from yours. Yours is in both God and the church."

"They are one and the same."

"God is perfect, but the church makes mistakes. You know this is true."

Matilda nodded ever so slightly, as if she was afraid someone might see her and punish her.

Jolenta smiled, hugged her friend and mentor, then stepped out of the convent. She had no possessions with her. She couldn't take the habits she'd worn over the last few years and she couldn't wear the clothes she'd had on when she'd arrived, because she'd outgrown them. Instead, she wore a simple faded, blue dress, a gift from one of the nuns who had been large for her age when she'd entered God's service. The loose dress fit the full-grown Jolenta well enough. She wore nothing else, not even shoes.

Jolenta paused, still a short distance outside Grimsby Nunnery. Her body felt heavy, as if she'd gained twenty pounds with each of the steps she'd taken from the convent door. Her plan was to head to Croyland where she would find her father, observe him, then help his victims in any way she could. There were a few problems with this plan. First, she didn't know if she could recognize the man, whom she hadn't seen since she was an infant. Second, she had no idea if he had victims. She hoped he didn't, but a cruel nature is not something people grow out of. Third, she had to survive. She would be hungry again in a few hours.

"Jolenta!"

She heard the shout from behind and turned to see Matilda following her. It took a moment to recognize her mentor, because the older nun was no longer wearing her habit. Instead, she dressed in a light green frock, which had belonged to the same friend who had given Jolenta the blue one. Matilda was wearing leather, wrap shoes and carrying a similar pair. Jolenta took a few steps back.

When the two women were face to face, Matilda asked, "May I walk with you?"

Jolenta reached out, touched Matilda's cheek, then shifted her hand to the woman's gray hair. This was the first time she'd seen her friend without a head covering. Matilda's hair was cut short and her receding hairline made her seem as if she was going bald. Jolenta wondered if all the nuns wore their hair this way. The girls in the dormitory didn't. Matilda looked unlike any woman Jolenta ever saw.

"May I walk with you?" Matilda repeated.

Jolenta smiled wide. "Of course."

"I want to continue our conversation."

"I see. And does your dress mean you are also leaving Grimsby?" Jolenta asked.

Matilda nodded. "You aren't the only one God calls."

Matilda handed Jolenta the shoes she carried, then gestured toward the trunk of a fallen tree where she could sit to put them on. They were a little large, but much better than barefoot. Once she covered her feet, they walked in silence, listening to the sounds of the woods: bird calls, leaves rustling, sticks cracking under their steps. Jolenta felt peaceful and secure as she walked beside the woman who had cared for her after her mother had died, a calm feeling that left the younger woman with a sense of unity with her older friend.

"I thought you would go to Croyland," Matilda said.

"I'm looking for my father, or rather, his victims."

"There are plenty of victims. Luken, the priest you met when you first arrived at Grimsby, is a violent man who has hurt many women and he's not alone. But there are good people as well, people who share your ideals, people who can guide you toward ways to help the victims."

"Can the good people lead us to the ones who need our help?"

"That won't be a problem," Matilda told her, "since I'm one of the women in trouble."

"You!"

"There's another reason I had to leave the nunnery. I am with child."

Jolenta stopped, then grabbed Matilda's arm. "How?"

"A priest forced me. Nothing can be done about that now, but he begged for my forgiveness and gave me a house and some money."

"Really? What happened to his vow of poverty?"

"He's too important to worry about that, at least that's what he says. When I heard you speak about your calling, I knew my purpose was to help you. We can use the place he gave me to hide women who've been hurt, until we find a safe place to send them. I think that will serve God's justice. As for me, I'll hide until the child comes. After that, I'll dress like a man and pretend to be your husband. We'll be another farm family to anyone around us, a family with runaways in the back room."

Chapter Eighteen
Elfgar
(Years earlier – When he was a child)

Fishing would be good, since it had rained the night before. Elfgar and his father, Halig, ate what was left of the eel and potatoes they'd had for dinner, then went out. "You will do well," Halig told his son. This was the first day the ten-year-old boy would have his own net. "You are strong and know how to cast as well as I do."

Elfgar smiled, but was aware his father was flattering him. He would be lucky to catch half of what his father caught. His mother, Sarnat, spent days weaving a strong fishing net from nettle Elfgar had helped gather and prepare. She attached stone weights, creating a net that was as good as his father's, better, since the cordage was new, but there was more to fishing than having good equipment, more even than knowing how to loop the net over his left arm and toss it so it would open up when it landed. Elfgar's father had a sense of where the fish were swimming, which made him one of the best fishermen north of Dublin.

It took very little time for Elfgar to be proficient in working his own net, since he'd been practicing with his father's net for months. He found the main difference in the fact that his father now stood away from him, to avoid the two nets interfering with each other. Since shouting across that distance would scare the fish, they couldn't talk as they had previously. He missed their conversations.

Elfgar stood on a flat rock in a pile of boulders at the edge of the Irish Sea. He couldn't imagine such large stones being washed in by the waves. The boulders must have been one enormous rock broken into pieces from years of bashing waves. His father said the rough shore was good fortune, because it kept the Vikings away. But Elfgar didn't believe it was necessary. *They would never raid here,* he thought. *My father and I would chase them away.*

He glanced at his father, who was throwing his net further out than Elfgar's and pulling it back full of fish. This would be a good day for them both. Elfgar took a few pollock and a dogfish from his net. He killed them with his club, then put them on his pile, which was smaller than his father's. He would get better, even as good a fisherman as his father someday, yet Elfgar couldn't help but wonder if this was all he would ever do with his life.

For close to two years, Elfgar was certain his doubts about living the life of a fisherman were private. He learned otherwise when his mother told him, "You are meant for something more than the life your father and I live. Promise me you'll open your eyes to your destiny." She spoke these words from her sick bed.

Elfgar and his father still fished together after Sarnat became too weak to help prepare the fish they brought home. But they had to stop earlier, because it took time to cut, then dry or smoke the fish.

One day his mother did not get up from the straw bedding where she slept, his father did the fishing while Elfgar stayed home. He tried to feed her, even when she didn't want to eat. He cooled her head with a damp cloth when her fever grew. He listened to everything she had to say, which was mostly about her dreams for him. When she died, he cried for days. Yet he never stopped helping his father. It wasn't their way to give into grief.

About a month after his mother died, Elfgar's father spoke with him about Sarnat's dreams for him. Halig told Elfgar he was sending him to live on his uncle's farm, two days walk from their home.

"I don't know if your mother was right about fishing," Halig told him. "It's been a fine way for me to make a living and you could be good at it. But your mother saw other qualities in you and I do not believe I can nurture those, if I raise you alone."

"I'll go where you send me," Elfgar replied, "but I'll miss both the sea and you."

***

At first, farm work seemed harder than fishing, but gradually, the tasks became routine, he lost himself in feeding goats and gathering the eggs. His thoughts drifted as they had while he stood by the sea, but now his dreams were more likely to be about his future than about fighting Vikings.

Shortly after Elfgar turned fourteen, his uncle told him he had picked a wife for him: Philona, a twelve-year-old who lived on one of the neighboring farms. She didn't thrill him and, at first, there didn't seem to be much interest in the marriage on her part, either.

"Do you have plans to start your own farm?" This was the longest sentence he had ever heard her utter. She'd surprised him with the question, asking it after supper one evening, when they were sitting outside his uncle's house waiting for Philona's parents to take her home.

Philona was a skinny, pimply-faced girl, who rarely spoke. Elfgar figured she was worried about a husband who might go back to fishing for a living. She didn't want to spend the rest of her life breathing the odor of a man who pulled his living from the sea. He told her, "I don't plan to stay on a farm forever. Life is better by the sea. The fish just circle around, waiting to be caught."

Elfgar wasn't afraid of marriage, just marriage to Philona. The birth of a colt had opened his eyes to the wonder of life even as it had exposed him to the pain and mess. He had watched a brown mare lie on her side as she contorted her body into the perfect position to push her newborn out into the world. Then he had seen the young horse wiggle out of the filmy sac and struggle to rise up on his feet.

Elfgar was appalled by the image of little Philona pushing a tiny version of him out of her scrawny body. He wanted a larger, more durable woman for a wife.

Philona, however, seemed encouraged, rather than put off by his assertion that "Life is better by the sea." She told him she thought a change might make her life exciting. She started showing up at the barn as Elfgar was finishing his chores, then walking to his house to sit with him and talk. He was polite at first, but after she started appearing regularly, he began to avoid her. Once he climbed a fence behind the barn and circled around to enter the house without passing her. Another time, he finished his work quickly and ran into the woods, so he wasn't there when she arrived.

Finally, he began to pray.

Elfgar wasn't raised with religion, but he was desperate. His aunt and uncle were Christians and taught him the basics of their beliefs. So, he spoke to God, one on one, asking Him to do something about Philona, something to prevent this marriage from taking place.

Five days after Elfgar began to pray Philona stepped on a poisonous snake. Two days later, when Elfgar heard of Philona's death, he grew sick with guilt. *Is the Christian God that powerful?* he wondered. *There has to be something I can do. This horror was created by prayer, so shouldn't the answer be found there?*

He started in the barn, speaking out loud among the goats. The animals noticed him briefly, then went back to their regular activities, which included eating, drinking, and leaving their droppings everywhere. Elfgar prayed there each day for Philona's return from death, but never felt at ease mixing prayer and dung. Still, Philona remained dead.

He moved to the woods, to the place where the snake had bitten her.

"Hail to you, Christian God! You raise the sun in the morning and the stars at night. You make the plants grow and the animals thrive. You are all powerful. You answered my prayer, even though what I asked of you was wrong. I pray for your forgiveness and now ask you to bring Philona back. She is an innocent who never had a chance at life."

His voice cracked and his legs shook. He fell to his knees and looked up at the branches of a tall oak beside the path. He began to weep. "Take me. I was too angry, too caught up in myself." He tilted his head down until he was again looking forward, tears now running down his face.

With his prayer done, he walked on to the farm where Philona's family lived and asked where she was. Philona's father's shoulders drooped and his arms lay limp by his side. He said, "Why would you ask such a thing? You know she has passed."

"But I prayed!" Elfgar received no answer, neither from Philona's father nor from the Christian God.

***

Elfgar crossed the sea to Britannia and entered Croyland Abbey in the Kingdom of Lindsey, during the winter following Philona's death. He was depressed over his inability to bring the girl back to life and thought the Christian God would listen better if he dedicated his life to contemplation and ritual. He gave up on the belief he could restore Philona to life but he prayed to the Virgin Mary, hoping her understanding of pain might help her explain what he couldn't understand. No answers came.

During the three and a half years Elfgar spent in Croyland, he learned many of the monks broke their vows of chastity by requiring sexual favors for penance. He knew the women, who had come to the abbey seeking forgiveness, would leave with more serious problems than the ones they'd brought with them. Already disillusioned by the permanence of Philona's death, Elfgar began to indulge in another vice he had picked up from the monks – alcohol. There was, however, a blessing in this, because mead gave him the strength to leave Croyland Abbey and find another direction for his life.

His only possessions were the clothes he was wearing and three skins of apple wine he had taken from the monastery cellar before stepping out the door. He needed to seek help and since he wasn't about to return to his uncle's farm or his father's seaside, the only friends he had were a few craftsmen who donated supplies to the monks. Among those was Cuthbert, a smithy who had forged some of the tools the monks used in their gardens.

"I will work for food," Elfgar told the smithy. "Whatever you ask of me, I will do it. I've been a fisherman and I've worked on a farm. I am used to hard labor."

"I work alone," Cuthbert told him, looking away from Elfgar's eyes, at the forge. "I would help if I could."

He wanted to argue, but his words caught in his throat. Cuthbert's work area started to spin and Elfgar had to take a step backwards to keep from falling.

"Are you sick?"

"No, it's just..."

"You are hungry and tired. I can tell."

Elfgar nodded, but didn't speak. He scratched the back of his neck. Two crows landed on the thatched roof over the smithy's shop, and tilted their heads. They appeared to study the men.

"Stay for supper and spend the night here. Perhaps, I spoke too quickly. We can talk later."

The smithy's work place was a tiny enclosed structure with a roof that extended over an open area where he kept his forge and anvil. He was sheltered from the rain when he worked, but the smoke from his fire could drift into the sky. Yet the entire area smelled of smoke and sweat, especially inside. The enclosure must have been for tools, iron bars, and finished products waiting for final payment, although Cuthbert kept some tools outside: a hammer, tongs, the bellows, and a bucket of water he used to quench the hot metal.

They walked past the shop as Cuthbert led Elfgar to what appeared to be his home, a small building behind his shop. He didn't sleep or eat at his shop.

Dinner, a meager portion of pottage with beans and turnips, seemed a feast to Elfgar. After they split one of the skins of apple wine, they both enjoyed the evening more than they had thought they could. "I want you to speak with someone tomorrow who may provide a solution to your problems. You might know her. She's been at the abbey."

The following morning, after breakfast, Cuthbert and Elfgar left the smithy's home and set off on foot back toward Croyland Abbey. After a few hours, Cuthbert took an unexpected turn.

"That's not the way," Elfgar told his companion. "I just came from Croyland and I know it's down that road." He pointed toward a massive oak with a split trunk. "I rested by that tree, closed my eyes and dreamed of venison stew."

"Have you ever eaten venison?"

"No, but I've dreamed about it before."

"I thought as much." Cuthbert kept walking away from the abbey. Elfgar shook his head then followed. "The woman I spoke of lives in this direction. She can help you find a place to stay."

They walked side by side, without speaking, while the sun continued to rise. The day was warm for spring.

"She lives alone?" Elfgar asked. He heard a sound in the branches above them and turned in time to see a red squirrel jump from one branch to another. It was quite a distance for such a small animal. Elfgar wondered if this might be God's way of telling him he was right to take a leap of faith when he left the abbey. But that thought was silly. Squirrels were always leaping around in the trees.

"She lives with her daughter. Her husband died about a year ago. He was working on the abbey roof, which is why I thought you might have met his wife."

"I remember that accident," Elfgar now wondered if this story of a man falling might be a sign that he should *not* have left the abbey. "He shouldn't have been out there. The weather was bad and the roof was icy."

"The monks wanted the work done quickly. They had ways of getting what they wanted."

"This woman we're going to see must have been quite bitter."

"Too practical to be bitter. After the accident all she was concerned about was getting her husband back to his home. She had his body on a cart before the noon sun was at its height and home before sunset. I heard she had him buried the next day, in unconsecrated ground that was frozen. She had to build a fire on the spot before she could dig."

***

Jolenta was a muscular woman in her early thirties, a few inches shorter than Elfgar, with brown hair and dark eyes like most of the people Elfgar knew. She aged poorly and looked weathered, compared to others of her age.

"I've met you," she told Elfgar, "at the monastery."

"After your husband died?"

"No."

He didn't remember, which was odd since the solitary life of a monk kept him from meeting many outsiders, especially women. Then she reminded him of a time she had arrived with Cuthbert. They were bringing newly forged tools. He placed her after that. She hadn't stayed with Cuthbert. Instead, she had gone to speak with a group of visiting nuns, while he and Cuthbert discussed the gardens.

"I guess you didn't like life as a monk," she said.

Elfgar didn't respond, but felt his heart beat faster. He stared down at his rawhide shoes.

"I'm not criticizing. I wouldn't like life in the abbey, either.

The conversation continued in this strange manner. The nature of Jolenta's questions bothered Elfgar at first, but the thought came to him that she might be looking for someone to help on her farm in exchange for food and shelter. He hoped so, due to his limited options.

"The Benedictines took me in. I can't fault them for that," he said. He looked at Cuthbert, who was quietly allowing the talk to remain between Jolenta and Elfgar.

"I can understand your gratitude," she said, "but still you left. There had to be a reason." His legs felt weak. He stepped away from her and took a seat on the bench by the wall. She followed, still speaking. "The problems aren't from the church. If they were, convents would suffer the same failings."

"What do you want from me?" he asked, starting to shake. He managed to control his body, hopefully before Jolenta noticed.

"I want you to help some of the women the church has hurt." After her words there was silence. Jolenta stared at Elfgar, giving him the impression she was waiting for a response.

He stared back then spoke softly saying, "I could use a drink. I've got two more skins of apple wine."

Before either one answered, Elfgar heard someone else enter Jolenta's small hut. He turned to see a younger version of Philona, smaller, but identical in stature, coloring, and pimples. Philona's image stuck in Elfgar's mind since her death, growing in clarity rather than fading. He felt no doubt this girl was as much like Philona as one raindrop was like another.

Jolenta turned, glancing up at the underside of the thatched roof before looking at the child. "Duette, please stay outside. I will call you when we're done."

The young girl turned and left, without saying a word.

"Please," Jolenta said to Elfgar. "Open the wine. There are a few more questions I have."

"Who was that?" Elfgar asked.

"So, you have questions, too." Jolenta smiled. "Her name is Duette. She's my daughter."

"Duette?"

"I am a strong woman and I want my child to be the same. I named her Duette because I knew we would be two of a kind."

"Let us share wine," Elfgar said as he reached for the skin. *She doesn't seem at all like her mother,* he thought. *Her name might mean she is like Philona, rather than her mother. If so, this could be a sign about where my life needs to go.*

He liked that idea. "I'll do whatever you ask," he told her.

The next day, Elfgar was told his assignment was to return with Cuthbert to learn the blacksmith trade. He explained to Jolenta he was already an experienced farmer and an excellent fisherman and asked why he needed a new trade. She made an expression halfway between a smirk and a smile. "You are also to spend time with Cuthbert's neighbor. She's a healer who can teach you her trade as well."

"You want me to be a doctor?"

"I want you to be a blacksmith who can heal the people who deserve healing."

Elfgar turned his attention to Duette, who was sitting on a bench, spinning. She seemed much older than she had the day before. Perhaps it was the way she handled the spindle, feeding the wool and turning the shaft without any trouble. Although he had never watched Philona at her daily tasks, the evidence of Duette's skill made the comparison stronger in his heart. Elfgar was confident God had answered his prayer. It was time for his own part of the bargain, which meant he needed to follow Jolenta's instructions without question.

***

The work at Cuthbert's was hot and hard, but no more or less difficult than fishing or farming. He needed to build strength in his arms. Even if he hadn't grown weaker during his time in the abbey, the muscles a smithy used were different from the ones he'd built during his other occupations. Once his body was up to the task, Elfgar switched his focus to another need - alcohol.

Cuthbert brewed ale in his home, but it was sludge compared to the quality Elfgar had drunk at the abbey. When he was a monk, he had his choice of ale, beer, apple or grape wine, although the latter drink was rare. Now he had to buy his alcohol through the friends he still had in Croyland. He generally chose apple wine, ale and added the decent mead Cuthbert made.

Elfgar hadn't become a polished blacksmith when, twenty days later, Jolenta visited Cuthbert's shop. He had, however, learned enough to make rough items like garden tools or horseshoes. His limited skills seemed to satisfy her.

The first question she asked was, "Why did you leave the abbey?"

They were standing close to the forge, so Elfgar took a few steps away from the heat and Jolenta followed. He wasn't sure how he should reply. He had been disillusioned with the behavior of some of the monks, but most were not bad. The good ones spent their time in worship and service, working hard when required to do so. He still had friends among them. The real reason he left was a combination of the monks' sins and his own lack of faith. His faith was restored when he met Duette, but he couldn't tell Jolenta that reason.

"My reason is between me and God," Elfgar said. Jolenta's eyes narrowed, causing Elfgar to add, "I don't mean to offend you, but the reason has to do with faith. Talking about it would diminish its power."

"You don't want to work with me?"

"That's not what I said."

"You would rather drink yourself to death than help those in need?"

"You're not being fair."

"Should I be?" Jolenta was breathing hard now, her nostrils flaring.

Elfgar wished he could start over. He looked at Cuthbert, who was trying his best to ignore the discussion, then Elfgar turned his eyes down at the dirt floor. Jolenta paused until he looked up. "Forget about why you left. Tell me what you think of the monks."

Jolenta appeared to have a defined opinion about the church, which would make it difficult to explain his own. Yet he had no choice. "I think most of them are trying to understand life and I think some know where to look for the answers, but others get caught up in their own desires."

"And those desires hurt people?"

"Sometimes." Elfgar's stomach churned.

"*Too often* would have been a better answer. Tell me what the monks think of the people they hurt. Then explain how they rationalize the things they do."

"It's not all of them."

"Of course. The higher up you look in the church structure, the more corruption you find. I'm glad you see that as well."

"Can I have a drink?"

Cuthbert looked at Jolenta. She nodded, so he brought out a clay mug, which he filled with mead from a matching jug. Elfgar accepted it and immediately drank about a third of the contents. There was a sense of release as his body loosened and he breathed easier. He looked at Jolenta then Cuthbert, but closed his eyes before he started to speak.

"There were a few monks at Croyland who could read. I talked to one of them about the event that had sent me crawling there, told him God wasn't listening. He said to look to the Bible, quoted a verse and translated so I could understand. It's from Proverbs. *He who shuts his ear to the cry of the poor will also cry himself and not be answered.* I had no idea what it meant when he first read it, but now I believe I understand. You wanted to know why I left the abbey? Well, that is it. I thought about what I was doing for others and came up empty. I don't know exactly what you are asking of me, Jolenta, but I want to help people in need. If that's what you want, I'm in."

Elfgar finished the mead in his cup and looked at Jolenta. She was smiling.

Chapter Nineteen
Abigail

Abigail lay still after the rapists were gone. *Were they coming back?* She tried to breathe evenly and concentrate on the other question, *What now?*

Goda was near. She had watched them tie him and leave Holt nearby. She needed to free him and make sure they weren't hurt. Abigail tried to sit up, but there was a sharp pain in her lower abdomen. She also realized she was sitting in a puddle, naked in the wetness with her dress still around her neck. She reached to her crotch, felt the sticky substance, then pulled her hand back to see. It was blood, mixed with their semen no doubt, but mostly her own blood. They'd ripped her open, inside, and out. No wonder she felt so weak.

There was no noise other than the sound of birds and the honking of geese, probably swimming about on a nearby pond. Life was going on as if nothing had happened. She shook the thought out of her head. She needed to gather the strength to concentrate.

She had to free Goda, so Abigail rolled over, ignoring the pain as much as she could. She got up on her knees, but knew she couldn't rise any further. It wasn't the pain, it was exhaustion. She looked, found the tree where the slumped figure of Goda was tied, and started to creep forward, crawling, the way Holt would move toward her – if he could.

Her body told her to lie down. It said, "Stay on your back until death wraps you in a blanket of peace." But her heart told her she had to help the two people she loved or they would die with her.

When she reached Goda, Abigail shook him. He hadn't been punched or strangled, hadn't had a gang of men force themselves into his body, but he was the one who had to be roused.

"Are you all right?" she asked, when his eyes opened.

"I couldn't stop them," he muttered, his voice cracking.

"No, you couldn't, but God will damn them to Hell!" She was breathing heavily, like a horse who had been worked too hard.

She started to dig at the knots that tied his wrists. Her nails were short and broken and the knots were tight from his attempts to free himself. She kept picking at them as best she could, willing them loose.

"I'm like the pig," Goda said, "tied up and scared. Remember the pig, the little one father tied to a post so Waso and I could watch him slaughter it? You were only two, but I remember. You told me how you loved that little pig and I remember you following me behind the house. That's when I fell in love with you. I was too young to know it at the time, but I do now. You were my sister. I would have loved you anyway, the way I love Waso. But that day I knew I never wanted to leave you. I couldn't have imagined we would have a child together, but my heart knew we would share a life."

She was tired, too exhausted to say how she felt. Instead, she poured all the energy she had left into her fingers, finally forcing the knot to come loose. She fell back to the ground as Goda pulled the rope off his hands. He began to work on the tie binding his feet.

Holt was crying now, just a soft whimper and she could hear his breathing. As she gave in to exhaustion, the sound told her Holt was alive and consoled her with the knowledge that he and his father would survive.

***

Goda

Untying the knot that bound his ankles seemed to be taking Goda five hundred times longer than it had taken Abigail to free his hands. Holt's whimper had turned into a wild sound, like the wail of a trapped fox.

He finally managed to free himself then rushed to Abigail only to find her body limp and lifeless. He picked her head up and held his cheek against her mouth. He couldn't feel her breath! Could she be dead? She was talking just moments earlier. Her skin wasn't stiff. It didn't make sense. God couldn't be this cruel.

Goda shook her body trying to get some sign of life, but the blood that drenched her from waist down made it clear that the rape had killed her. This was his fault. He was the man. He was supposed to protect her. He'd done nothing when the priests had scarred her, nothing when the robbers raped her, nothing to keep her alive.

There was too much guilt, too much sorrow, too much loneliness to go on without her. He looked around for a weapon to end his life, but they'd taken his knife. He couldn't even kill himself properly. Then the screaming started again, the shrill sound he wanted to ignore as he held the woman he loved. The screeching spun him around as if he'd been hit with a club. Holt was alive and crying out for help. The child, their son, the person who was half Abigail, was lying beside the tree. Goda needed to free the boy.

Goda went to Holt, then lifted and brought him back to his mother. For a moment, as he held Holt over Abigail, Goda thought again that this tragedy was his own fault. God had punished him for having relations with his sister. Yet Abigail had been possessed with an unwavering need to have a child and, although they both had known incest was as grave a sin as anyone could commit, what they had done had brought Holt to them.

"It is not my fault and not yours, either," Goda told Holt. "The robbers did this to her and we will find revenge. I've got to get you to a safe place. After that I will come back, I will track them, and I will kill them, one by one. I make this promise to you and to the soul of your mother, for if God doesn't forgive, why should I?"

Goda started to lower Holt to the ground, but the boy's legs pushed down and touched the ground with intent. Goda realized his son was trying to stand. He held Holt up briefly, then released him. The child took one, two, three steps, and fell on his mother. His first steps were to the body of the woman who was supposed to guide him through the early years of his life. This was a sign. Goda wondered if this was Holt's way of saying he also wanted revenge.

***

Goda didn't know how to bury Abigail without tools to dig her grave, but he couldn't bear the thought of leaving her body in the forest, unprotected. He found a shallow ditch, dragged her to it, then gathered as many rocks as he could, enough to build a mound over her. He considered making a cross to mark where her head lay, but decided against it. God hadn't accepted her profession of faith while she was alive, so why would He now? She was better off lying unknown in an unmarked grave.

By the time Goda was ready to leave, he had decided where he would take his child. "We're going to see Elfgar," he told Holt.

The boy tilted his head and looked at his father in a way that indicated he was trying to understand, even though he was too young to know words.

"He's a good man. He helped us in the past and he'll help us now."

It took them a day and a half to reach Elfgar's home and when they arrived they found him on the floor, sleeping in a puddle of vomit and mead.

***

Elfgar

When Elfgar opened his eyes, he discovered he was on the floor. This was the third time since the last full moon he'd woken somewhere other than on the straw pallet where he normally slept. He would have a sore neck most of the day, but it wouldn't bother him after a couple of cups of mead. He stood, feeling a little dizzy, but he had no morning-after headache. He hadn't suffered from one of those since he'd started drinking regularly.

He took a step out of the pool of mead and vomit, looked around, and gasped. "What are you doing here?" he shouted at a man who was staring at him from the bench by his medicine table. Elfgar thought he recognized his uninvited guest, but he wasn't certain, until he noticed the child with the scarred nose.

"Where's your..." Elfgar's words trailed off. He didn't know if he should say wife, lover, or sister.

"Abigail is dead. That's why I'm here. I was looking for a safe place to leave Holt while I kill the gang of robbers who murdered her. It appears I may have made a mistake."

Goda's words surprised Elfgar. This was not a man he'd thought of as either brave or a lying braggart, but to say such a thing he had to be one or the other.

"They raped her," Goda continued, "and left her bleeding. I couldn't save her life, but I thought I could avenge her death, until I saw you lying in your own filth."

"You don't trust me to take care of your son? Is that what you're saying?"

"How often are you like that?" Goda pointed to the puddle of vomit.

Elfgar frowned. "I can take care of myself and I can take care of Holt while you're away. But what if they kill you? I don't want him here for the rest of my life. Raising your son is what Abigail would have wanted you to do."

"They were hiding. They surprised us while we were traveling. This time I will surprise them."

"Not after the first one dies."

Goda paused, took a couple of steps away from Elfgar, then turned back.

"Robbers in the forests have stolen from me a few times," Elfgar said, "They've also attacked victims of church abuse I was relocating to safe areas. The world would be better off without them, but Holt would *not* be better off without you."

"You sit with Holt while I go back to where I buried Abigail. I'll find the ones who attacked us and I'll kill their leader. I'll do it when he's alone and vulnerable. After that, I'll leave before any of his companions know what happened."

Elfgar thought about Goda's idea. It might work, if he was careful and quiet before he attacked and quick once he was done. Goda wasn't the man Elfgar would have chosen for such a plan, but Goda loved Abigail and perhaps all she had suffered had finally pushed him to a point where he had to strike back.

"All right," Elfgar told him. "You do what you have to do. Holt will be here when you return."

***

Goda

The first part of Goda's trip back to where Abigail had been killed was not difficult. Other than finding a safe place to sleep after the sunset, the walk there was just the reverse of the journey away. However, when he was getting close to the place where the attack took place, Goda abandoned the trail. The robbers would be watching the trail and Goda's plan would be ruined if they saw him before he found them. Off trail was a challenge. There were fallen trees and numerous gullies, but the biggest problem was knowing which way to go. Goda had to stay far enough from the trail to avoid being seen and that meant he was too far away to use it as a guide. He depended on the position of the sun, when the canopy of branches was thin enough to see through. He also depended on luck, which for the first time in as long as he could remember, came down on his side. He came up to the robber's camp without being noticed.

Goda had borrowed two weapons from Elfgar. The first was a spear, a wooden shaft as long as he was tall with an iron head sharpened to a point. The second was a knife, cast-iron like the spearhead, but with a short handle and a sharpened cutting edge. The spear was good for attacking from a distance, but the knife was better up close.

Goda watched the robbers, to learn their habits. He wanted to know when and where they ate, pissed, and shat, as well as how much time they spent away from the camp. But darkness came shortly after he reached them, so Goda picked a tree to lean against and settled there for the night. He found a stone the size of his fist and held it. Each time he dozed off, he dropped the stone and woke. As he had told Elfgar, this time he would not be the one caught unaware.

He was awake in the morning when the leader of the gang rose. The robber walked to a creek near their camp. Goda followed.

The killing was easy. Goda waited until the murderer was relieving himself, until he heard the man's piss hit the leaves of a bush. Then he stepped out from behind a large oak, moving as quietly as he could. He grabbed a handful of the man's hair, pulled his head back, and slit his throat open like a biscuit waiting for butter. The man had no time to yell. The only sound he made was a gargling noise as air from his lungs mixed with blood from his heart. His body twitched a few times, then slumped. Goda let him fall to the ground.

He made his way back to the place where he'd left his spear, then kept walking into the woods. Escaping seemed as easy as the killing had been. Goda watched his step, avoiding sticks that might break and piles of leaves or low branches that might rustle. It wasn't long before he had traveled far enough to move onto the trail. There were no signs that anyone was following.

Goda expected a rush of satisfaction as he walked toward Elfgar's home. He hadn't been able to protect Abigail when she was attacked, but there was no better way to honor her memory than to prevent her rapist from attacking other women. Yet the revenge wasn't what filled his thoughts, instead it was the small pig his father had slaughtered so many years ago, the one he and Abigail had spoken of. Goda had been listening from behind his house back then and had heard his father say to Waso, "...first we have to bleed it or the meat will go bad. I'll show you the cut." He was repulsed, but now, when he made a similar cut on a man, he felt a gentle high, as sweet as the day he and Abigail had basked in the sun, before the farmer caught them and changed their lives.

He thought about the skin of a man and how similar it is to the skin of a hog, with only the thinnest hair covering most of his body. He told himself that cutting human flesh is the same as cutting a hog. Then he remembered grabbing hold of the man's thick, brown head hair and the shock in the man's wide eyes as Goda pulled his head back. Goda remembered bringing the knife up and into the man's neck. "...bleed it or the meat will go bad." his father had said. He knew his father would have approved of, even praised, the killing, but would Abigail have felt the same? This was the woman who had adopted a stoat, who loved all life. Was it possible his own need for revenge had caused him to do something Abigail would not have wanted?

"No," he said out loud. "Sometimes killing is the only path to justice and the only way to ease the pain of grief."

Goda stepped to the side of the trail to pee. The closest bush had small, oval leaves, each with a slight point at the tip. As his water ran down the bush, he recognized the plant. It was the same type Abigail's murderer had been pissing on when Goda killed him. This was a sign. God was telling him killing a killer was a worthy act – a life for a life.

He felt another wave of pride, until he asked himself the same question he had asked before. What would Abigail say? This time he heard her answering with a different question. "Why didn't you say goodbye?"

"But I did," he said aloud, feeling a flutter in his stomach. "I said all I could say when I buried you."

But that wasn't good enough. He hadn't stopped by her grave this time. He'd been so close and hadn't given her body a thought. He looked up, then down the trail. There was no choice. It would be dangerous to go back, but if he didn't, he would regret his decision for the rest of his life.

Once again Goda walked the trail for a short distance, then stepped into the woods where he could continue his trip to Abigail's grave without revealing himself to the gang of robbers. Because this was the third time he hiked through this area, finding his way was easier. He recognized a few landmarks, such as a large boulder with a crack down the middle and a thin tree that was growing in a giant arc. The familiar places meant he didn't have to stop to determine which way to walk, allowing him to move much faster.

He found the robbers, still camped where he had killed their leader. This was unexpected. They knew someone had found and attacked one of their own. Goda had expected them to move to another campsite, deeper in the woods. He looked around, fearful that they might have set up guards around the perimeter, but the security around the site did not appear any greater than the last time.

He made a wide circle, then headed on toward Abigail's grave. He had to cross the trail near the place where the robbers had attacked them, making his way as cautiously as possible, checking for motion up in the trees as well as all the potential hiding places at ground level. He didn't see anything unusual until he was close enough to the mound of rocks to see two bodies, spread out on top of the stones.

He stopped to look again, thinking it could be a trap. The bodies weren't moving and he was close enough to be certain they were dead. One was a full-grown man, the other a child, slightly older than Holt. They were most likely victims of the gang, but why had the robbers dumped them on the grave? They'd left Abigail dying and had left Goda tied, without any concern for what would happen to their bodies. So, why would they move these?

Goda took a few more steps toward the grave for a closer look when a chill flashed through his body. The man had a thin stature, similar to his own and dark brown hair the same length and color as his. He looked more like Goda's twin than Waso ever had. *That's why they killed this man and his son,* Goda told himself, *and why they brought them here. The robbers thought these two were Holt and me. They didn't move their camp because they thought they'd killed the only man who knew its location.*

***

Elfgar

Before Holt arrived, each of Elfgar's days had seemed slower than the last. After Goda left him with the responsibilities of caring for a child, Elfgar found most days rushed by. This was good, but not all good. Having a naked child crawling around the house meant a lot of cleaning, but Elfgar was used to cleaning up after his own drunken activities, so he could take care of that. Elfgar loved the way alcohol helped him lose reality, but realized he wouldn't be able take care of a baby in that state, so he cut way back on his drinking.

On the fourth day after Goda left, Elfgar decided to take advantage of a warm, clear day to show Holt his favorite place. It was a spot by the river near his home, a place where tall grasses grew between the water and a line of trees. There was a large, flat rock where he liked to sit as he watched the river roll on.

One of the rules Jolenta had for everyone who helped her find homes for the victims of church abuse, was the requirement to pick a special place, somewhere they could think, pray, and remember the goodness of God. This was Elfgar's place. He'd never shared it with anyone, not even Jolenta.

Elfgar wrapped Holt in swaddling blankets. He packed salted pork, a wineskin of water for them both, and a knife to chop Holt's meal into pieces he could swallow.

The walk to the river seemed shorter than it had before, probably because Elfgar had someone to talk to along the way, even if that someone couldn't understand what he was saying. Once they arrived, he took Holt out of his blanket, which was wet, and bathed the child in the cool water. Holt seemed to enjoy the plunge so much Elfgar decided to join him. He carefully held the child's head above water as he waded waist deep. After their dip, Elfgar placed Holt next to him on the rock. They let the warm sun dry them.

The pork made a good midday meal, but eventually Elfgar knew it was time to head home. He carried Holt back in time to prepare a full dinner, before the sun went down. They both had enjoyed their time together and Elfgar decided to bring Holt back in a few days, if the weather was nice and there were no clients looking for medicine or something from the forge.

***

Goda

When Goda returned, he went inside Elfgar's empty house. He wondered where Elfgar and Holt were. Perhaps Elfgar needed supplies.

Goda sat on a bench by the back wall of Elfgar's home. He leaned forward, resting the weight of his upper body by placing his forearms on his legs, then stared out the entrance. All he could do was wait and think. Two questions filled his thoughts. The first was about Holt and Elfgar. The second was more complicated. He thought about the bodies on Abigail's grave, wondering if his need for revenge was responsible for their deaths. He would never know for sure, but he did know his guilt was a weight he would carry for the rest of his life.

Elfgar and Holt returned, walking out of the forest in front of the house. When Goda saw them, he stood and walked in their direction. He reached for his son as he greeted them. Holt wasn't eager to return to his father's arms, which was a disappointment.

Elfgar also greeted him in a surprising way saying, "You don't look happy. Did something go wrong?"

Maybe that's why Holt didn't want me to take him, Goda thought, *my joy is missing*. But he said, "I found him, killed him, and none of his gang knew I was there. It couldn't have gone better. Why is Holt's hair wet?"

"We were swimming in the river."

"Swimming? Why would you do that?"

Elfgar took a step back before saying, "Holt likes the water."

Elfgar went to the river just because Holt likes water? Goda thought. *That sounds like something Abigail would have done.* Then he nodded and they went inside.

Chapter Twenty
Stateira

After the seventh time they made love, Waso told Stateira he wanted her for his wife. They were on the ground, in a forest beside a creek. The love making had been gentle rather than passionate, which felt right to her. She straightened her clothing, covering her legs with her skirt while he did the same with his trousers and tunic. He then lay on his back, staring at the stars as she curled up next to him, resting her head on his chest. She didn't speak.

His words of marriage were a statement rather than a question, but even so, she could tell he was waiting for an answer. It was a show of respect she'd never known in a man, not even her father, this consideration of her feelings and opinions. She would have loved Waso anyway, even without such respect, but with it she felt as if paradise could not be better than this moment on the ground. Yet it would be difficult to express how she felt about his proposal.

"I know I have nothing to offer." His words were soft, but firm, with a hint of pride. "But I promise you, my family had land and I will again someday."

"It's not that," she said. Her chest felt tight, causing her to force each breath. She tried to explain. "I have sinned a great deal in my life."

"I don't care about that. None of it was your fault and what's done is done. We can have a good life together. Abigail and Goda will love you. You'll see. We'll have a strong family. Maybe children."

Stateira wasn't certain how Waso would react to what she had to tell him, so instead she said, "It's hard to explain."

"Try." He lifted her, so they could sit up. She didn't want to look at him, but had no choice. He was staring in her eyes, his brow furrowed.

"I don't believe I can have a child. I told you of my daughter who was born dead. Something happened after that. I haven't been with child since, not with Omar nor the Abbot. Perhaps with you. It's too soon to know, but I doubt it. Maybe you don't care about my sins, but Allah does."

"Why would your God punish you for what you were forced to do?"

"I should have been stronger."

"You're saying you should have made them beat you or tie you down? That's foolish."

"I'm saying I should have prayed more. I should have followed the rituals, the ways of my people."

"You can do that as my wife. You can do whatever you believe is right."

Stateira stood and turned from Waso. "I will stay with you as long as you want me," she told him, with a quaver in her voice. "But I will only become your wife in a ceremony performed by an imam."

"An imam?"

"A leader in my religion, like a priest in yours."

"But where would we find this imam?"

"What I'm trying to say is – I want to marry in a place where people understand my faith."

***

Waso

They'd never spoken about religion. Waso had always believed in God, but with an unusual faith. He didn't fear God, because he believed God had no reason to hurt him. When Waso wanted to accomplish something, he did it himself. God gave him the ability and strength, but Waso depended on himself. He had thought Stateira's concept of her god was similar to his own.

"I don't understand," he told her. "At sea, it was your strength that kept us alive. Perhaps Allah was the source, but you were the one who brought us to Britannia - alive."

"I'm willing to give up my homeland to stay with you."

"Then is it marriage you object to?"

"Not at all. I want to marry you, in a mosque, with an imam. If we can't do that, I still want to spend the rest of my days with you."

"But not as man and wife."

Stateira nodded. "We've been through a lot together." She turned away from Waso, staring down at the water in the tiny creek. Her words began as a mumble, but became stronger as she continued. "I want my life to be more of the same. I want to spend more time with you, the rest of my life, if possible."

This was what Waso wanted to hear, but what she said still didn't explain Stateira's wish to marry in a mosque or not at all.

She smiled and looked up, bringing her stare back to Waso's eyes. "Yet, there was a time when I wasn't sure."

"There was?"

"It was right after we stole the boat, when we were crossing Lake Malaren and had to find a place where we could get the supplies we needed for the journey we were about to take."

"Yes. You're talking about the place where Wulfgyfe was a thrall. We were lucky I knew her."

"Exactly, the place where you found Wulfgyfe."

Waso noticed that Stateira rolled her eyes when she said Wulfgyfe's name. Was she jealous? This was a turn he hadn't expected, not given her history.

"We'd been together long enough for me to know you were different. The first man I was with was Omar. He was gentle, but had very little respect for me. He had three wives and didn't intend to marry me. After him there was the Abbot. He didn't hurt me, either, but he was a hypocrite and had no respect for any woman. You weren't like either of them. You not only accepted my opinion, you requested it. I thought I was more than a woman to you. I thought I was your world. But I wasn't, which you proved that night."

"You're my world now!"

"I didn't know there would come a time when you would say that. All I knew was that you wanted to find your brother and sister. I admired your goal, but it wasn't mine. I was there because something made me trust you and that something had been broken. So, I prayed."

"To Allah?"

"Of course." Her chin began to tremble and her eyes filled with tears. Waso could see that Stateira was opening to him in a way he hadn't imagined possible. She was telling him their relationship wasn't about the two of them. Whatever the name she called her God, it was clear she had brought Him with her and He had kept them safe. "I asked why I had been born in such a world, where love is so one sided. Then we struck a deal, Allah and me. He would guide me, keep me safe, and grant me the love I deserve, if I would always honor Him in our relationship."

"In our relationship? You mean us, not you and Allah?"

"That is the pact. I want to marry you, Waso, but only in a ceremony that honors Allah."

Chapter Twenty-One
Duette

Duette's work life had been mostly about wool, until Jolenta approached her on a spring afternoon while the young girl was using the distaff and spindle to spin.

"You're old enough now to start thinking about your future," Jolenta told her daughter. "Matilda wanted the best for you, but she realized what is best for one woman is not always best for another. Your life choices belong to you, not to me and not to Matilda's memory."

Duette knew her other mother had been forced to pretend she was a man, to compete in a world that wasn't fair to women. Although she wasn't sure what it was her mother considered unfair, she had a feeling she was about to find out.

The fact that Modig was not Matilda's real name was a family secret Duette had kept faithfully. Since she didn't like talking to adults and only knew one person her own age, the annoying son of the sheep farmer who sold them their wool, she had no problem keeping the secret.

"In a few years," Jolenta said to her daughter, "you will have to make a decision that will affect the rest of your life. If you want a husband, I will find one for you. I will look for a kind person, but no matter which man I choose, you will become his property as soon as you take your vows. He will have the right to tell you what to do and to hurt you if you disobey."

Duette clenched the distaff harder, but tried not to appear worried or scared.

"You could choose to join a convent," Jolenta continued. "If you do, no man will own you. Yet, your life will still be limited. You'll report to an Abbess who will control your daily life by assigning you a schedule of hard work, ritual, and prayer. I've been there, so I can tell you there are issues with that choice, as well."

Duette couldn't will her left leg to stop shaking, so she tried another tactic. She rested her free hand on it and applied pressure. The process worked with her leg, but she still felt a little dizzy.

"Unlike most young women, you have a third choice. You know some of what I do, but tonight I'm going to show you details of my choice. Matilda and I were lucky enough to provide for ourselves while helping others. I believe that choice has put us ahead of the priests in God's eyes, but we had to break a few rules to succeed and people would say we will suffer for what we did. That is something you have to keep in mind. If you choose to follow our path, I will train you. It is not a trade, like spinning and weaving, but it is a way to keep a roof over your head and food in your belly, while living a life with purpose."

Duette tried to return to her spinning after her mother walked outside, but her fingers felt fat and clumsy. She put the yarn down. She was ahead of where she needed to be for that project and it was time to think about making dinner.

***

Later that evening, an early moon provided light for Duette to watch her mother strap Polly, their brown cart horse, to the wagon. Duette witnessed this process often and each time it had preceded her mother leaving, sometimes for days. But this time would be different. She was going along. This was particularly exciting because this wagon wasn't used for regular farm work. Jolenta saved it, instead for her secret missions.

The cart was long enough that Jolenta could have lain in it with her feet at the back end and still have left plenty of room for Duette to lie down with *her* feet touching her mother's head. It was so wide, Duette couldn't reach both sides at the same time. It was filled with empty barrels.

When they both had climbed on the cart seat, Jolenta turned to Duette. "From this moment until we've returned home you will need to be quiet, no more sound than a flower makes when opening at dawn. Understand?"

Duette nodded. She knew how to be quiet as well as she knew how to breathe, having spent most of her life with no one but her mother to talk to. But she didn't know what good it would do. This old wagon would make more noise than a falling tree every time its wheels turned.

Jolenta shook the reins, causing Polly to move. Duette turned to see why the wagon was not as noisy as she'd expected. The barrels were lashed to the sides of the cart, so they couldn't bang against each other and the two axles must have been coated with chicken fat. Still, the wooden wheels against the stones in the path made enough sound to drown out the insects and frogs that normally sang throughout the night.

"As we make our way along the road, I will be praying for success," Jolenta told her daughter. "My prayers have always been answered in the past, which means God appears to believe in what I do. Remember that, even when our work seems misguided. I hope I've taught you how to tell good from evil without listening to false promises."

After they traveled for a while, the rocking motion of the wagon and the constant drone of the turning wheels caused Duette to grow sleepy. She rested her head against her mother's shoulder and drifted off. When Jolenta woke her with a gentle shake, the moon was high in the sky. They had pulled up in front of a large barn, the largest she'd ever seen.

The barn was a typical construction of rough wood sides and a thatched roof, but there were a few unusual aspects to this building. The first was its size. Then there was also the fact that it stood alone in the woods. Where did the farmer live? And what was most confusing was the large cross at the corner of the building nearest the wagon.

The barn was filled with grain, some in open piles still on the stalk, but most in barrels after the grain had been separated. Jolenta showed Duette how to dip her bucket into each barrel then carry it to the wagon and dump it in their own barrels. There was a word for what they were doing – stealing.

Even though Duette and her mother hadn't spoken to each other since shortly after they left home, it didn't take much thought to determine that the church owned this barn.

The priests hadn't stationed anyone here to protect their wealth, probably assuming no one would dare steal from God. That's why the cross was there, to let potential thieves know they were risking their souls. Or maybe it was more powerful than a warning. Maybe the cross called on God to punish the thieves. Maybe Duette would suffer for what she was doing this night. It came back to what Duette's mom had said earlier, that breaking rules to help others puts them ahead of the priests in God's eyes.

Duette reached into one of the barrels of barley to scoop more into her bucket. The container her mom had given her was half the size of Jolenta's and, since she was walking as far away as she could from the cross, it was taking Duette twice as long to make a trip out to the cart and back again. She was not contributing as much as she felt she should to the effort. But if God wasn't on her mom's side, then not contributing was a good thing. How can I know what's right and what's wrong? Duette wondered. I listen for God, but he doesn't speak.

This time, when Duette passed the cross while carrying another bucket of barley, she stopped to ask God what she should do. She didn't hear an answer, but she closed her eyes and a picture formed in her mind of one of the women who had come by the house to be relocated by Jolenta. It was almost a year ago. There was a hole in the woman's face, at the place where one of her eyes had once been. She must have witnessed something she wasn't supposed to see. Why else would the priests have gouged out an eyeball?

Duette opened her eyes and still saw the face of a one-eyed woman. It took her a moment to realize that the moon was behind the cross, off slightly to the right side, forming a picture of one eye and a long nose. This was a sign, but Duette wasn't sure what the sign meant. She continued on to the cart and dumped the barley into the appropriate barrel. Then she headed back to the barn, forming a wide circle around the cross.

She would ask her mother later, when she was allowed to speak again. Meanwhile, she would continue to help.

They rode in the cart until sunlight began to seep above the treetops. Duette felt nervous about what they'd just been through. The sensation had wiped out any thoughts of time. She was also too skittish to feel tired, but not so much she could avoid feeling guilty. Jolenta had taught her not to steal, yet that's what they had done.

"Are you all right?" Jolenta asked.

Duette must have been shaking. She struggled to control her limbs as she replied to her mother's question with one of her own. "Did the barn belong to the church?" When Jolenta didn't answer, she added, "I saw the cross."

"People who don't have other ways to pay, often give tithes in the form of grain or livestock. The church needs to keep those gifts someplace."

"So, you find out where those barns are and take what's there. Aren't you worried about God's vengeance?"

"The church hurt the people we help. They should pay. If God didn't understand, he would have struck me down years ago."

Jolenta's words made sense to Duette, but they hadn't been spoken by a priest. She wasn't sure her mother was right to draw a line between the church's will and God's. There was a lot she had to think over before she could know if joining her mother's work would be the right decision.

They rode the rest of the way home in silence.

***

Stateira

The trek through the forests of Britannia left Waso and Stateira tired every night. As a result, it had been five days since they'd had sex. She felt a tightening in her chest as she thought about their new-found celibacy. She wasn't certain it was all from exhaustion. Stateira knew they weren't abandoning the search for Waso's brother and sister, but she wasn't sure he was convinced, especially when she reached out for him during the night and he turned away.

The next evening Waso again fell asleep without touching her. Stateira lay awake, hugging herself as she tried to understand what was happening. After she was certain he was asleep, she rolled away from the man she loved, then stood and, feeling a need to hide, moved into the forest. This was not a safe choice. The canopy of leaves above her was thick enough to keep the moon and the stars hidden. The area was so dark she had to feel her way. Still, she crept away from the rock formation where they'd chosen to spend the night and kept going, because it hurt too much to stay near him. But as she started to make her way around a cluster of something with the texture of fir trees, she felt a hand on her shoulder.

Stateira dropped, first to a crouch then to her knees. She tried to crawl away, but the hand on her shoulder had gripped the material of her dress. She tried to break free, pulling until a familiar voice stopped her.

"It's me." She recognized Waso speaking in a whisper.

"Why did you follow?" she asked in full voice. She stood, but he kept his grip on her.

"There are people near," he said.

She fell back to a crouch and looked around, seeing only darkness.

"I heard them. Hold my tunic. We have to move before they find us."

Stateira held to Waso's clothing until they started to crawl. She kept so close to him, his legs were repeatedly touching her arms. Quiet was more important than speed, so they hadn't gotten far when something she heard caused a chill to shake her spine. It was a man's voice calling out a question. "What's going on?" She would recognize that voice anywhere – the Abbot's.

Stateira's eyes started to blink uncontrollably. The night was so dark open or closed eyes made no difference, but the involuntary movement made her realize how scared she was, which frightened her even more.

She had some relief in that Waso was in control and leading her to safety. When she heard the Abbot's voice the small comfort disappeared. Horrible memories swirled through her body, causing her arms to feel weak and her stomach to flip, as if she was about to lose the squirrel meat she'd eaten earlier that evening.

She froze for only the briefest moment, yet long enough for Waso to get away from her. When she reached out to touch him all she could feel was a few seedling trees. Now what, she thought. She had to keep moving, but if she lost her sense of direction she might crawl back under the control of the man who had repeatedly raped her in the name of God.

She pushed through the seedlings, scraping her bare knee on a stone. She pulled her skirt to her waist, but crawling was difficult. The dark had one advantage, the Abbot couldn't see her. Memories of that man flooded her thoughts, how many times he had her crawl to him, the way she was crawling now. She had to choose to come at him face first or to push her backside his way and if her choice matched his mood he'd give her things, mostly clothing or jewelry – sometimes extra freedom to leave the monastery on her own. The hardest part was to keep smiling. If her expression didn't match his mood, he wouldn't be happy.

Life had been hard since she'd met Waso, but she had dignity and felt loved for the first time since she was a girl on the surface of the Caspian. And if she could believe what Omar had told her, the love her father had shown was never true. Waso was the only one who cared unconditionally.

She crept forward again, but felt something touch her head. Stateira jumped slightly and nearly shrieked. She managed to keep her cool enough to realize this person had to be Waso. He'd returned for her. She reached up and touched his hand. He took hers and moved it to his trouser leg. This time she wouldn't let go, no matter how hard it was to crawl with only one hand touching the ground.

***

Waso

They stopped at a clearing where moonlight could break through allowing Waso and Stateira to see each other. They stood. Waso looked her over. She had scratches on her arms, legs, and face, but nothing deep enough to keep them from moving on. She checked him out in the same fashion, pointing to a few cuts on his neck, but nodding as if to say these would all heal.

Stateira gestured toward her mouth, indicating she wanted to speak. Waso shook his head because they had put very little distance between themselves and the people whom they had heard in the woods. He wanted to move farther to a place, any place, where they would be safe. But Stateira insisted she had something she needed to tell him. He stood still as she leaned in and whispered in his ear. "The Abbot."

Waso pulled back from her, while simultaneously grabbing both her upper arms. He felt as if he would fall without her support. But he knew he couldn't let her down. If he was shocked at discovering the Abbot in the middle of nowhere, how would Stateira feel? She had been the man's slave.

He signaled toward the forest on the other side of the clearing, taking a step. She followed without holding his arm. Waso turned, reached for her hand, and put it on his shoulder. They were heading back into the darkness, this time on their feet.

***

Stateira

They kept moving for the rest of that night and most of the following day. They stopped once, by a pond where they managed to find and catch two turtles, which they ate raw because it would take too much time to start a fire.

Other than two short water breaks, the turtle lunch was the only rest they allowed themselves. It was still light when they lay down together for the night, but they were too exhausted to keep moving.

Stateira was certain she would fall asleep as soon as she was horizontal, but Waso did something that stopped her. She was on her side with her back toward him. He put his left arm across her, pushed his fingers down the collar of her dress, and started to massage her skin just under her neck.

In an instant, she was awake and breathing hard. She turned to kiss him and he returned the kiss. All exhaustion was gone. She was filled with energy, driven by desire.

Waso was as good a man as had ever walked the world. He had saved her life, but she had loved him before that happened. This wasn't about gratitude or admiration. This was pure desire. She could feel her need for him throughout her body as she wrapped him with her arms and legs. He pulled away, which surprised her until she realized he was taking off his clothes. She did the same, then grabbed him again. He rolled to his back, so she was straddling him, then she leaned forward. Her breasts touched his chest as they kissed again.

When they were done making love, Stateira rested her head on Waso's chest. She loved lying in this position after their lovemaking. She felt as if she could stay on Waso forever, enjoying the feel of his body rising and lowering with his breathing. It was peaceful, as if they were the only two people in the world. She felt exhausted again and this time she fell asleep.

***

Waso

"Waso! My brother!"

He opened his eyes to see what had to be a dream. Goda was standing over him, looking down. His brother was holding a child. A man he didn't recognize was beside them.

"Elfgar?" Stateira called out as she sat up and tried to cover her nakedness as well as she could.

"Yes. That's my name." Elfgar replied, his eyes narrowing. Then he and Goda both turned while Waso scrambled to his feet and Stateira reached for her dress.

Everyone stood motionless for a moment, while Stateira slipped her clothing over her head. "I was at Nendrum," she said when she was done dressing. "You knew me."

"Stateira?" Elfgar said, turning back and taking a step forward. "What a surprise. Why are you and Goda's brother together?"

"We could ask the same question of you two," Waso said, as he pulled his clothes on. When he had his trousers in place he asked, "Who is this child? And where is Abigail?"

"The boy is Holt," Goda said, looking down at the ground as he answered Waso's first question. "We took him in, Abigail and I."

Waso noticed Elfgar's head jerk back slightly. For a moment, he wondered why the man seemed surprised, but his thoughts quickly turned to Abigail and Goda taking in a homeless child. He glanced at Stateira and nodded, as if to say, S*ee? That is so like my sister and brother.*

Goda then went on to answer the second question. The exact words he said didn't register in Waso's mind, but somehow their meaning did. Abigail was gone – dead.

What am I supposed to feel? Waso thought. He was emotionally numb. Wrapping his feelings around the death of his sister was harder than any task he'd ever accomplished or imagined.

From the time when they were children, Waso had been jealous of Goda's relationship with their sister. He never understood why she preferred their brother. Waso was stronger, braver, and quicker than Goda. He won at the games they played and was always done with his chores faster. So why had Abigail chosen Goda to be her favorite? Now that she was gone, Waso would never know. He would also never have a chance to prove to Abigail he could listen to her problems and keep her secrets as well as, or better than, Goda.

Waso had once caught Abigail climbing the tall oak that grew near a large boulder. He had been nine, so she must have been seven. The low branches could be reached from the top of the stone, which made it easy to get started. This was the best climbing tree anywhere near their farm. He'd climbed it himself more times than he could say. But he didn't like the idea of her up that high. She could hurt herself. He stopped her and made her go inside. He might have saved her life. But after that, she'd been whispering with Goda and they'd both scowled at him for days. He hated that memory.

Yet, there was also the time when Waso had to work outside, helping his father fix the side of the barn after a tree had fallen on it. It was raining hard. They couldn't stop, because the faster they patched the hole, the less water would reach the wheat they had stored for their winter bread. They saved most of it, but Waso turned sick the next day. Abigail tended to him, cooking for him, even feeding him when he was at his weakest. She stuck by his side after the illness was gone, until Goda had some other problem that stole her attention. Again, he had lost her to Goda.

Waso turned his back toward his friends. He didn't want them to see him cry, even Stateira - especially Stateira. Introducing her to Abigail had been in the back of his thoughts for what seemed forever, more a part of his being than a dream. That thought made him realize the truth about his sister's death as well. Losing her was losing a part of himself.

The world spun as tears streamed down his cheeks. He dropped to his knees and instantly felt a hand on his shoulder. "This world isn't all there is," Stateira whispered in his ear. She was right behind him. "You'll see her again."

Waso tried to thank her, but no words came out.

Chapter Twenty-Two
Duette

Most of the wheat Duette and her mother took from the church's barn was in the form of grain, but some was still on the stalk. It needed to be threshed, a task Jolenta assigned to Duette. Jolenta had brought home freshly harvested wheat from other raids, although never as much as they had this time. Duette wondered if there might be a message in her mother's choice.

Threshing was not an easy task. She had to spread the wheat on the barn floor, then beat it until she had separated most of the seeds from the stalks. She kept the seeds to make bread and the stalks for patching the thatched roofs of both the barn and their house. Gathering the seeds was a tedious task, but always somewhat of a relief from the exhausting work of threshing. Once she was done separating grain from stalk, she had to start over again with more wheat.

Most peasant girls Duette's age were used to this type of labor, but Duette was not. She wondered if that was the point her mother was trying to get across. A life centered on helping the victims of abusive priests would be less labor, more fulfilling, and a good deal less boring than a life as a farmer's wife.

When she had spread more stalks, she picked up the flail and started to swing it again. Over and over, she brought the loose bar attached to the handle down on the plants that would become their bread. The constant battering jiggled, knocked, and tore the seeds off, but the amount of dust raised caused Duette to have trouble breathing. She had to take a break, so she set the flail down and stepped out of the barn.

People were visiting Jolenta. Although Duette had heard crying while she was in the barn, she hadn't heard any shouting, a good sign, especially in combination with the knives the visitors had left on a stump outside the house. She walked to the entrance of her home and peered inside the open doorway.

Jolenta was there with five other people. She recognized Elfgar, but not the others. These were two men, one woman, and a crying baby. Since they were with Elfgar, they were probably people in search of new homes, victims of church or state abuse.

The men looked like farmers, who could have come from any neighboring village. They both had scruffy beards, like most of the men Duette had met, but one of them had longer hairs on his chin. That one was shorter than the other, thin, with a pot belly. The taller one had more muscular arms and stronger shoulders.

They were sitting on the benches along the back wall, the tall man, and the woman next to each other, close enough to give the impression they were a couple. This surprised Duette because the woman looked foreign. She dressed normally, in a simple brown shift, but her dark hair and skin made her look special. How did such different people find each other?

"Duette," Jolenta called. "I want you to clean up after the baby, then take him outside. His name is Holt." The baby was on the floor at the feet of the shorter man.

Duette smelled an odor in the room, like an outhouse. She couldn't determine where the stink came from, until she looked at Holt and saw he'd soiled his clothing. He was dressed in a gown, open at the bottom for just such a problem. The problem was, he hadn't been on his feet when he'd emptied his bowels. The hem of the gown was almost as wet and dirty as his body was. The man should have lifted his gown and held him out where he could drop his waste on the floor, instead of setting him down to take care of himself. But she didn't mind. She supposed Jolenta and Matilda had done the task for *her*, before she was old enough to use the outhouse.

She didn't remember ever seeing a child this small and was fascinated by the way his little hands worked, grasping at the air. Holt had a scar on his nose, but other than that mark and his dirty clothes, he seemed fine.

Holt kept crying as Duette took a wet cloth to his bottom. He didn't stop until she picked him up and carried him outside. There was still some odor from what remained on his gown, but she wondered if there was another smell as well. Matilda had once told her babies have a unique scent, one that seems to linger in a woman's nose then swirls to the back of her head. This was the first chance she'd had to smell that special odor. She had seen other babies before, but because she had no close friends, she'd never known a mother well enough to hold her child. Matilda had said she remembered the odor clearly. She had said it left her wanting more, like waiting to watch the sun rise on a cloudy morning.

Duette stepped around the house, where Jolenta and the visitors couldn't see her. She lifted his gown and buried her nose in his belly. He still smelled of his own waste more than anything else. She held him at arms distance and looked at his little round body. He had a tiny penis, smaller than her thumb. She wondered if that was normal for male babies, as it was for baby goats, whose male parts were so small she had to look for the absence of female parts to know what sex they were. Of course, the goats had hair between their legs. Like her, this little one had nothing. Jolenta had told her she would grow hair there someday. Maybe men had to wait like she did.

She leaned in and took one more deep inhale of Holt's belly. There was still no magical smell, but the little boy reached out and touched the side of Duette's face. She liked his touch and the smooth feel of his body. She pulled the gown down and headed back to the front of the house. She would sit on a stump out there and let him rest on her lap. Maybe he wouldn't mind if she played with his feet. They were so cute.

***

Jolenta

"You've raided this barn more than once?" Elfgar asked. He wasn't looking at Jolenta when he spoke to her, rather out the door where Duette was sitting with Holt. "Wasn't that dangerous?"

"I believe God is fair and I've been at this a long time without being wrong."

Waso tipped his head slightly. "Are you saying you protect yourself through prayer?"

"I'm saying the church blessed the ground where they built the barns, then erected crosses. The priests think that's enough to keep thieves away, but God isn't on their side. He's on the side of the women they abused, so a cross doesn't drive me away, it beckons me."

Everyone remained quiet until Jolenta continued, "I spent years in a convent. I know God, and He knows me. He wants me to live the life I live. And Matilda, Duette's other mother, was a nun. She understood God more than anyone I've ever known, certainly better than Duette's horror of a father, Luken."

"Luken?" Stateira whispered, her voice shaking.

Jolenta could see sweat on the woman's forehead. "You understand which man I'm speaking about, don't you?"

"He didn't allow me to use his name, but I was in Nendrum for a long time."

"He forced himself on Matilda, just as he forced himself on you."

"Are you...are you saying the Abbot is Duette's father?" Waso lifted his hand to his throat as he spoke, as if he was trying to keep his words inside.

Jolenta looked back and forth between Waso and Stateira. "Before he was sent to Nendrum, years before."

Elfgar leaned forward, drawing Jolenta's attention. "And now he's in this area." She noticed his brow was furrowed and his hands balled into fists. "And probably looking for the person who took his grain. We need to think of a way to handle him before he realizes you're the thief, Jolenta."

"What do you suggest?"

"Should we hide the grain?" Elfgar asked.

"Or dump it somewhere," Waso added.

Jolenta shook her head. "I need to sell it, to buy resettlement houses."

That's when Goda, who had been quiet for most of the conversation, finally spoke. "I could kill him." No one said a word until Goda added, "I've killed before."

Jolenta wondered if doing God's will was about to cross over to mortal sin, but she stayed quiet. It would certainly help if the man was gone.

"We should determine what he's up to before we take action," Waso suggested.

Jolenta looked at Stateira to see her reaction. Waso had just dismissed the suggestion to kill the man who had raped Stateira repeatedly, but she wasn't showing any emotion. Jolenta had heard of Stateira when the woman had been one of Elfgar's contacts inside Nendrum. At the time, she knew the Persian beauty was brave enough to betray the man who owned her.

"I agree with Waso," Elfgar said. "Stateira just heard his voice. She didn't see him, so she could have made a mistake. The first thing we need to do is confirm we're dealing with Luken. After that, we need to know what he's up to. Is he going to the barn? Is he on his way here? What does he know about us?"

Stateira and Jolenta started to speak at the same time. They looked at each other and Stateira nodded, giving Jolenta the right to speak first. "He knows nothing about me."

"You can't be sure," Elfgar argued. "You've helped many victims and people talk, especially if they're threatened."

"They wouldn't..."

"What did you want to say?" Elfgar asked Stateira.

"The Abbot's voice rings in my ears night and day and will probably stay there for the rest of my life. I can't stamp it out or burn it or bury it in some far-off pile of sheep dung. And when I heard him in the forest, the sound of that voice matched the terror in my head. There is no chance I was mistaken."

"We still need to find him and the men he's traveling with."

A sound broke into the house as if it was thrust at them, like a spear. Goda turned to Jolenta and asked what the noise could be. "It sounded like a tree falling," he said.

Jolenta heard a second crash, not quite as loud as the first. "We have to leave. Now! It's Duette, signaling us!"

"Where do we go?" Elfgar asked.

"What about Holt?" Goda shouted before Jolenta could answer Elfgar's question.

"He'll be safe. Duette will know where to meet us in the woods. She'll take care of him."

"Where in the woods? Where do we go?" Elfgar repeated.

"We'll move together, behind the barn. If everything seems safe, we'll head into the forest from there."

"You're certain Duette will take care of Holt?" Goda yelled as they all stood.

"What you heard was Duette hitting one of the grain barrels with a thick branch we keep in the barn, probably breaking the barrel given how loud the sound was. We've planned this escape for years. Holt will be fine, but you won't, not unless you do what I say, right now."

***

Stateira

Faith in an afterlife kept Stateira fearless. She had shown how she was willing to face hardships on land and sea, but the thought of returning to the Abbot's control terrified her. He had never hurt her physically, but instead had beaten her psychologically. He had thrown his words of God, of humanity, and of her worthlessness at her every day, until she broke. She couldn't explain why, but if he wanted her to cook for him, she cooked. To sew for him, she sewed. To dress for him, she dressed. To *undress* for him, she undressed. When he wasn't in her presence, she was capable of betraying him, but every time she saw him, she fell like cut wheat.

She was more terrified than she had ever been, so Stateira prayed as she ran, prayed the noise was not the Abbot. And if it was, that he wouldn't catch her. Waso came up behind her, as they crossed the yard toward the barn. When she felt his presence beside her, she felt guilt for not including him in her prayers.

"It is the Abbot, right?" she asked Jolenta when they were hidden behind the barn.

The woman ignored her question, first staring at the woods, then commanding the others to follow as she began running again.

***

Goda

It was painful for Goda to run as if Abigail never existed. He told himself he was not running for his own life, but for Holt's. Abigail would have wanted him to do what he was doing. Yet his fear seemed a betrayal. Goda was glad he had volunteered to kill the priest, but more than that he needed to take Holt to a safe place where he could raise him. Yet, when Goda had seen Duette playing with his son, he had realized Holt needed more than safety. Holt needed family, especially now that he'd lost his mother. If they both survived this day, he would do something to fix that.

Chapter Twenty-Three
Duette

There was a story Jolenta and Matilda used to tell about a fox who had to run from his uncle, the wolf. It should have been easy to escape the witless wolf, because he was about to kill and eat a bunny. But the bunny was a friend of the fox, so Reynard (that was the fox's name) felt he had to save the innocent animal. He made a loud noise, then, while the wolf was distracted, picked the bunny up by the scruff of his neck and carried him to safety.

As Duette grew older, she convinced herself that her two mothers had made up that story to explain why they helped the victims of the abusive priests. But now the story seemed all too real. She was the fox. Holt was the bunny. And the wolf? Hopefully, they would get away without discovering his identity.

Duette picked up Holt and jumped for the pile of wheat stalks waiting to be threshed. She slipped behind the pile then got on her back, holding Holt on her chest. She pulled wheat over herself and the child. He was as quiet as a scared bunny, which surprised her. She knew next to nothing about babies, but she did know they were supposed to cry.

Two men came in the barn, which caused the goats to bleat. It was unusual for them to react to people, but they were probably still scared from the noise Duette had made when she broke the empty barrel. She was glad for the distraction, because Holt began to whimper slightly. She moved her left hand to cover his mouth, but since her attention was on the men, she missed slightly and stuck her thumb in Holt's mouth. She could feel the tension drain from his little body as he started to suck, like a kid on a mama goat's teat.

The goats drew the attention of the two men, who were armed with axes, until a tall, bald man with a thick, gray beard stepped into the building and ordered them out. The first two men were dressed in trousers and tunics, like most men she knew. This third man was wearing a long, robe, similar to the clothing she'd seen on priests. If he was from the church, then he may have been looking for the thieves who stole the grain.

"This is where the noise came from," one of the original men said. He pointed at the broken barrel with the tree branch beside it.

"I can see that, but nobody's here now. Look around outside and move quickly. It had to be a warning of some sort. I want to find out who did it and why."

They all left the barn. Duette gave them a short time to move away from the door, then followed them out of the building. She could see the back of the tall man, but decided to run anyway. Hopefully, he wouldn't turn around. She circled the barn to the back, where the woods were close. Jolenta and the others had been in the house. These men had been walking in their direction when Duette had made the noise that had pulled them away. She hoped her mom, Holt's dad, and the people with them had escaped while they were looking for her. Now, she hoped she and Holt could also get away.

She reached the house, but didn't go inside. Instead she went around to the back, near the outhouse, then crossed the narrow field to the woods. The men would go inside first and were certain to find signs that people had just been there. It would take them some time to decide what to do next. By the time they circled the house, she and Holt would be in the protection of her forest, where she knew every stone, tree, and creek. Once there, the men would never catch up with her.

They made it to the woods, but when Duette looked back, she saw a group of five men running in their direction. This wouldn't be as easy as she had thought, especially since she was still holding Holt with her right arm while allowing him to suck her left thumb.

The men would hear them if they tried to run, letting them know which way to follow. And Duette couldn't outrun them, even if she left Holt behind, which she would never do. They had to hide. She knew the perfect place, if they could get there before the men reached the woods. She turned slightly to her left and made her way deeper into the forest. A portion of the creek that ran through their farm was this way and a short distance upstream, a large oak stood beside the running water. Something must have rerouted the creek years ago, because the roots of the tree stuck out over the water. The part of the root structure over the water had been washed clean of dirt, leaving a thick mass of tangled roots, half in the water and half in the air.

Duette had played fort with that tree a few times and knew the way to get inside. They would have to get wet to do it, but it was their best chance. Her plan depended on how quickly she moved and on how well she could keep Holt quiet, even when she had to dunk him in the brook.

Her thumb was getting sore. She pulled it out of Holt's mouth and let him suck on two of her fingers. She knew his mother was dead and he hadn't had the breast in a while. Duette had seen goats who were weaned too soon react that way, so maybe people did, too. But for now, as she ran through the woods, she was grateful she had a way to keep him quiet.

She found the tree and saw that weeds and small floating branches were wrapped around more than half of the root cage. This would help block Duette and Holt from the sight of the men, even if the group walked close to the side of the creek.

Duette brought water to Holt's lips and took some herself. She was thirsty and could tell Holt was as well. After they drank, Duette moved quickly, stepping down into the sloped surface under the moving water. Holt was no longer sucking. He was restless, but still quiet. She rocked him and quietly hummed in his ear as she stepped further in, until the stream was waist high. The water was colder than she'd expected. Duette placed her hand behind Holt's head, moved his face against her shoulder, bent her legs, and dipped beneath the surface.

She carried him along the rocky creek bottom, walking through the water because her hands were not free to help by paddling. She made it to the space among the roots and rose up where they could both breathe. Holt didn't complain. He stopped his squirming and stared in her eyes, still not making a sound. It was as if the child was used to water.

The men must have looked in other directions first, because it took them some time to reach the tree. When they did, they tramped by without any notice of her and Holt under it. Duette waited for the men to pass again, on their way back, then, after giving them sufficient time to leave the woods, she left the shelter of the root cage by repeating the underwater walk.

Although the creek had been cool, the work required for Duette to carry a child kept her blood flowing and her body warm. She was sweating and her arms began to ache, forcing her to stop. She set Holt on his back and stepped away, to sit on a stone. She watched him wave his arms and legs as she thought how important it was to save this innocent child from the terror chasing them. She wondered if he understood the need to escape. He turned over and crawled toward her until he was close enough to sit and hold his arms out. She smiled, thinking, *I guess he does*. After running with him, dipping him in water, and jostling him for so long she'd probably bruised his little body, he still looked to her to keep him safe.

Duette picked Holt up, but then returned to the rock to sit and rest with the baby on her lap. She thought of the stories Jolenta had told her of growing up in the home of a wet nurse, what life had been like in a house filled with infants. Jolenta generally started with complaints about the children, but she would add something to the effect of, "It was different with you. You were our own."

Once Duette had learned about birthing from watching the goats, Jolenta would tell her that Matilda was the one who had brought her into this world, but they had always considered her to be a daughter to both. Their shared love didn't stop after Matilda's death.

Duette knew where Jolenta would be waiting, but to go there would require walking in the same direction as the men who had been chasing them. Instead, she decided to go the opposite way, to a neighbor's orchard. She could get a few apples there. After they ate, they could head to the meeting place. Her mom had said not to hurry if there was any danger. They would both keep checking until they found each other.

When they reached the orchard, Duette put Holt down near the edge of the woods, so she could keep an eye on him while she picked. She took a few steps toward the fruit trees, then turned back to check on the baby. He was crawling, following quite fast. She turned around and picked him up. This presented a problem. Duette needed to pick and carry the apples back to the woods. She couldn't do that while carrying Holt. She thought about eating in the open, by the trees, but if the men came back they'd see her before she saw them.

Instead, Duette set Holt down long enough for her to take off her dress and place it on the ground beside one of the trees. She straightened it until it was flat, then she ran after Holt who had started to crawl again. She picked him up, shifted him to her right arm, then started picking apples and placing them on her dress. It was too early for ripe fruit, so what she got were small, green apples. When she had twelve on the makeshift tarp she'd created, she wrapped the material around the fruit, lifted it without putting Holt down, and headed back to the shelter of the forest.

Holt was sucking again, this time on her naked chest, which wasn't any more productive than her thumb had been. Yet, he didn't seem to mind. When they got back to the woods, Duette dressed then chewed a couple of the apples and spit the mush onto a flat rock, a technique she'd learned from Jolenta's stories. The process took some time, because the apples were hard. When she had enough soft food, she placed Holt on her lap with his face up and used her fingers to feed him the mush.

Enough time had passed for Duette to head to the meeting place. She planned to be cautious as she carried Holt, moving slowly and keeping her head up so she would hear the men before they could hear her. However, her plan was spoiled when Holt began to cry. He'd been perfect until this point, but now he was loud. If the men had traveled slowly or were distracted by something along the way, Holt and she would have a problem. She needed to stop his wailing, which meant she needed to figure out why he kept crying

As she rocked him, she noticed that his stomach was gurgling between his cries. At first, she thought the sound was her own belly, because she felt something swirling in there. When she set Holt on the ground she could hear the complaining from his stomach, until her own seemed to reply. "The apples," she said out loud.

A strong smell came from Holt as the lower part of his tunic turned brown. In response to the sudden stink, her own body gurgled louder and she could tell that tightening her bottom wasn't going to be enough to keep everything inside. She stepped away from the baby, lifted her skirt, and relaxed. Her own smell was worse than Holt's, but at least she hadn't soiled her clothes. She let her skirt fall back into place as she stood, then picked up Holt.

It had been the apples. Her mother would have known better. Hopefully, all the good from their meal hadn't flushed out of their bodies. They would need to cross the same creek where they'd hid in the root fort. Although they'd be further upstream, there would still be plenty of water to clean themselves.

The water was cool, as Duette expected. They stepped in the stream the way they had before. This time the purpose was to wash their clothing and themselves. Their clothes would dry, as they had before, while they walked. This time Duette didn't drink. When they got out of the brook they headed toward the meeting place.

Chapter Twenty-Four
Waso

When Waso heard someone approaching, he was walking the perimeter of the meeting place, guarding against the possibility of a surprise attack. He was alone. Stateira and Jolenta were hunting small animals such as squirrels or weasels, hoping to find something to cook on a small fire Elfgar was trying to start. Meanwhile, Goda had gone back toward Jolenta's home, looking for Duette and Holt and trying to find out something about the Abbot's plans.

The sound was one set of footsteps with an unexpected lightness that indicated less weight than a full-grown adult. But Waso hid cautiously until the young girl and the baby in her arms were close enough to be certain. When his body relaxed, he stepped out to greet them. "You made it, as your mother said you would. We were worried." He noticed they were both wet. "What happened?"

"We were followed," she told him when he took Holt from her. "We couldn't come here until we knew it was safe."

Waso nodded, thinking how Jolenta had trained her daughter well. "Your mother said that was what was happening. The rest of us weren't certain. Goda went back to your home, to check on the Abbot and to look for you and the baby."

Duette turned away from Waso as she told him, "Holt got sick. Both of us did. But I worry about him. He's so tiny."

"Sick?"

"We ate green apples."

"You'll both be all right. We should have fresh meat soon. It will settle his stomach and yours. When Goda gets back, we'll talk about getting you and Jolenta home."

**

Life in the camp settled into a routine. Jolenta was the best hunter, so she went after small game, accompanied by a different person each day. The others stayed back to watch for the Abbot and to keep the fire going. It was hard to keep the smoke down and the embers hidden at night, but easier than starting a new fire each day. They had built rough shelters for themselves and makeshift walls to hide the flames.

Goda hadn't returned, so Duette, who was too young to help with camp security, was given the task of caring for Holt.

"She's good with the boy," Stateira said, as she and Waso watched the young girl from the edge of the camp.

Waso turned his gaze at the woman he loved. "It's not Holt I'm worried about. It's Goda."

"We better worry about Holt as well. He lost his birth parents and then the only mother he knew. Goda is all he has left."

Waso touched his thigh with his fist and stood straight. "Of course. But Abigail was my sister and I couldn't bear losing Goda after her. I'm going to look for him."

"I should be the one," she told him. "The Abbot won't kill me."

"I'd rather die than see you back with him."

"Don't say that. Don't ever say that. If you die, I die." He could feel her hands shaking, as she grabbed and held his fist. She pulled him close and touched his forehead with hers. "I love you."

Waso felt her chest rise and settle as she breathed. The rhythm of her body was like the flow of a gentle river. "And I, you."

***

Jolenta's home was gone, no doubt burned by the men who had chased them. A few blackened logs stood at odd angles where the walls had once been. Smoke still rose from the ashes, but Waso could see no glowing coals.

The rest of the property, including the barn was undamaged. Waso saw this fact as confirmation that the Abbot's purpose was to punish Jolenta for stealing and to warn her not to commit further acts against the church.

He walked around the yard and approached the barn, looking through the open door to see if there were any signs of the men. Something was hanging there, an object in shadow. It appeared to be a small body, perhaps a child.

He was moving toward the barn when he heard someone behind him. He spun, dropped to the ground and rolled behind a cart. When he felt safe enough to look at the person, he discovered Duette standing alone in the yard, staring at the remains of her home.

Waso rose and walked toward her. "Why are you here, Duette?"

"They burned my home."

"Yes, they did. Houses can be rebuilt, but you are alive. Following me could change that."

"Where will we go?"

"Right now, you need to go away from here, into the woods where you can hide. I saw something in the barn and have to look closer. Don't worry about what will happen after that. Jolenta will take care of you."

Waso stepped away from Duette, toward the barn. He turned to see if she was heading back to the forest. She wasn't. She was standing still. He waved his arm, indicating she needed to go, then stared at her until she turned.

In the barn, Waso discovered the chickens and goats had all been slaughtered and Polly, the cart horse was missing. Blood and bodies were everywhere. The hanging carcass was one of the smallest goats, strung by its neck as a warning of sorts.

"No!"

Waso looked back when he heard Duette's scream. She had followed him, after he had told her not to. "What?" he shouted.

"She was the sweetest of all. Why would he kill her?"

"They're warning us. But they didn't take the grain, which means they're coming back, probably soon. We need to leave." He found a few loaves of bread. The Abbot's men hadn't taken those, either. Waso put them in a sack and handed it to Duette, then he turned and left the barn, but only after he was certain she was following him.

Danger could be behind any of the countless trees they were passing and she was only ten. Yet, Waso's thoughts were not focused entirely on the girl beside him. He was also thinking of Abigail and Goda. He'd struggled so hard to find them only to learn that his sister was dead and now his brother was missing. They'd hardly had time to speak.

Waso sensed Duette stop. He glanced back to see her holding her head high, like a dog sniffing out something unexpected. She pointed into the woods. Waso quietly looked. He saw what appeared to be a man, resting on his back, his head held up by a small fallen tree. Fortunately, the man appeared to be asleep, which meant he hadn't noticed them.

They backed up a few steps before they turned and walked away.

"What now?" Duette asked, when they were far enough to whisper to each other without being heard. "Should we sneak by before he wakes?"

"You should," Waso told her. "I need to follow him. He could lead me to my brother."

Duette slowly exhaled a deep breath before she said, "I'll help you."

Waso felt suddenly cold. The last thing he needed was a girl getting in his way.

"Can't you find your way back alone?"

"I know this forest better than anyone, even Jolenta. I can go back to the camp or I can stay and help you." She stared in his eyes, without blinking. "I can be as quiet as any animal, quieter than most. And if you don't want me to walk with you, I'll walk behind."

Waso frowned. There didn't appear to be an easy way out of this situation. "We don't know anything about him. It's possible he isn't one of the Abbot's men. If so, we'll be wasting our time."

Duette smiled and shook her head. "Hardly anyone comes out this way, except me and the animals. If this man is not looking for us, he's either a squirrel or a weasel."

Waso hated when children acted smart and sassy, but Duette was different. Her relationship with Holt had warmed him to her. Duette felt like family.

"Then we watch him together. We have to stay ready, because when he wakes and starts to move, we follow."

"Why is he sleeping during the day?" Duette asked.

Waso could see the man's belly rising and falling, like a resting dog, so he wasn't dead. "I'm not certain," he told his young companion.

"Do you think he's injured?" she whispered, her voice wavering slightly, but her gaze clearly fixed on the man.

"I don't see wounds or blood. He might have twisted an ankle or broken a leg." But Waso believed the man could walk, since there was no sign that he had crawled into his prone position. "And there is more I don't understand about this. Why would he be separate from the rest of the Abbot's men? Even if they split up to search for us, he'd have at least one other man with him, to protect each other."

Duette touched Waso's shoulder and they both crouched lower. The man was stirring.

***

Duette

The man stood, then stretched both arms toward the sky. When he was upright, Duette could see him better. He wasn't much older than she was, maybe a few years. He dropped to his knees and began to pray. *If he knew we were here, he'd run*, Duette thought. She didn't know if he would run away or toward them. The man didn't look like her idea of a soldier, especially when he was on his knees, but there was no need to take chances. She crouched lower and tugged on Waso's tunic.

After the man finished praying, he turned away from them and stepped over a small knoll. Waso started to follow, but Duette hung to his clothing. "Should we follow?" she asked. She wasn't scared, but if they got caught in a trap they couldn't get back to warn the others. Waso was bigger than the young man who didn't appear to have a weapon, but there could be others hidden somewhere.

"You stay," Waso told her. "I'll see what's going on."

She didn't want to be left alone, so she followed him despite his command. Waso looked back once, shook his head, but kept moving. He dropped to his stomach and crawled as he reached the top of the knoll. She did the same, a short distance behind him.

Waso looked beyond what Duette could see, then lunged up and forward, charging at the man. Duette scrambled to her feet to see Waso grab and knock the man down, his fists flying at the stranger's face. There was someone else there. It took her a moment to recognize Goda. It was his voice she knew. He was trying to yell, but his voice was strained and weak. "Waso! Let him go!"

After landing a couple of solid punches, Waso stopped and rolled off his victim.

"His name is Pax." Goda said, his weak voice quieter now. "He saved my life."

"One of the Abbot's men?" Waso asked.

"I was, before I saw what he was doing to Goda."

"He's training to be a priest," Goda told his brother, then he repeated, "He saved my life."

Duette looked at Holt's father. His face was swollen, his clothing was torn, and there were lash marks on his arms, back, and chest.

"Saving him will be for naught, if we make too much noise," Pax said, glancing at Goda. Waso helped the man to his feet, but didn't look guilty for the brutal way he'd attacked. Duette ran to Goda, to see if she could help tend to his wounds.

"We aren't far from a branch of the creek," she told Goda. "I could go wet a cloth and clean the cuts."

"That's a good idea, if you can get there safely," Pax said. "We also need water to drink. I brought Goda here. I wasn't sure how long he would last if I kept carrying him, so I found this hidden spot. I put him down where he could rest, then went over the mound there to watch for the Abbot's men. I was more exhausted than I realized and fell asleep. Thank God you are the ones who found us."

"How did this happen to him?" Waso asked Pax, as he knelt beside his brother.

"The Abbot had suspected someone was stealing our grain, but he wasn't certain until the quantities grew so big there could be no other explanation. When the same barn was targeted multiple times, we came out this way to look for the thieves. We found Jolenta's farm. Some of us sneaked into the barn when she was busy in her house. We found more grain in that livestock barn than any single wheat farmer would harvest in a year. We regrouped outside, then decided to punish Jolenta and her friends, which I guess included both of you. But we held off when we heard loud noises, a decision that apparently gave you enough time to get into the woods. We looked for you, but we didn't know the area well enough. So, we stayed at the farm until we caught Goda spying on us. Goda wasn't the only person the Abbot was after, so he had him beaten, trying to get him to tell where Jolenta was. Goda didn't break. They stopped whipping him for the night, but told him they would start up again the next day. This action didn't seem like God's will, not to me at least, and I decided to do something about it. I rose in the middle of the night and helped Goda get away from the camp, but as you can see, he's in bad shape."

Waso shifted to a sitting position and lifted Goda's head to his lap. Waso's face was bowed, but Duette could tell he was crying.

Duette turned away from Waso to look at Pax. "Do you have anything I can use to carry water?" she asked.

Pax pulled out a knife, a medium size blade with an undecorated, wooden handle. He went to where Goda was lying and, after asking Waso to lean back, cut three strips of cloth from the injured man's torn shirt. As he stepped back toward Duette, he picked up a wineskin, then handed Duette the items she needed to take to the creek.

"I'll be back," Duette called out to Waso.

"You better be."

Chapter Twenty-Five
Stateira

Jolenta had been pacing in circles since Duette disappeared, her face puffy and red from crying. This woman, who had been strong and capable, was now unable to help the group survive, hardly able to think on her own. Stateira took over caring for Holt, while Elfgar switched to handle the hunting and cooking. The cooking only happened over a late-night fire when it was too dark for the Abbot's men to venture into the woods.

While Jolenta walked around them, Elfgar and Stateira, with Holt on her lap, sat by the coals they had lit the night before, when they had cooked the last squirrel Jolenta had caught. So here they were, staring at lumps of burnt wood, trying to talk about anything other than the fate of their missing friends, especially Duette.

"Tell us about her," Stateira said to Jolenta. "Sit by me and tell us of the way Duette came into your life. It was a wonderful day, right?"

Jolenta stopped moving, turned to Stateira and sat beside her, so close their hips were touching. She didn't speak, just kept pulling on her hair where it reached her shoulder. Stateira handed Holt to Elfgar, then put her arm around Jolenta.

"Duette will be fine," Stateira told her. "She's a brave and resourceful young woman."

"She takes after her moms," Elfgar said, "both of them."

Jolenta smiled ever so slightly at his comment and Stateira asked her to tell the story of Duette.

Jolenta said, "I can't tell about the day Duette came to me without including the woman who brought her into this world."

***

Jolenta

*M*atilda *was pregnant when she caught up to me on the path leading from the convent. The pregnancy wasn't her choice. A priest had raped her, once, which was enough to leave her with child. She had been a virgin, had dedicated years of her life to Christ: praying, teaching, and working at physical labor. That woman was gone now.*

Yet, for me there was a convenience. Luken, the priest who had attacked her, apologized and provided Matilda with a home. Since I was with her, I also had a place to stay. Luken gave her some of the church's supplies and money, which meant we could eat.

I need to make this clear – Luken is the man we now know as the Abbot. As is often the case, he was rewarded for his corruption with advancement in the church. Now, I'll continue.

The next few months were pleasant. Luken stayed away from us, choosing instead to send servants to bring us what we needed and to report back about Matilda's condition. I imagine they reported on me as well, but Matilda was the woman carrying his child.

After Duette was born, Luken came himself. I thought he would continue to ignore us when he discovered the child was a girl, but he surprised me. I suppose it's different for a man of the church. He didn't need another field worker as much as he needed someone else to help wash and sew.

The Matilda I knew at that time was different from the nun who had guided and taken care of me in the convent. She was my friend rather than my teacher, but it wasn't until after Duette was born that her relationship with the church changed.

Let me tell you about Duette's birth before I get into all that.

I didn't have any idea what to do, but Matilda did. "Prayer," she told me. "Women die when giving birth, if it's God's will. If you want me to survive, you need to ask Him to protect me. There are ointments and stones, but those are nothing compared to the will of God."

"I want to use whatever will help you survive."

"I suppose you do. Some women use gemstones, while others use rose oil or eagle's dung. I don't want those heathen items at my child's birth, even if they ease my pain. I want a crucifix by my bed and I want you there, of course, with your head bowed."

It might have helped if I'd had a few of those icons and potions. It definitely would have helped if Matilda had told me what to expect before she started screaming.

Her pain came in surges, so when Matilda was able to talk she told me what to do and I did it. There were no complications.

When the birth was done, we'd both discovered how much we loved Duette, but also how much we loved each other. It wasn't the rape that drove Matilda from the church. How could it be? The rape gave us Duette. It was her relationship with me that turned her. "Why would God fill me with this love, then tell me it's wrong?" she asked many times. I never found the right answer.

Matilda was on her feet the day after the birth, but moving slowly. It took some time before she was back to normal. Meanwhile, Luken started showing up – every day. His servants must have informed him of Duette's arrival. He started taking charge of everything, even issuing orders about when Matilda should feed her baby. Like a farmer, he'd planted his seed and had returned to harvest the bounty. The talk was his way of letting us know he was in charge. Since he was the one giving us food and shelter, there was nothing we could do about it.

The weather was starting to turn cold when Luken arrived with a second infant. When Matilda saw the child, she was upset, but not for the reason I was. "He forced himself on another nun," she said, "then took her baby. She might have been someone I know."

"I think there's more to it than that."

"What?"

"Luken gets you pregnant, then offers what you need to keep you and the baby alive. You can't say no when he starts bringing other babies, because you're dependent on the church. Soon there are three, plus Duette – four babies you have to care for while always carrying one of them with you, a child always hanging on your chest like a giant boil. The church ends up with money, while you lose your freedom. 'The life of a milk goat' is what my mother used to say."

"What can I do?" Matilda asked.

"We can go," I told her.

There was no way we could leave in midwinter, so we waited for spring and planned while we waited. When the time came, Matilda had three infants in addition to Duette, just as I had suspected. We traded grain for a cart and farming tools: hand plow, sickle, pitchfork, shovel, rake, axe, and a couple of knives. Matilda and I ate less bread that winter, to have enough to trade and some left over to plant at our new home. Matilda was feeding four infants, so she couldn't give up as much, but that worked in our favor because the church was expecting her to need a lot. I did some sewing for one of our neighbors who lived alone. He was generous and practically gave us the hand plow. I think the man was trying to impress me and I believe he would have asked me to marry him if I'd stayed. But I didn't and I would guess he's still alone.

Matilda dressed like a man. She was tall and big boned, so she could easily pass. We left in the middle of the night and went to the nunnery where we left the three babies at the door. The cart was noisy, but no one confronted us. They must not have known we were there until they found the infants the following morning.

We eventually found land we could farm, then built a small shelter and lived there as we built what you saw. We hadn't traveled far, but we were sure nobody recognized us. Since she appeared to be getting away with the deception, Matilda picked up extra work at Croyland. After that, there was the accident that killed her, which is how I became Duette's only mother.

I've never been certain it was an accident. The Abbot was capable of violence, which he used to accomplish what he claimed was God's will. I'd known people who had been killed at his command and no one had seen Matilda fall. She'd arrived early that day and was on the roof alone.

Duette and I continued on, but with a few changes. We'd already been helping the victims of the church; women Matilda knew while she was a nun. What happened next was intense. I dedicated my life to helping more and more of those victims. I stopped all attempts at serious farming and took up stealing to support myself, taking only from the church. I had grown to the point where I understood that the church's purpose was not to spread the word of God. It was to use the word to achieve riches and power. This was and is a corruption that extends beyond life. Stealing from the monsters I was fighting seemed a good idea.

***

Jolenta looked at her companions. Elfgar was still holding Holt, but sitting up, stiff as stone, his eyes as wide as a field of grain. Stateira, however, didn't seem surprised by Jolenta's suspicion.

***

Staetira

Stateira understood as well as anyone alive, what the Abbot can do. There was no way Matilda's disguise could have been enough to prevent him from recognizing her and there was no way he didn't have a hand in her death.

Chapter Twenty-Six
Duette

When Duette returned with the water-filled wineskin and the wet rags, she discovered Goda still lying where he had been when she left. Waso and Pax were standing over him, arguing. They were speaking in hushed tones, but with strength and a hint of anger.

They hadn't noticed when Duette walked over the tiny hill that hid them. If she had been one of the Abbot's men, they would have been just as unaware and would probably have been killed. Duette was upset they were careless.

"I know my brother," Waso told Pax. "He doesn't care about consecrated land."

"You can't possibly know what he cares about now. We're talking about eternity in Hell. The burial soil can make a difference. I can bless this land."

"Can you? Even though you're not yet a priest?"

"I know the words. God will listen."

"Even if that's right, it's not where Goda would want to be. Abigail is buried in a ditch in the forest, covered with stones. He would want to be in a similar grave, rather than in land blessed by the church that hurt both of them so much."

"God is always good. The church is his voice on Earth."

Waso stepped back. He raised his eyebrows. "If God is good and, as priests often say, all powerful, then why is Goda dead?" He lifted his hands toward his head, as if it hurt to even consider the idea of God's goodness. "Why is Abigail dead?" he spoke faster, raising his voice. "Why is Matilda dead? And why is the Abbot alive and continuing to wreck the lives of innocent people? What about Holt? The child has lost both his parents. Who knows what will happen to him now? Why would a good God allow such horrible things?"

Pax turned his eyes down, away from Waso. "I can't explain everything God does. If I could, I would *be* God."

"Then explain one thing. Why do *you* still believe after watching what Goda went through?"

"That wasn't God's work, that was Luken's."

Waso let out a short, sharp laugh. "You call him Luken?"

"You asked me what I felt. I don't honor Luken with his title."

"But you believe enough in the church to think of Abbot as an honorable title?"

"Yes. I honor what is good in the church, even when the human failings of the leaders deny it."

"Goda is dead?" Duette asked. She thought of Holt. This was his father! She felt so dizzy she sat, right there, on the ground. "What happened?" She already knew the answer. The Abbot had beaten him so thoroughly, he *couldn't* recover.

Waso looked at the young girl, back at Pax, shook his head, then stared up at the tree tops. "All right," he said in a voice so soft Duette had trouble hearing him, "then bless the land before we bury him. It's too late for Goda to know what we do. If you're right about God, it may save his soul. If you're wrong, it can't hurt anyone now."

Pax stepped toward Duette and looked down at her. "May I have the water, please."

She handed him the wineskin. He turned back toward Goda's body, placed the wineskin on the ground, held his hands over it, then said. "Praise the Lord, you his angels, you mighty ones who do his bidding, who obey his word. Praise the Lord, all his heavenly hosts, you his servants who do his will. Praise the Lord, all his works everywhere in his dominion. Praise the Lord, my soul." Pax then picked up the wineskin. He paced around the ditch where Goda's body lay, sprinkling water on the body and on the land.

"That's all there is to it," Pax told both Waso and Duette. "Hopefully, it will do some good."

"Do we go back to Jolenta now?" Duette asked Waso.

"First, we collect stones," he told her. "We will bury him the way he buried Abigail."

"I'll help," Pax said. "After that, I'd like to go with you."

"You would?"

Duette could hear the suspicion in Waso's reply. She also wondered about this man.

"There is no other place left for me," Pax told them both.

"Won't God take care of you?" Waso asked.

"God sent me Goda and Goda brought you to me."

What Pax said seemed true, but Duette was scared. She wished they knew him better.

***

Jolenta

Waso and Duette returned, but with the wrong man. Apparently, Goda had been killed. In his place they had one of Luken's warriors. Jolenta didn't know this one and certainly didn't trust him. He was barely older than a boy.

"Tell me something about yourself," Jolenta demanded.

"I tried to save Goda."

She looked at Waso, who nodded back at her.

"I'm destined for something," Pax told her, "something good. Helping Goda didn't work out, but maybe helping you is what I'm supposed to do."

This is a weird turn, Jolenta thought. She shrugged then asked, "Destined?"

Pax stood tall and stared at her. She studied the bruises on his face from Waso's fists, before he believed in this young man. "Why do you think that?" she added.

"I almost died as an infant," Pax told her in a steady, low-pitched voice, without breaking eye contact. "I was one of four babies placed with a church wet nurse. When the woman died, her daughter saved my life by packing us in a cart and hauling us to Grimsby Nunnery."

"You're lying," Jolenta could feel her body tense as she confronted this impostor. "That's my story."

"I believe him," Elfgar told her. "The priests talked about you when I was at Croyland. One of the infants was a boy named Pax."

"How do we know Pax is your real name?" Jolenta asked the young man.

Pax took a step back, "It is my name and what I told you is what my mother told me. It's why she said I was destined for something good or, in her words, something mighty."

"Tell me about her."

"All right. She was strong and kind, a great mother. My father disappeared shortly after I was born and she was left with nothing but the hut we lived in. To survive, she had to weave and sew when the weather was bad and work in our neighbor's field when it was better, which is why she had to pay the church to board me with one of their wet nurses. I was old enough to be weaned when I was brought to the abbey, so they sent me back to her. I went to the abbey two years ago to try to live up to her expectations."

"You think killing Goda was the way to do that?" Jolenta asked.

"I didn't..."

Waso broke in over Pax's protest, stepping between him and Jolenta and saying, "Goda swore Pax tried to save his life. That's good enough for me."

Waso continued to speak, explaining how Pax had risked his life to get the wounded Goda away from the Abbot. Jolenta didn't respond, but she wondered if the situation might have been better had Pax put loyalty to the Abbot over loyalty to God, as the others had. Goda would still have died, but he wouldn't have suffered as long and there would be no confusion as to where Pax stood. Now, Jolenta would need to treat him with the caution of a rabbit watching a circling hawk.

Holt, who had been resting in one of the three temporary shelters they'd built out of branches and grass, started to cry. The sound drew Elfgar away. As soon as he left, Waso took his place beside Jolenta and spoke in a soft, near whisper. "I'm going to kill him."

Jolenta knew which man Waso planned to kill and why. The Abbot had enslaved and repeatedly raped Stateira, then his men had beaten and murdered Goda. And other priests had disfigured Abigail as a punishment for an act they had no right to judge. Waso had plenty of reasons to hate the church in general and the Abbot in particular.

Jolenta had her reasons to hate the Abbot, too. He'd raped Matilda, before he'd been promoted to Abbot and he was very likely responsible for Matilda's death, when she was working at the abbey. "Can I help?" she asked. She felt breathless as she spoke, but forced her words out.

"Yes," Waso replied quickly. "Pax has agreed to go with me, to help find the Abbot's camp. We can surprise him, if we go alone. But I need you to watch Duette, so she doesn't follow me again. And would you also keep an eye on Stateira. I didn't tell her of my plan. I need her to be here when I return. I intend to spend the rest of my life with that woman, to marry her, if we can get back to her home in Persia."

He's taking Pax with him? Jolenta thought, to kill the Abbot? I wonder if that is a good idea.

Chapter Twenty-Seven
Waso

The camp wasn't hard to find, since the men had fires burning all day. Once there, Pax and Waso hid in the woods and spied on the Abbot and his men. The Abbot's men had set up seven tents, all pure white except the largest one, decorated with blood red crosses. That tent had to be the Abbot's. The white tents were positioned in a circle around the tent with the crosses, like bees protecting their queen.

"The Abbot's a canny man," Pax whispered. "He could be spending his nights in one of the other tents, but I doubt it. He doesn't have a reason to fear us."

"We better watch, to know for certain. I've packed supplies for ten days." Supplies meant only bread and water, but enough to keep them going. Shelter would be in a bush or behind a fallen tree, with the emphasis on keeping out of sight rather than keeping warm and dry. They were in for a hard time, but if they killed the Abbot, it would be worth the sacrifice.

Waso and Pax had to be careful to avoid the men who left the camp. Most of the time those men were just stepping into the woods to relieve themselves. They went alone, except for the Abbot who always brought armed men for protection. However, each morning five men would venture further, probably to search for Jolenta. Whatever five went out, always returned before dark, indicating they hadn't found her.

"They're not trained killers," Pax told Waso as they watched the Abbot lead his men in prayer. "They're priests who believe God is speaking to them through the Abbot. I was the same until God opened my eyes to see what the

Abbot was doing was not following the teachings of our Lord and Savior, Jesus Christ."

Pax was lying beside Waso. They were both on their stomachs, trying to watch the camp without being seen. Pax kept balancing on his left arm as he lifted his hand to his forehead and stroked his brow. Waso touched his shoulder to get him to lie still. If any of those priests saw movement, they'd be reaching for their axes and spears before Waso and Pax could get to their feet.

"I'd rather face a trained knight than anyone who believes he's fighting for God," Waso whispered.

"Here's what we do." Waso's mouth was so dry, he had trouble forming the words. "We need to get the Abbot alone. There are two of us, so one distracts his protectors while the other kills him."

"Is there another way?"

Waso thought this might be an issue for Pax. The priest had agreed to lead him to the Abbot's camp, but they hadn't spoken of what Waso intended to do once they were there. "Another way?" Waso asked, his stomach tightening as he spoke. It would be much harder to carry out the attack without Pax's help, but it had to be done. "We can't kill him if we don't get him alone. We're two. They have ten or twelve, at least."

"I'm wondering if we can convert him," Pax whispered, "convince him there's a better way."

Waso almost laughed out loud at that idea, but he forced himself to stay quiet, avoiding any sound that might bring the Abbot's men out. "Priests are always trying to convert people, but this time we're not talking about bringing a heathen to God. The Abbot is a corrupt, murdering hypocrite and that means he's more typical than you are. Men of the church are as corrupt as the royalty."

"You might be right about the Abbot," Pax said, "but we're not all corrupt. We need to follow Christ's teachings, if we are to reach His side in Heaven. All the priests in that camp know that."

How could anyone be so naive? Waso thought, but when he spoke he said. "If you don't want to be the one who kills him, then you distract while I do it. After everything the Abbot has done, eternal life is the last thing on my mind."

"Your plan still has a problem," Pax told Waso. "I could make noise or let the priests see me, but they'll never empty the camp. They'll send a few men to chase me down and I'll be gone. That happens and you'll be stuck on your own."

Waso knew Pax wouldn't be the only one to die if his plan failed and Pax was right about it having little to no chance for success. What would happen to Stateira if he was gone? What would happen to Holt? But they had to stop the devil. "Have you got a better idea?" he asked.

"I believe I do."

That was encouraging. "What is it?"

"We leave a message for the priests, one that scares them and tells them the Abbot's way is not God's way. They're believers. If we make the sign strong enough, they'll abandon the Abbot, just as I did."

Was he suggesting a sign from God? Waso wondered. *How could they do that? They were just mortal men. Unless Pax was suggesting something that a mortal man could do, something shocking enough to force the priests to see the error of their ways. This also seemed impossible.* "You were the only one in the Abbot's camp to get upset enough to leave. How can we make a sign that's stronger than Goda's beaten body?"

"By using his *dead* body." Pax said.

Waso felt a chill. Just a few days earlier, they'd left Goda under a pile of rocks. His body might have started to deteriorate, but it would still be recognizable. The idea of lifting the rocks, to see his brother's distorted face, terrified him.

He turned toward Pax. They'd only met recently, but Waso had believed him when he had described his effort to save Goda. Pax had risked his own life because his God would want him to live a life with respect for others. Then, when he had blessed the land, he had said he was concerned about Goda's eternal soul. If the land where Goda was buried affected his soul, what would happen when they took him out of that land?

Waso had no way of knowing what his brother would have wanted. They had never spoken about God.

Stateira had the strongest faith of anyone he knew. If he could imagine what she would say, he might have something to go by. He tried to picture her on a sandy shore, back before they crossed to Britannia, the day he'd killed Olaf.

Waso concentrated, carefully recalling the image of her expression as Waso pulled his knife from Olaf's body. It was a mixture of shock and fear, but something else as well. She looked to the sky, to heaven.

The soul and the body are one during life, but after death they are separate. The body should be honored, but the soul should be honored more. That's what Goda would want and what better way to honor his soul than to use his body to achieve his wishes.

"Let's go," Waso said, as he rose to his knees and started to crawl, as quietly as possible. "He would have wanted this, so it's what we'll do."

"Can you catch a squirrel?" Pax asked as they began their walk away from the Abbot's camp. "Or some other small animal? A few mice might do."

Waso was having trouble jumping from the thought of retrieving his brother's body to considering Pax's strange question. "We don't have time to cook, if that's what you're thinking,"

"I need fresh blood for my plan," Pax told him.

"Goda's body and fresh blood?" Waso felt tense, his heart racing. "Is this witchcraft? You can't use Goda's body for witchcraft!"

"You need to trust me. I spent enough of my life living with priests to understand what they think about -- and what they fear."

He would trust Pax, but if it ever appeared the man was about to defile Goda, Waso would react quickly with whatever force it took to stop him. "I can make a snare," Waso told him, answering his question about catching a squirrel, "if you have twine."

"I have some."

"I'll make one, or more if you have enough material. We'll set them along our way to get Goda's body and see what we have when we return. *Blood*, you say. I do trust you, but what you are asking for, makes it hard."

Pax had enough twine for Waso to set two snares. Waso had to find a pair of saplings for each trap. He set two: one early on in their walk to Goda, another a bit later. Each snare needed a thin, young tree to bend for the force and another to cut low enough to use for the release. After that he had to whittle a framework to hold the twine. He was no expert, but when he was done both snares appeared ready to work. With a little luck they would have a couple of dead squirrels when they returned.

Removing the stones was not as difficult as digging up a deep, dirt grave would have been, but the job still took time. Pax worked with Waso and did not appear to have any trouble keeping up. Apparently, all the prayer and meditation in a religious life had not softened him.

When they reached the last layer, Goda's body was revealed a little at a time. Although it had only been a few days since they had buried him, there were places where he had begun to decay: the flesh along his side and a few small spots near his nose and eyes. Waso considered how a body buried under stones is protected from crows and foxes, but not from worms and insects. He had to scrape some parts clean.

Yet, Goda was still recognizable, which shook Waso at the same time as it left him with a sense of relief. Whatever Pax's plan was, everything seemed to be in place. If Pax deserved the trust he asked for, there was a good chance the Abbot would be left alone and unprotected. And if that happened, Waso could kill him.

Goda's body was stiff, with some places where the stones had caused dents and the flesh was unable to bounce back. But Pax said the body was positioned well. Waso wondered what "well" meant. Goda was on his back with his hands crossed in front of his chest.

"He looks like himself," Pax said.

Waso nodded. He noticed a couple of bald spots on his brother's head, but the hair that remained looked strong. That was good, if looking like himself was important.

Waso still wished Pax would explain what he intended. If there had been any other plan with even a small possibility of success, Waso would have insisted. But since he had no other choice, he decided to go with whatever the young man had in mind. Trust was a peculiar emotion, in this case as much a result of the situation as Pax's character.

The walk back seemed to be going well, until they checked the first snare. The bread they'd used for bait was gone and the sapling had snapped to its original position. Yet, nothing had been caught. The twine loop was not tightened around the neck of an animal as Waso had hoped, instead it was hanging loosely from the sapling.

Waso got down on one knee, to study the snare. The animal had approached from the side, springing the trap without getting caught in the loop. Waso had built barriers of twigs and grass on the sides, which, apparently, weren't enough.

"Is this a problem?" Waso asked, turning to Pax, who was standing beside Goda's body.

He was scowling. "Not if the other one worked."

Waso rubbed his forehead with two fingers. "And if it didn't?"

"I don't want to think about it."

They picked up Goda and started walking again. Neither of them had spoken much on the way to the grave site, but now the *only* sounds they made were their breathing and their footsteps.

When they reached the other snare, it became clear it wasn't in their destiny to catch an animal. This bait hadn't been touched. Pax and Waso stood still for a moment, studying the failed trap, before they set Goda's body down. Waso found a straight stick and pushed it, first through the snare, then against the trigger. It snapped up, tightening the noose around the stick, pulling it out of his hand.

"It should have worked," Waso told Pax. "Just bad luck."

"No such thing as luck. God has told me what I have to do. It's my job to do it."

***

They approached in silence. "Set him here," Pax whispered when they reached a small clearing near the camp's perimeter. If the priests caught them, they would be accused of sacrilege for removing a body from its grave.

Goda's body had been easy to carry. He had been thin and light in life and death hadn't changed that. With his arms frozen in place, across his chest, Waso had to hold him from under the body's shoulders. Pax had held the feet, the lighter end, but was still huffing a bit.

"We need to build a cross," Pax said to Waso, as soon as they set the body down. "It will lie flat on the ground with his body on top."

Waso didn't have tools other than a knife. He glanced around for broken branches, already the right size.

Pax must have known what Waso was thinking because he said, "We won't need to cut anything, just arrange loose sticks and stones, maybe even leaves, anything that will show up against the ground. What matters is that when we lay Goda on top, it is clear he's on a cross."

Waso gathered the materials while Pax watched the camp. When the cross was ready, the two men lifted Goda's body and put him in place.

"Now for the most important step," Pax said. "Stigmata." He pulled his knife from his belt and cut holes in the body: in Goda's side, his hands, and his ankles. During this process it was Waso's responsibility to watch the camp, but it was difficult to tear his gaze from Pax's actions. It seemed as if Pax was butchering Goda. Waso needed to stop thinking of this body as his brother.

When the last hole was cut through, the one in Goda's left ankle, Pax leaned back, kneeling before the body. He prayed, "God give me the knowledge that what I am about to do is Your will and the strength to do it." Pax then slit his wrist and leaned forward to use his own blood to transform the holes he'd just cut into the wounds of a living man.

When Pax was finished, he was still dripping blood -- on Goda's body and on the ground around it.

"Hold your hand over the cut and press!" Waso instructed as he grabbed Pax by the upper arm. The man was starting to sway slightly, as if he was about to faint. "Keep awake. Put one foot in front of the other and walk. I'll keep you from falling."

"I can't stop the bleeding. It's too...too..."

They stopped where they stood while Waso bent over and picked up a handful of dirt. "Rub this in. It will help."

Pax had lost blood, but not so much he should pass out. Most of his weakness had to be from fear. But that could be just as dangerous.

"God is with you. Hold that thought in your heart."

"We've got to make noise," Pax told him, grabbing for Waso's hand. "They've got to see the body before the blood dries."

Waso was scared by how cold Pax's hand felt, his skin like the flesh of a newly slaughtered piglet. "Put your hand back over the cut. Press the dirt in place and hold it there." Waso watched while Pax did as he was told, then they started walking again. "I'll make them notice, once you're in a safe place. But they know you carried Goda away. They'll assume you set his body there and they'll be right."

"That doesn't matter," Pax said in a voice so quiet Waso could barely hear it. "These are priests. When they look at a cross, they don't think of the carpenter or stone mason who built it. They think of Christ." Pax leaned toward Waso and stared. "They know the difference between right and wrong. They just need to be reminded their oaths of obedience are to God, not to the church and its Abbot. This tableau of God's suffering will be enough. They will remember Goda suffered from their actions as Christ suffered at the hands of the Roman soldiers. I promise that's how they will think."

"I'm not sure."

"I knew you wouldn't be. That's why I didn't want to tell you what I had in mind. Now, I say to you one more time, you need to trust me!"

Trust in Pax's knowledge of the Abbot's priests was Waso's only option. He had to follow through with this strange plan. He brought Pax to a place where he could hide behind a cluster of large boulders. Pax could rest there. He could regain some strength in case they had to run.

As he walked back toward the Abbot's camp, Waso found six stones the size of pebbles rather than rocks. They were all he could find, other than boulders that weighed more than he did. He stepped to the edge of the forest, tossed the handful of stones at the closest priest, then turned and ran.

He jumped a small ravine and began to head up a hill. The ground was covered with leaves and small branches, causing Waso's footfalls to make as much noise as a rushing stream. He was trying to draw the priests in his direction. The noise was good, but he wanted to stay out of the reach of the men who would likely kill him.

He ducked behind a thick tree, covered in vines. Most of the trees in this area were thin, birch trees and saplings so small they bent when he stepped on them. The tree where he was hiding was one of the few places where he could get out of their view, but, for the same reason, the priests were likely to look there. Hopefully, they would stop looking when they found Goda's body.

For the first time since he started to run, Waso looked back. He could see a few groups of priests, searching through the woods, sticking their spears into piles of leaves large enough to cover him. Two things were wrong. First of all, one of the groups was heading toward the place where he'd left Pax. Secondly, the groups had all managed to bypass the clearing where they would find Goda.

Waso had to make a choice. If he avoided the men chasing him, they would likely find and kill Pax, then fall back to protect the Abbot. That outcome would mean failure.

Waso rolled out from behind the tree, jumped to his feet, and began running down the hill. He headed between two of the search groups, certain they both could see him. Men on either side of him were shouting, but he kept running. Someone threw a spear which fell behind him. The throw had been weak and off the mark.

Waso broke through a bush then lunged in to Goda's clearing. There was his brother, still lying on his back. The sun shone through the tops of the trees, creating a patchwork of light among the darkness of the forest shadows. One of the spots of light was directly on Goda's face. Waso knew his brother was dead, but the light seemed to argue against that reality. The skin of his face looked moist and soft, the way it had when Goda was a child.

Waso fell to his knees. Pax had positioned Goda like Christ on the cross to remind the priests of their Lord and His teachings. But this vision had captured Waso instead. Suddenly he understood his brother's innocence as well as his love for their sister. For a moment Waso believed this understanding was all there was to life. He was ready to die. But then he looked up and saw a vision of an angel hovering above his brother. He knew his life was not over. He knew he would not die. He knew this because the angel was the image of Stateira, his own love.

Waso heard the priests break through the vines and enter the clearing. He didn't turn, but he could tell they all had stopped, all three groups. He looked at the angel and saw them reflected in her eyes. They lowered their weapons and lowered their eyes.

"Kill him!"

Waso raised his eyes to see the Abbot had entered the clearing. He was standing on Goda's opposite side, looking at Waso across the body. The angel was gone.

"What you see on the ground before you is a sacrilegious abomination created by heathens, not by God or His representatives on Earth! Purify your souls by acting against the one who made it! Kill him, now!"

The Abbot's words were elegant, but they were lies. The crucifix had been created by Pax, a man whose life was an example of what was holy about this Christian religion, while the Abbot's life was the opposite. Goda's body held the power at the center of this image. Waso believed in Goda more than he believed in any god.

Waso heard a few weapons drop behind him. He didn't turn away from the Abbot, so he didn't know if the weapons were spears or swords or axes, but he could tell from the sound that they were on the ground. He also heard bodies moving away, through the vines surrounding the clearing.

"Stop!" the Abbot shouted. "Remember your vows. You can't turn your back on God."

All the priests hadn't left, but some had. The Abbot looked to the heavens, then jumped over Goda's body. Waso turned to see what was happening. The Abbot did not attack any of the men who were disobeying his orders. Instead, he grabbed a spear and pointed it at Waso.

"Who are you?" the Abbot shouted. "Why have you acted against God?"

Waso clenched his fists and stood tall. "You should ask the same of yourself," he said in a steady, even voice.

The Abbot started forward, as if he was about to run his weapon through Waso, but someone grabbed him from behind and slit his neck. The Abbot dropped to the ground, blood spurting out of the wound under his jaw. Pax stood over him.

"Thou shall not kill," Pax said, as he stared at the body lying at his feet. "I just broke God's commandment."

Waso's muscles felt weak and his knees shook, but he stood firm. He caught Pax's eye and nodded. "You saved my life and you saved the world from whatever this cruel man would have done to others." Waso turned to look at the other priests. They had all left. "We can talk about all this later. Now we have to get you back to Elfgar, so he can look at that cut of yours."

Epilogue

At first, the herbal mixture Elfgar provided did not seem to have any effect on Pax's wrist infection. The painful, red skin color kept growing, creeping up his arm like ivy. But Duette was a careful nurse. She kept the wound as clean as possible and continued to apply the herbs. Eventually, the cut healed and Pax regained his strength. Waso complained to Pax, saying he had stayed sick just long enough to avoid working on the rebuilding of Jolenta's house.

After his physical healing, Pax was able to concentrate on his spiritual health. He'd broken one of God's commandments and had done so by killing a church leader. The Abbot had been selfish, cruel, and hypocritical, but God had blessed him with life until Pax's action.

When Pax was able to walk, he left Jolenta's home, but not before Jolenta apologized for doubting him and told the young man she was glad she had once saved his life.

He returned to Croyland Abbey, where a new, reform-minded Abbot had been appointed. After he heard Pax's confession, the holy man offered absolution. Pax was able to return to his former life of prayer, meditation, and peace.

***

Since Holt's parents were gone, Jolenta took the baby into her home. Stateira and Waso helped with his care, but Jolenta was best suited to step in as his new mother. Duette became like a sister to him. Elfgar stayed by Jolenta's side. He taught her a smithy's trade and, in later years, taught

Holt the same skills. Elfgar didn't replace Matilda in Jolenta's heart, but he turned out to be a reliable partner.

Jolenta could no longer help victims of the church, because so many people knew her methods. Yet, she was not as upset as she thought she would be. The death of the Abbot meant fewer women were hurt. What she would say to anyone who would listen was, "It's someone else's turn to save the world."

***

A couple of months after Pax left, he returned to Jolenta's house riding Polly, their cart horse. Apparently, the priests who stole her had brought her to the abbey. Pax received permission to bring Polly to Jolenta, but he'd ridden her bareback. The bit and bridle he used on the animal were the only tack he left with Jolenta. Although, they didn't need a saddle, they did need a cart harness and long reins.

Jolenta sent Duette to the tanner to trade for the required leather. The tanner liked the knives Elfgar had made, but the tanner's son, a young man of about fourteen years, was more interested in Duette than in the tools she'd brought to trade.

"It's about time I found a wife for Ulric," the tanner told her. "You're a little young, but you look sturdy. Do you have a husband?"

Duette looked at Ulric, who was tall, but a bit scrawny.

"He's stronger than he looks," the tanner told her, "and he'll inherit this place." The man gestured around at the small house and barn. Duette saw and smelled the urine pits where the leather was soaking. However, she also noticed the house was well maintained and there were animals in the barn: goats and chickens.

Ulric, in what appeared to be an effort to prove his father right, stepped to Duette and picked her up.

"Put me down!" she said, laughing as she spoke. He did as she requested and she added, "I think he might do." It wasn't as if she had many other offers.

"Keep your knives," the tanner told her. "You can have the leather. Just tell your family of our proposal. If they're willing and you still are, we will have a marriage. You'll live here, of course, and help with the tanning. Maybe there will be a son or two in a couple of years, God willing."

Duette said goodbye then turned to leave for home. The day was half gone. If she didn't start walking immediately, she would still be on the path after sundown. She turned to look at Ulric one more time, wishing he had said something, anything. Hopefully, she would know how his voice sounded before they married.

On her second trip to the tanner home, she discovered Ulric could speak well – when his father wasn't near. At night, when they were alone, she discovered talking wasn't his only skill.

***

A small house with seven people bothered Stateira. Perhaps because she was used to living alone, with only Waso. Living with the others made it hard to have private conversations. It was even harder to find a space for private prayer, which was becoming much more important to her because they had survived with Allah's help.

After the weather turned warmer, Stateira would often step outside after dark, to have time alone.

One night, Elfgar followed her. "Waso spoke to me," Elfgar told Stateira, "and I spoke to Jolenta."

"About what?"

"What do you know about Spain?"

Stateira was confused. She knew maps, so she knew the country's location, but that was all. She shrugged and shook her head.

"Jolenta knows some women down there, people who needed a safe place far from Britannia."

"She moved them there?"

"Yes. But safe might not be the right word. There are conflicts in that land between Christian controlled areas and Muslim controlled areas. Sometimes the conflicts turn violent."

"Muslim?" she asked, trying to keep her voice from shaking. She took a step back.

"Yes. The land has Islamic areas and Jolenta can resettle you in one of them. Waso wants to go there with you."

Stateira wondered why Waso had sent Elfgar to tell her this, instead of approaching her himself. Perhaps he wanted her to look into her heart, rather than seeking an answer in his eyes. Or maybe Jolenta and Elfgar wanted her to know they understood her needs.

"It's a big decision for Waso," Stateira told Elfgar, "leaving his homeland."

"Not as hard a choice now that Goda and Abigail are gone."

"Holt is still here."

"Jolenta can take care of him and I'll be with her for as long as she wants me."

Spain wasn't Persia, but it might do. She could marry there, without breaking her promise to Allah. Marriage was important to Waso and maybe to her as well. She just hadn't admitted it.

"You don't have to decide now," Elfgar said as he turned to leave her.

"I don't need to wait," she said, causing Elfgar to turn back to her. "Tell Jolenta I want to go, but don't tell

Waso. I want to speak to him myself." As soon as she gave her answer, she felt lighter, as if Allah was lifting her up.

***

Elfgar had not had a drink since his days of living alone.

There was the time in the woods, when all they had to drink was creek water. Then there were the weeks of work, rebuilding Jolenta's home. They had no fermenting honey in the barn and not much worth trading with a neighbor, so while they worked, water continued to be their only option.

Elfgar waited until spring to set up a smithy shop near the barn, because during winter the frozen ground was too hard to find the stones he needed for his forge. He traded his healing skills and some meat for a few basic tools and some raw iron, but, once again, he didn't ask for mead or wine.

More than a year later, Elfgar finally had another drink. Jolenta had caught an abundance of eels, some of which she traded for a jug of mead. Elfgar wasn't sure why she brought it home, but she did say she intended to share it with him. Maybe she was testing him. Maybe she just wanted to say thank you.

After Jolenta poured a cup for each of them, Elfgar took a drink from his. One gulp was not enough to affect him, yet he felt the bite when the alcohol slid down his throat. The sensation reminded him of the way drink can dull the sadness, but he wasn't sad. He also remembered how drink allowed him to overcome nervousness, but he wasn't nervous.

He took another, smaller drink, then watched as Jolenta drank. Life can be good, he thought.

***

The boat Waso and Stateira were to take to Spain was huge when compared with either of the small ferries they had used to cross the Baltic and North Seas. All ten of the crew could have lain head to toe, from bow to stern, with room left for Stateira and Waso to stand at either end. The sail was about four times the size of a ferry sail and there were oars for multiple rowers, although Waso couldn't see how many from the shore. This boat would be safer than the others, but Waso would have felt better if Stateira was to be one of the sailors rather than a passenger.

There would be so much to learn in this new land. It was good they would be staying with people who spoke their language, but he had promised Stateira they would learn the language of the land together. He hadn't promised her anything about her religion, except for his agreement that they would be married by an imam, but he intended to learn what he could about that part of Stateira's life, as well.

They were leaving Holt with Jolenta, Duette, and Elfgar, even though he had come to believe the child was more than an orphan his brother and sister took in. Holt had their mother's eyes and the round shoulders of their father. He also had their father's nose, hidden behind that large scar.

He doubted the boy was Goda's, because Goda would have dedicated his entire life to their sister. Waso could not envision him taking a wife. So that left Abigail. Her face had been butchered, which would have kept most men away, but maybe the damage to her appearance drove her to find someone willing to take her for a night or two. Still, leaving Holt was the right choice. Jolenta, Duette, and Elfgar would raise him properly.

"It's time," Stateira told Waso, as she took his hand. One of the crewmen was signaling to them from the boat.

They walked hand in hand, up the ramp and on to a new life together.

***

Over the following years, Duette and Ulric had three healthy children, although she lost two others along the way. One was born dead. Another died in her sleep, just two months after her birth.

Duette named the surviving boys Waso and Goda and the girl Abigail.

About Steve Lindahl

Steve Lindahl's first two novels, *Motherless Soul* and *White Horse Regressions*, were published in 2009 and 2014 by All Things That Matter Press. His third novel, *Hopatcong Vision Quest,* published by Solstice Publishing, won a CIPA 2017 Evvy merit award in historical fiction. His short fiction has appeared in *Space and Time*, *The Alaska Quarterly*, *The Wisconsin Review*, *Eclipse*, *Ellipsis*, and *Red Wheelbarrow*. He served for five years as an associate editor on the staff of *The Crescent Review*, a literary magazine he co-founded. He is currently the managing editor for *Flying South*, a literary magazine sponsored by Winston-Salem Writers and is also a board member of that organization.

His Theater Arts background has helped nurture a love for intricate characters in complex situations that is evident in his writing. Steve and his wife Toni live and work together outside of Greensboro, North Carolina. They have two adult children: Nicole and Erik. *Under a Warped Cross* is Steve Lindahl's fourth novel, his second with Solstice Publishing.

Social Media

Website: http://www.stevelindahl.com/

Blog: http://stevelindahl.blogspot.com/

Facebook: https://www.facebook.com/steve.lindahl.3

Twitter: https://twitter.com/lindahlst @lindahlst

Amazon author page: https://www.amazon.com/Steve-Lindahl/e/B0031GLA5Y/ref=sr_ntt_srch_lnk_1?qid=1512223939&sr=8-1

Goodreads author page: https://www.goodreads.com/author/show/3117087.Steve_Lindahl

Acknowledgements

I would like to credit my wife, Toni, my daughter, Nicole, and my son, Erik. They give me constant encouragement and are the best critics any author could have. I also want to thank the writers in my critique group: Joni Carter, Robert Shar, and Ray Morrison, talented people who are fun to be around and have improved my work in ways too numerous to list.

Source Material

Viking Age: Everyday Life during the extraordinary era of the Norsemen by Kirsten Wolf, published by Sterling Publishing Co., 2013

The Normans told chiefly in relation to their conquest of England by Sarah Orne Jewett, published 1898

Monasticism in late medieval England, c.1300-1535 by Martin Heale, published by Manchester University Press, 2009

Avalon by Anya Seton, published by Mariner Books, 2013

Medieval Chronicles – Medieval History (website)
http://www.medievalchronicles.com/medieval-history/

Medieval Chronicles: Anglo Saxon Farming (website)
http://www.medievalchronicles.com/medieval-history/medieval-history-periods/anglo-saxons/anglo-saxon-farming/

The History Learning Site – Medieval Farming (website)
http://www.historylearningsite.co.uk/medieval-england/medieval-farming/

Regia Anglorum – Food and Drink (website)
https://regia.org/research/life/food.htm

The English Companions – Anglo-Saxon clothes (website)
http://www.tha-engliscan-gesithas.org.uk/education/anglo-saxon-clothes-men and http://www.tha-engliscan-gesithas.org.uk/education/anglo-saxon-clothes-women

Hurstwic Viking Age – History (website)
http://www.hurstwic.com/history/text/history.htm

Hurstwic Viking Age – Viking Ships (website)
http://www.hurstwic.org/history/articles/manufacturing/text/norse_ships.htm

The Viking Museum (website)
http://www.thevikingmuseum.com/index.html

The Viking Answer Lady (website)
http://www.vikinganswerlady.com/

Sword Fighting As It Was For the Vikings (website)
https://www.youtube.com/watch?v=xFiIDl_mt2c

Short axe fighting techniques (website)
https://www.youtube.com/watch?v=IUYXceCWRTQ

Megalithic Ireland – Nendrum Monastery (website)
http://www.megalithicireland.com/Nendrum%20Monastery
.html

Encyclopedia Britannica – Persia (website)
https://www.britannica.com/place/Persia

History World – History of Iran (Persia) (website)
http://www.historyworld.net/wrldhis/PlainTextHistories.as
p?ParagraphID=FGJ

Wikipedia - Nendrum Monastery (website)
https://en.wikipedia.org/wiki/Nendrum_Monastery

If you enjoyed this story, check out these other Solstice Publishing books by Steve Lindahl:

Hoptacong Vision Quest

"An enticing, engaging novel" / "...deftly plotted and extremely well written" / "A fascinating view of ancient tribal beliefs bleeding into the present day."

With the help of a hypnotist, Diane, Ryan, and Martha look into their hidden memories, hoping to use past life experiences to solve the murders of two people they loved. The trail to the justice they seek runs through a life they shared hundreds of years earlier, in a Native American village.

Oota Dabun, Diane's counterpart in her past life, always dreamed of having a vision quest, a rite normally reserved for the young men of her village. This Lenape woman reaches for her dream in an unusual and compassionate fashion which teaches Diane a great deal about the capacity of the soul they share.

https://myBook.to/HVQ_Kindle

www.ingramcontent.com/pod-product-compliance
Lightning Source LLC
Chambersburg PA
CBHW052030020726
47501CB00004B/1339